AND YOU SHALL KNOW THEM...

"...There is a race that has three times broken out to overrun this mapped area of our galaxy and dominate other civilized cultures—until some inherent lack or weakness in the individual caused the component parts of this advance to die out. The periods of these outbreaks has always been disastrous for the dominated cultures and uniformly without benefit to the race I am talking about. In the case of each outbreak, though the home planet was destroyed and all known remnants of the advancing race hunted out, unknown seed communities remained to furnish the material for a new advance some thousands of years later. That race," said the academician, and coughed —or at least made some kind of noise in his throat, "is your own.

"...There *must* be something more in you, some genius, some capability above the normal, to account for the fantastic nature of your race's previous successes. But the legend says only—*Danger, Human! High Explosive. Do not touch*—and we find nothing in you to justify the warning."

*forthcoming

GORDON R. DICKSON
THE MAN FROM EARTH

A JIM BAEN PRESENTATION

TOR

A TOM DOHERTY ASSOCIATES BOOK

THE MAN FROM EARTH

Copyright © 1983 by Gordon R. Dickson

A Tor Book
Published by Tom Doherty Associates, Inc.
49 West 24th Street
New York, N.Y. 10010

Cover art by David Egge

ISBN: 0-812-51007-0

First Tor printing: June 1983

Printed in the United States of America

0 9 8 7 6 5 4 3

Acknowledgements: The stories published herein were first published and are copyright as follows:

CALL HIM LORD, *Analog Science Fiction*, copyright©1966 by The Conde Nast Publications, Inc.

THE ODD ONES, copyright©1955 by Quinn Publishing Co., Inc.

IN THE BONE, copyright©1966 by Galaxy Publishing Corporation.

DANGER, HUMAN, *Astounding*, December 1957, copyright©1957 by Street and Smith Publications, Inc.

TIGER GREEN, copyright©1965 by Galaxy Publishing Corporation.

THE MAN FROM EARTH, *Galaxy*, June 1964, copyright © 1964 by Galaxy Publishing Corporation.

ANCIENT, MY ENEMY, copyright©1969 by Univeral Publishing and Distributing Corporation.

THE BLEAK AND BARREN LAND, copyright©1952 by Standard Magazines, Inc.

STEEL BROTHER, *Astounding*, February 1952, copyright© 1952 by Street & Smith Publications, Inc.

LOVE ME TRUE, copyright©1961 by Street and Smith Publications, Inc.

CALL HIM LORD

There are many characteristics desirable in an Emperor that can be done without if necessary. But there is one that any true ruler absolutely must possess.

"*He called and commanded me*
—Therefore, I knew him;
But later on, failed me; and
—Therefore, I slew him!"

"Song of the Shield Bearer"

The sun could not fail in rising over the Kentucky hills, nor could Kyle Arnam in waking. There would be eleven hours and forty minutes of daylight. Kyle rose, dressed, and went out to saddle the gray gelding and the white stallion. He rode the stallion until the first fury was out of the arched and snowy neck; and then led both horses

7

around to tether them outside the kitchen door. Then he went in to breakfast.

The message that had come a week before was beside his plate of bacon and eggs. Teena, his wife, was standing at the breadboard with her back to him. He sat down and began eating, rereading the letter as he ate.

". . . The Prince will be traveling incognito under one of his family titles, as Count Sirii North; and should not be addressed as 'Majesty'. *You will call him 'Lord' . . .*"

"Why does it have to be you?" Teena asked.

He looked up and saw how she stood with her back to him.

"Teena—" he said, sadly.

"Why?"

"My ancestors were bodyguards to his—back in the wars of conquest against the aliens. I've told you that," he said. "My forefathers saved the lives of his, many times when there was no warning—a Rak spaceship would suddenly appear out of nowhere to lock on, even to a flagship. And even an Emperor found himself fighting for his life, hand to hand."

"The aliens are all dead now, and the Emperor's got a hundred other worlds! Why can't his son take his Grand Tour on them? Why does he have to come here to Earth—and you?"

"There's only one Earth."

"And only one you, I suppose?"

He sighed internally and gave up. He had been raised by his father and his uncle after his mother died, and in an argument with Teena he always felt helpless. He got up from the table and went to her, putting his hands on her and gently trying to turn her about. But she resisted.

He sighed inside himself again and turned away to the weapons cabinet. He took out a loaded slug pistol, fitted it into the stubby holster it matched, and clipped the holster to his belt at the left of the buckle, where the hang of his leather jacket would hide it. Then he selected a dark-handled knife with a six-inch blade and bent over to slip it into the sheath inside his boot top. He dropped the cuff of his trouser leg back over the boot top and stood up.

"He's got no right to be here," said Teena fiercely to the breadboard. "Tourists are supposed to be kept to the museum areas and the tourist lodges."

"He's not a tourist. You know that," answered Kyle, patiently. "He's the Emperor's oldest son and his great-grandmother was from Earth. His wife will be, too. Every fourth generation the Imperial line has to marry back into Earth stock. That's the law—still." He put on his leather jacket, sealing it closed only at the bottom to hide the slug-gun holster, half turned to the door—then paused.

"Teena?" he asked.

She did not answer.

"Teena!" he repeated. He stepped to her, put his hands on her shoulders and tried to turn her to face him. Again, she resisted, but this time he was having none of it.

He was not a big man, being of middle height, round-faced, with sloping and unremarkable-looking, if thick, shoulders. But his strength was not ordinary. He could bring the white stallion to its knees with one fist wound in its mane—and no other man had ever been able to do that. He turned her easily to look at him.

"Now, listen to me—" he began. But, before he could finish, all the stiffness went out of her and she clung to him, trembling.

"He'll get you into trouble—I know he will!" she choked, muffledly into his chest. "Kyle, don't go! There's no law making you go!"

He stroked the soft hair of her head, his throat stiff and dry. There was nothing he could say to her. What she was asking was impossible. Ever since the sun had first risen on men and women together, wives had clung to their husbands at times like this, begging for what could not be. And always the men had held them, as Kyle was holding her now—as if understanding could somehow be pressed from one body into the other—and saying nothing, because there was nothing that could be said.

So, Kyle held her for a few moments longer, and then reached behind him to unlock her intertwined fingers at his back, and loosen her arms around him. Then, he went. Looking back through the kitchen window as he rode off on the stallion, leading the gray horse, he saw her standing just where he had left her. Not even crying, but standing with her arms hanging down, her head down, not moving.

He rode away through the forest of the Kentucky hillside. It took him more than two hours to reach the lodge. As he rode down the valleyside toward it, he saw a tall, bearded man, wearing the robes they wore on some of the Younger Worlds, standing at the gateway to the interior courtyard of the rustic, wooded lodge.

When he got close, he saw that the beard was graying and the man was biting his lips. Above a straight, thin nose, the eyes were bloodshot and circled beneath as if from worry or lack of sleep.

"He's in the courtyard," said the gray-bearded man as Kyle rode up. "I'm Montlaven, his tutor. He's ready to go." The darkened eyes looked almost pleadingly up at Kyle.

"Stand clear of the stallion's head," said Kyle. "And take me in to him."

"Not that horse, for him—" said Montlaven, looking distrustfully at the stallion, as he backed away.

"No," said Kyle. "He'll ride the gelding."

"He'll want the white."

"He can't ride the white," said Kyle. "Even if I let him, he couldn't ride this stallion. I'm the only one who can ride him. Take me in."

The tutor turned and led the way into the grassy courtyard, surrounding a swimming pool and looked down upon, on three sides, by the windows of the lodge. In a lounging chair by the pool sat a tall young man in his late teens, with a mane of blond hair, a pair of stuffed saddlebags on the grass beside him. He stood up as Kyle and the tutor came toward him.

"Majesty," said the tutor, as they stopped, "this is Kyle Arnam, your bodyguard for the three days here."

"Good morning, Bodyguard . . . Kyle, I mean." The Prince smiled mischievously. "Light, then. And I'll mount."

"You ride the gelding, Lord," said Kyle.

The Prince stared at him, tilted back his handsome head, and laughed.

"I can ride, man!" he said. "I ride well."

"Not this horse, Lord," said Kyle, dispassionately. "No one rides this horse, but me."

The eyes flashed wide, the laugh faded—then returned.

"What can I do?" The wide shoulders shrugged. "I give in—always I give in. Well, almost always." He grinned up at Kyle, his lips thinned, but frank. "All right."

He turned to the gelding—and with a sudden leap was in the saddle. The gelding snorted and plunged at the shock; then steadied as the young man's long fingers tightened expertly on the reins and the fingers of the other hand patted a gray neck. The Prince raised his eyebrows, looking over at Kyle, but Kyle sat stolidly.

"I take it you're armed good Kyle?" the Prince said slyly. "You'll protect me against the natives if they run wild?"

"Your life is in my hands, Lord," said Kyle. He unsealed the leather jacket at the bottom and let it fall open to show the slug pistol in its holster for a moment. Then he resealed the jacket again at the bottom.

"Will—" The tutor put his hand on the young man's knee. "Don't be reckless, boy. This is Earth and the people here don't have rank and custom like we do. Think before you—"

"Oh, cut it out, Monty!" snapped the Prince. "I'll be just as incognito, just as humble, as archaic and independent as the rest of them. You think I've no memory! Anyway, it's only for three days or so until my Imperial father joins me. Now, let me go!"

He jerked away, turned to lean forward in the saddle, and abruptly put the gelding into a bolt for the gate. He disappeared through it, and Kyle drew hard on the stallion's reins as the big white horse danced and tried to follow.

"Give me his saddlebags," said Kyle.

The tutor bent and passed them up. Kyle made them fast on top of his own, across the stallion's withers. Looking down, he saw there were tears in the bearded man's eyes.

"He's a fine boy. You'll see. You'll know he is!" Montlaven's face, upturned, was mutely pleading.

"I know he comes from a fine family," said Kyle, slowly. "I'll do my best for him." And he rode off out of the gateway after the gelding.

When he came out of the gate, the Prince was nowhere in sight. But it was simple enough for Kyle to follow, by dinted brown earth and crushed grass, the marks of the gelding's path. This brought him at last through some pines to a grassy open slope where the Prince sat looking skyward through a singlelens box.

When Kyle came up, the Prince lowered the instrument and, without a word, passed it over. Kyle put it to his eye and looked skyward. There was the whir of the tracking unit and one of Earth's three orbiting power stations swam into the field of vision of the lens.

"Give it back," said the Prince.

"I couldn't get a look at it earlier," went on the young man as Kyle handed the lens to him. "And I wanted to. It's a rather expensive present, you know—it and the other two like it—from our Imperial treasury. Just to keep your planet from drifting into another ice age. And what do we get for it?"

"Earth, Lord," answered Kyle. "As it was before men went out to the stars."

"Oh, the museum areas could be maintained with one station and a half-million caretakers," said the Prince. "It's the other two stations and you billion or so freeloaders I'm talking about. I'll have to look into it when I'm Emperor. Shall we ride?"

"If you wish, Lord." Kyle picked up the reins of the stallion and the two horses with their riders moved off across the slope.

". . . And one more thing," said the Prince, as they entered the farther belt of pine trees. "I don't want you to be misled—I'm really very fond of old Monty, back there. It's just that I wasn't really planning to come here at all— *Look at me, Bodyguard!*"

Kyle turned to see the blue eyes that ran in the Imperial family blazing at him. Then, unexpectedly, they softened. The Prince laughed.

"You don't scare easily, do you, Bodyguard . . . Kyle, I mean?" he said. "I think I like you after all. But look at me when I talk."

"Yes, Lord."

"That's my good Kyle. Now, I was explaining to you that I'd never actually planned to come here on my Grand Tour at all. I didn't see any point in visiting this dusty old museum world of yours with people still trying to live like they lived in the Dark Ages. But—my Imperial father talked me into it."

"Your father, Lord?" asked Kyle.

"Yes, he bribed me, you might say," said the Prince thoughtfully. "He was supposed to meet me here for these three days. Now, he's messaged there's been a slight delay—but that doesn't matter. The point is, he belongs to the school of old men who still think your Earth is something precious and vital. Now, I happen to like and admire my father, Kyle. You approve of that?"

"Yes, Lord."

"I thought you would. Yes, he's the one man in the

human race I look up to. And to please him, I'm making this Earth trip. And to please him—only to please *him*, Kyle—I'm going to be an easy Prince for you to conduct around to your natural wonders and watering spots and whatever. Now, you understand me—and how this trip is going to go. Don't you?" He stared at Kyle.

"I understand," said Kyle.

"That's fine," said the Prince, smiling once more. "So now you can start telling me all about these trees and birds and animals so that I can memorize their names and please my father when he shows up. What are those little birds I've been seeing under the trees—brown on top and whitish underneath? Like that one—there!"

"That's a Veery, Lord," said Kyle. "A bird of the deep woods and silent places. Listen—" He reached out a hand to the gelding's bridle and brought both horses to a halt. In the sudden silence, off to their right they could hear a silver bird-voice, rising and falling, in a descending series of crescendos and diminuendos, that softened at last into silence. For a moment after the song was ended the Prince sat staring at Kyle, then seemed to shake himself back to life.

"Interesting," he said. He lifted the reins Kyle had let go and the horses moved forward again. "Tell me more."

For more than three hours, as the sun rose toward noon, they rode through the wooded hills, with Kyle identifying bird and animal, insect, tree and rock. And for three hours the Prince listened—his attention flashing and momentary, but intense. But when the sun was overhead that intensity flagged.

"That's enough," he said. "Aren't we going to stop for lunch? Kyle, aren't there any towns around here?"

"Yes, Lord," said Kyle. "We've passed several."

"Several?" The Prince stared at him. "Why haven't we come into one before now? Where are you taking me?"

"Nowhere, Lord," said Kyle. "You lead the way. I only follow."

"I?" said the Prince. For the first time he seemed to become aware that he had been keeping the gelding's head always in advance of the stallion. "Of course. But now it's time to eat."

"Yes, Lord," said Kyle. "This way."

He turned the stallion's head down the slope of the hill they were crossing and the Prince turned the gelding after him.

"And now listen," said the Prince, as he caught up. "Tell me I've got it all right." And to Kyle's astonishment, he began to repeat, almost word for word, everything that Kyle had said. "Is it all there? Everything you told me?"

"Perfectly, Lord," said Kyle. The Prince looked slyly at him.

"Could you do that, Kyle?"

"Yes," said Kyle. "But these are things I've known all my life."

"You see?" The Prince smiled. "That's the difference between us, good Kyle. You spend your life learning something—I spend a few hours and I know as much about it as you do."

"Not as much, Lord," said Kyle, slowly.

The Prince blinked at him, then jerked his hand dismissingly, and half-angrily, as if he were throwing something aside.

"What little else there is probably doesn't count," he said.

They rode down the slope and through a winding valley and came out at a small village. As they rode clear of the surrounding trees a sound of music came to their ears.

"What's that?" The Prince stood up in his stirrups. "Why, there's dancing going on, over there."

"A beer garden, Lord. And it's Saturday—a holiday here."

"Good. We'll go there to eat."

They rode around to the beer garden and found tables

back away from the dance floor. A pretty, young waitress came and they ordered, the Prince smiling sunnily
at her until she smiled back—then hurried off as if in
mild confusion. The Prince ate hungrily when the food
came and drank a stein and a half of brown beer, while
Kyle ate more lightly and drank coffee.

"That's better," said the Prince, sitting back at last. "I
had an appetite . . . Look there, Kyle! Look, there are
five, six . . . seven drifter platforms parked over there.
Then you don't all ride horses?"

"No," said Kyle. "It's as each man wishes."

"But if you have drifter platforms, why not other
civilized things?"

"Some things fit, some don't, Lord," answered Kyle.
The Prince laughed.

"You mean you try to make civilization fit this old-
fashioned life of yours, here?" he said. "Isn't that the
wrong way around—" He broke off. "What's that they're
playing now? I like that. I'll bet I could do that dance."
He stood up. "In fact, I think I will."

He paused, looking down at Kyle.

"Aren't you going to warn me against it?" he asked.

"No, Lord," said Kyle. "What you do is your own
affair."

The young man turned away abruptly. The waitress
who had served them was passing, only a few tables
away. The Prince went after her and caught up with her
by the dance floor railing. Kyle could see the girl pro-
testing—but the Prince hung over her, looking down
from his tall height, smiling. Shortly, she had taken off
her apron and was out on the dance floor with him,
showing him the steps of the dance. It was a polka.

The Prince learned with fantastic quickness. Soon, he
was swinging the waitress around with the rest of the
dancers, his foot stamping on the turns, his white teeth
gleaming. Finally the number ended and the members of

the band put down their instruments and began to leave the stand.

The Prince, with the girl trying to hold him back, walked over to the band leader. Kyle got up quickly from his table and started toward the floor.

The band leader was shaking his head. He turned abruptly and slowly walked away. The Prince started after him, but the girl took hold of his arm, saying something urgent to him.

He brushed her aside and she stumbled a little. A busboy among the tables on the far side of the dance floor, not much older than the Prince and nearly as tall, put down his tray and vaulted the railing onto the polished hardwood. He came up behind the Prince and took hold of his arm, swinging him around.

". . . Can't do that here," Kyle heard him say, as Kyle came up. The Prince struck out like a panther—like a trained boxer—with three quick lefts in succession into the face of the busboy, the Prince's shoulder bobbing, the weight of his body in behind each blow.

The busboy went down. Kyle, reaching the Prince, herded him away through a side gap in the railing. The young man's face was white with rage. People were swarming onto the dance floor.

"Who was that? What's his name?" demanded the Prince, between his teeth. "He put his hand on me! Did you see that? *He put his hand on me!*"

"You knocked him out," said Kyle. "What more do you want?"

"He manhandled me—*me!*" snapped the Prince. "I want to find out who he is!" He caught hold of the bar to which the horses were tied, refusing to be pushed farther. "He'll learn to lay hands on a future Emperor!"

"No one will tell you his name," said Kyle. And the cold note in his voice finally seemed to reach through to the Prince and sober him. He stared at Kyle.

"Including you?" he demanded at last.

"Including me, Lord," said Kyle.

The Prince stared a moment longer, than swung away. He turned, jerked loose the reins of the gelding and swung into the saddle. He rode off. Kyle mounted and followed.

They rode in silence into the forest. After a while, the Prince spoke without turning his head.

"And you call yourself a bodyguard," he said, finally.

"Your life is in my hands, Lord," said Kyle. The Prince turned a grim face to look at him.

"Only my life?" said the Prince. "As long as they don't kill me, they can do what they want? Is that what you mean?"

Kyle met his gaze steadily.

"Pretty much so, Lord," he said.

The Prince spoke with an ugly note in his voice.

"I don't think I like you, after all, Kyle," he said. "I don't think I like you at all."

"I'm not here with you to be liked, Lord," said Kyle.

"Perhaps not," said the Prince, thickly. "But I know *your* name!"

They rode on in continued silence for perhaps another half hour. But then gradually the angry hunch went out of the young man's shoulders and the tightness out of his jaw. After a while he began to sing to himself, a song in a language Kyle did not know; and as he sang, his cheerfulness seemed to return. Shortly, he spoke to Kyle, as if there had never been anything but pleasant moments between them.

Mammoth Cave was close and the Prince asked to visit it. They went there and spent some time going through the cave. After that they rode their horses up along the left bank of the Green River. The Prince seemed to have forgotten all about the incident at the beer garden and be out to charm everyone they met. As the sun was at last westering toward the dinner hour, they came finally to a small hamlet back from the river, with a roadside inn mirrored in an artificial lake beside it, and guarded by oak and pine trees behind.

"This looks good," said the Prince. "We'll stay overnight here, Kyle."

"If you wish, Lord," said Kyle.

They halted, and Kyle took the horses around to the stable, then entered the inn to find the Prince already in the small bar off the dining room, drinking beer and charming the waitress. This waitress was younger than the one at the beer garden had been; a little girl with soft, loose hair and round brown eyes that showed their delight in the attention of the tall, good-looking, young man.

"Yes," said the Prince to Kyle, looking out of corners of the Imperial blue eyes at him, after the waitress had gone to get Kyle his coffee. "This is the very place."

"The very place?" said Kyle.

"For me to get to know the people better—what did you think, good Kyle?" said the Prince and laughed at him. "I'll observe the people here and you can explain them—won't that be good?"

Kyle gazed at him, thoughtfully.

"I'll tell you whatever I can, Lord," he said.

They drank—the Prince his beer, and Kyle his coffee—and went in a little later to the dining room for dinner. The Prince, as he had promised at the bar, was full of questions about what he saw—and what he did not see.

". . . But why go on living in the past, all of you here?" he asked Kyle. "A museum world is one thing. But a museum people—" he broke off to smile and speak to the little, soft-haired waitress, who had somehow been diverted from the bar to wait upon their dining-room table.

"Not a museum people, Lord," said Kyle. "A living people. The only way to keep a race and a culture preserved is to keep it alive. So we go on in our own way, here on Earth, as a living example for the Younger Worlds to check themselves against."

"Fascinating . . ." murmured the Prince; but his eyes had wandered off to follow the waitress, who was glowing and looking back at him from across the now-busy dining room.

"Not fascinating. Necessary, Lord," said Kyle. But he did not believe the younger man had heard him.

After dinner, they moved back to the bar. And the Prince, after questioning Kyle a little longer, moved up to continue his researches among the other people standing at the bar. Kyle watched for a little while. Then, feeling it was safe to do so, slipped out to have another look at the horses and to ask the innkeeper to arrange a saddle lunch put up for them the next day.

When he returned, the Prince was not to be seen.

Kyle sat down at a table to wait; but the Prince did not return. A cold, hard knot of uneasiness began to grow below Kyle's breastbone. A sudden pang of alarm sent him swiftly back out to check the horses. But they were cropping peacefully in their stalls. The stallion whickered, low-voiced, as Kyle looked in on him, and turned his white head to look back at Kyle.

"Easy, boy," said Kyle and returned to the inn to find the innkeeper.

But the innkeeper had no idea where the Prince might have gone.

". . . If the horses aren't taken, he's not far," the innkeeper said. "There's no trouble he can get into around here. Maybe he went for a walk in the woods. I'll leave word for the night staff to keep an eye out for him when he comes in. Where'll you be?"

"In the bar until it closes—then, my room," said Kyle.

He went back to the bar to wait, and took a booth near an open window. Time went by and gradually the number of other customers began to dwindle. Above the ranked bottles, the bar clock showed nearly midnight. Suddenly, through the window, Kyle heard a distant scream of equine fury from the stables.

He got up and went out quickly. In the darkness outside, he ran to the stables and burst in. There in the feeble illumination of the stable's night lighting, he saw the Prince, pale-faced, clumsily saddling the gelding in the center aisle between the stalls. The door to the stallion's stall was open. The Prince looked away as Kyle came in.

Kyle took three swift steps to the open door and looked in. The stallion was still tied, but his ears were back, his eyes rolling, and a saddle lay tumbled and dropped on the stable floor beside him.

"Saddle up," said the Prince thickly from the aisle. "We're leaving." Kyle turned to look at him.

"We've got rooms at the inn here," he said.

"Never mind. We're riding. I need to clear my head." The young man got the gelding's cinch tight, dropped the stirrups and swung heavily up into the saddle. Without waiting for Kyle, he rode out of the stable into the night.

"So, boy . . ." said Kyle soothingly to the stallion. Hastily he untied the big white horse, saddled him, and set out after the Prince. In the darkness, there was no way of ground-tracking the gelding; but he leaned forward and blew into the ear of the stallion. The surprised horse neighed in protest and the whinny of the gelding came back from the darkness of the slope up ahead and over to Kyle's right. He rode in that direction.

He caught the Prince on the crown of the hill. The young man was walking the gelding, reins loose, and singing under his breath—the same song in an unknown language he had sung earlier. But, now as he saw Kyle, he grinned loosely and began to sing with more emphasis. For the first time Kyle caught the overtones of something mocking and lusty about the incomprehensible words. Understanding broke suddenly in him.

"The girl!" he said. "The little waitress. Where is she?"

The grin vanished from the Prince's face, then came

slowly back again. The grin laughed at Kyle.

"Why, where d'you think?" The words slurred on the Prince's tongue and Kyle, riding close, smelled the beer heavy on the young man's breath. "In her room, sleeping and happy. Honored . . . though she doesn't know it . . . by an Emperor's son. And expecting to find me there in the morning. But I won't be. Will we, good Kyle?"

"Why did you do it, Lord?" asked Kyle, quietly.

"Why?" The Prince peered at him, a little drunkenly in the moonlight. "Kyle, my father has four sons. I've got three younger brothers. But I'm the one who's going to be Emperor; and Emperors don't answer questions."

Kyle said nothing. The Prince peered at him. They rode on together for several minutes in silence.

"All right, I'll tell you why," said the Prince, more loudly, after a while as if the pause had been only momentary. "It's because you're not *my* bodyguard, Kyle. You see, I've seen through you. I know whose bodyguard you are. You're *theirs!*"

Kyle's jaw tightened. But the darkness hid his reaction.

"All right—" The Prince gestured loosely, disturbing his balance in the saddle. "That's all right. Have it your way. I don't mind. So, we'll play points. There was that lout at the beer garden who put his hands on me. But no one would tell me his name, you said. All right, you managed to bodyguard him. One point for you. But you didn't manage to bodyguard the girl at the inn back there. One point for me. Who's going to win, good Kyle?"

Kyle took a deep breath.

"Lord," he said, "some day it'll be your duty to marry a woman from Earth—"

The Prince interrupted him with a laugh, and this time there was an ugly note in it.

"You flatter yourselves," he said. His voice thickened. "That's the trouble with you—all you Earth people—you flatter yourselves."

They rode on in silence. Kyle said nothing more, but

kept the head of the stallion close to the shoulder of the gelding, watching the young man closely. For a little while the Prince seemed to doze. His head sank on his chest and he let the gelding wander. Then, after a while, his head began to come up again, his automatic horseman's fingers tightened on the reins, and he lifted his head to stare around in the moonlight.

"I want a drink," he said. His voice was no longer thick, but it was flat and uncheerful. "Take me where we can get some beer, Kyle."

Kyle took a deep breath.

"Yes, Lord," he said.

He turned the stallion's head to the right and the gelding followed. They went up over a hill and down to the edge of a lake. The dark water sparkled in the moonlight and the farther shore was lost in the night. Lights shone through the trees around the curve of the shore.

"There, Lord," said Kyle. "It's a fishing resort, with a bar."

They rode around the shore to it. It was a low, casual building, angled to face the shore; a dock ran out from it, to which fishing boats were tethered, bobbing slightly on the black water. Light gleamed through the windows as they hitched their horses and went to the door.

The barroom they stepped into was wide and bare. A long bar faced them with several planked fish on the wall behind it. Below the fish were three bartenders— the one in the center, middle-aged, and wearing an air of authority with his apron. The other two were young and muscular. The customers, mostly men, scattered at the square tables and standing at the bar wore rough working clothes, or equally casual vacationers' garb.

The Prince sat down at a table back from the bar and Kyle sat down with him. When the waitress came they ordered beer and coffee, and the Prince half-emptied his stein the moment it was brought to him. As soon as it was completely empty, he signaled the waitress again.

"Another," he said. This time, he smiled at the waitress

when she brought his stein back. But she was a woman in her thirties, pleased but not overwhelmed by his attention. She smiled lightly back and moved off to return to the bar where she had been talking to two men her own age, one fairly tall, the other shorter, bullet-headed and fleshy.

The Prince drank. As he put his stein down, he seemed to become aware of Kyle, and turned to look at him.

"I suppose," said the Prince, "you think I'm drunk?"

"Not yet," said Kyle.

"No," said the Prince, "that's right. Not yet. But perhaps I'm going to be. And if I decide I am, who's going to stop me?"

"No one, Lord."

"That's right," the young man said. "That's right." He drank deliberately from his stein until it was empty, and then signaled the waitress for another. A spot of color was beginning to show over each of his high cheekbones. "When you're on a miserable little world with miserable little people . . . hello, Bright Eyes!" he interrupted himself as the waitress brought his beer. She laughed and went back to her friends. ". . . You have to amuse yourself any way you can," he wound up.

He laughed to himself.

"When I think how my father, and Monty—everybody —used to talk this planet up to me—" he glanced aside at Kyle. "Do you know at one time I was actually scared—well, not scared exactly, nothing scares me . . . say *concerned*—about maybe having to come here, some day?" He laughed again. "Concerned that I wouldn't measure up to you Earth people! Kyle, have you ever been to any of the Younger Worlds?"

"No," said Kyle.

"I thought not. Let me tell you, good Kyle, the worst of the people there are bigger, and better-looking and smarter, and everything than anyone I've seen here. And I, Kyle, I—the Emperor-to-be—am better than any of them. So, guess how all you here look to me?" He stared at Kyle, waiting. "Well, answer me, good Kyle. Tell me the truth. That's an order."

"It's not up to you to judge, Lord," said Kyle.

"Not—? Not up to me?" The blue eyes blazed. "*I'm* going to be Emperor!"

"It's not up to any one man, Lord," said Kyle. "Emperor or not. An Emperor's needed, as the symbol that can hold a hundred worlds together. But the real need of the race is to survive. It took nearly a million years to evolve a survival-type intelligence here on Earth. And out on the newer worlds people are bound to change. If something gets lost out there, some necessary element lost out of the race, there needs to be a pool of original genetic material here to replace it."

The Prince's lips grew wide in a savage grin.

"Oh, good, Kyle—good!" he said. "Very good. Only, I've heard all that before. Only, I don't believe it. You see—I've seen you people, now. And you don't outclass us, out on the Younger Worlds. *We* outclass *you*. We've gone on and got better, while you stayed still. And you know it."

The young man laughed softly, almost in Kyle's face.

"All you've been afraid of, is that we'd find out. And I have." He laughed again. "I've had a look at you; and now I know. I'm bigger, better and braver than any man in this room—and you know why? Not just because I'm the son of the Emperor, but because it's born in me! Body, brains and everything else! I can do what I want here, and no one on this planet is good enough to stop me. Watch."

He stood up, suddenly.

"Now, I want that waitress to get drunk with me," he said. "And this time I'm telling you in advance. Are you going to try and stop me?"

Kyle looked up at him. Their eyes met.

"No, Lord," he said. "It's not my job to stop you."

The Prince laughed.

"I thought so," he said. He swung away and walked between the tables toward the bar and the waitress, still in conversation with the two men. The Prince came up to the bar on the far side of the waitress and ordered a new stein of beer from the middle-aged bartender. When it was given to him, he took it, turned around, and rested his elbows on the bar, leaning back against it. He spoke to the waitress, interrupting the taller of the two men.

"I've been wanting to talk to you," Kyle heard him say.

The waitress, a little surprised, looked around at him. She smiled, recognizing him—a little flattered by the directness of his approach, a little appreciative of his clean good looks, a little tolerant of his youth.

"You don't mind, do you?" said the Prince, looking past her to the bigger of the two men, the one who had just been talking. The other stared back, and their eyes met without shifting for several seconds. Abruptly, angrily, the man shrugged, and turned about with his back hunched against them.

"You see?" said the Prince, smiling back at the waitress. "He knows I'm the one you ought to be talking to, instead of—"

"All right, sonny. Just a minute."

It was the shorter, bullet-head man, interrupting. The Prince turned to look down at him with a fleeting expression of surprise. But the bullet-headed man was already turning to his taller friend and putting a hand on his arm.

"Come on back, Ben," the shorter man was saying. "The kid's a little drunk, is all." He turned back to the Prince. "You shove off now," he said. "Clara's with us."

The Prince stared at him blankly. The stare was so fixed that the shorter man had started to turn away, back to his friend and the waitress, when the Prince seemed to wake.

"Just a minute—" he said, in his turn.

He reached out a hand to one of the fleshly shoulders

below the bullet head. The man turned back, knocking the hand calmly away. Then, just as calmly, he picked up the Prince's full stein of beer from the bar and threw it in the young man's face.

"Get lost," he said, unexcitedly.

The Prince stood for a second, with the beer dripping from his face. Then, without even stopping to wipe his eyes clear, he threw the beautifully trained left hand he had demonstrated at the beer garden.

But the shorter man, as Kyle had known from the first moment of seeing him, was not like the busboy the Prince had decisioned so neatly. This man was thirty pounds heavier, fifteen years more experienced, and by build and nature a natural bar fighter. He had not stood there waiting to be hit, but had already ducked and gone forward to throw his thick arms around the Prince's body. The young man's punch bounced harmlessly off the round head, and both bodies hit the floor, rolling in among the chair and table legs.

Kyle was already more than halfway to the bar and the three bartenders were already leaping the wooden hurdle that walled them off. The taller friend of the bullet-headed man, hovering over the two bodies, his eyes glittering, had his boot drawn back ready to drive the point of it into the Prince's kidneys. Kyle's forearm took him economically like a bar of iron across the tanned throat.

He stumbled backwards choking. Kyle stood still, hands open and down, glancing at the middle-aged bartender.

"All right," said the bartender. "But don't do anything more." He turned to the two younger bartenders. "All right. Haul him off!"

The pair of younger, aproned men bent down and came up with the bullet-headed man expertly handlocked between them. The man made one surging effort to break loose, and then stood still.

"Let me at him," he said.

"Not in here," said the older bartender. "Take it out-side."

Between the tables, the Prince staggered unsteadily to his feet. His face was streaming blood from a cut on his forehead, but what could be seen of it was white as a drowning man's. His eyes went to Kyle, standing beside him; and he opened his mouth—but what came out sounded like something between a sob and a curse.

"All right," said the middle-aged bartender again. "Outside, both of you. Settle it out there."

The men in the room had packed around the little space by the bar. The Prince looked about and for the first time seemed to see the human wall hemming him in. His gaze wobbled to meet Kyle's.

"Outside . . . ?" he said, chokingly.

"You aren't staying in here," said the older bartender, answering for Kyle. "I saw it. You started the whole thing. Now, settle it any way you want—but you're both going outside. Now! Get moving!"

He pushed at the Prince, but the Prince resisted, clutching at Kyle's leather jacket with one hand.

"Kyle—."

"I'm sorry, Lord," said Kyle. "I can't help. It's your fight."

"Let's get out of here," said the bullet-headed man.

The Prince stared around at them as if they were some strange set of beings he had never known to exist before.

"No . . ." he said.

He let go of Kyle's jacket. Unexpectedly, his hand darted in towards Kyle's belly holster and came out holding the slug pistol.

"Stand back!" he said, his voice high-toned. "Don't try to touch me!"

His voice broke on the last words. There was a strange sound, half grunt, half moan, from the crowd; and it swayed back from him. Manager, bartenders—watchers —all but Kyle and the bullet-headed man drew back.

"You dirty slob..." said the bullet-headed man, distinctly. "I knew you didn't have the guts."

"Shut up!" The Prince's voice was high and cracking. "Shut up! Don't any of you try to come after me!"

He began backing away toward the front door of the bar. The room watched in silence, even Kyle standing still. As he backed, the Prince's back straightened. He hefted the gun in his hand. When he reached the door he paused to wipe the blood from his eyes with his left sleeve, and his smeared face looked with a first touch of regained arrogance at them.

"Swine!" he said.

He opened the door and backed out, closing it behind him. Kyle took one step that put him facing the bullet-headed man. Their eyes met and he could see the other recognizing the fighter in him, as he had earlier recognized it in the bullet-headed man.

"Don't come after us," said Kyle.

The bullet-headed man did not answer. But no answer was needed. He stood still.

Kyle turned, ran to the door, stood on one side of it and flicked it open. Nothing happened; and he slipped through, dodging to his right at once, out of the line of any shot aimed at the opening door.

But no shot came. For a moment he was blind in the night darkness, then his eyes began to adjust. He went by sight, feel and memory toward the hitching rack. By the time he got there, he was beginning to see.

The Prince was untying the gelding and getting ready to mount.

"Lord," said Kyle.

The Prince let go of the saddle for a moment and turned to look over his shoulder at him.

"Get away from me," said the Prince, thickly.

"Lord," said Kyle, low-voiced and pleading, "you lost your head in there. Anyone might do that. But don't make it worse, now. Give me back the gun, Lord."

"Give you the gun?"

The young man stared at him—and then he laughed.

"Give *you* the gun?" he said again. "So you can let someone beat me up some more? So you can not-guard me with it?"

"Lord," said Kyle, "please. For your own sake—give me back the gun."

"Get out of here," said the Prince, thickly, turning back to mount the gelding. "Clear out before I put a slug in you."

Kyle drew a slow, sad breath. He stepped forward and tapped the Prince on the shoulder.

"Turn around, Lord," he said.

"I warned you—" shouted the Prince, turning.

He came around as Kyle stooped, and the slug pistol flashed in his hand from the light of the bar windows. Kyle, bent over, was lifting the cuff of his trouser leg and closing his fingers on the hilt of the knife in his boot sheath. He moved simply, skillfully, and with a speed nearly double that of the young man, striking up into the chest before him until the hand holding the knife jarred against the cloth covering flesh and bone.

It was a sudden, hard-driven, swiftly merciful blow. The blade struck upwards between the ribs lying open to an underhanded thrust, plunging deep into the heart. The Prince grunted with the impact driving the air from his lungs; and he was dead as Kyle caught his slumping body in leather-jacketed arms.

Kyle lifted the tall body across the saddle of the gelding and tied it there. He hunted on the dark ground for the fallen pistol and returned it to his holster. Then, he mounted the stallion and, leading the gelding with its burden, started the long ride back.

Dawn was graying the sky when at last he topped the hill overlooking the lodge where he had picked up the Prince almost twenty-four hours before. He rode down towards the courtyard gate.

A tall figure, indistinct in the pre-dawn light, was waiting inside the courtyard as Kyle came through the gate; and it came running to meet him as he rode toward it. It was the tutor, Montlaven, and he was weeping as he ran to the gelding and began to fumble at the cords that tied the body in place.

"I'm sorry . . ." Kyle heard himself saying; and was dully shocked by the deadness and remoteness of his voice. "There was no choice. You can read it all in my report tomorrow morning—"

He broke off. Another, even taller figure had appeared in the doorway of the lodge giving on the courtyard. As Kyle turned towards it, this second figure descended the few steps to the grass and came to him.

"Lord—" said Kyle. He looked down into features like those of the Prince, but older, under graying hair. This man did not weep like the tutor, but his face was set like iron.

"What happened, Kyle?" he said.

"Lord," said Kyle, "you'll have my report in the morning . . ."

"I want to know," said the tall man. Kyle's throat was dry and stiff. He swallowed but swallowing did not ease it.

"Lord," he said, "you have three other sons. One of them will make an Emperor to hold the worlds together."

"What did he do? Whom did he hurt? Tell me!" The tall man's voice cracked almost as his son's voice had cracked in the bar.

"Nothing. No one," said Kyle, stiff-throated. "He hit a boy not much older than himself. He drank too much. He may have got a girl in trouble. It was nothing he did to anyone else. It was only a fault against himself." He swallowed. "Wait until tomorrow, Lord, and read my report."

"*No!*" The tall man caught at Kyle's saddle horn with a grip that checked even the white stallion from moving.

"Your family and mine have been tied together by this for three hundred years. What was the flaw in my son to make him fail his test, back here on Earth? *I want to know!*"

Kyle's throat ached and was dry as ashes.

"Lord," he answered, "he was a coward."

The hand dropped from his saddle horn as if struck down by a sudden strengthlessness. And the Emperor of a hundred worlds fell back like a beggar, spurned in the dust.

Kyle lifted his reins and rode out of the gate, into the forest away on the hillside. The dawn was breaking.

THE ODD ONES

Said the Snorap, sitting down with a thump, "This I do not understand."

"They are young," replied the Lut, settling on his haunches beside the Snorap. "Young and stupid."

"I agree they are young," said the Snorap. "I am not yet convinced they are stupid. But how can they expect to persist?"

They were of different races these two; but equally old and experienced in the ways of the universe. Both had evolved to cope with the varying conditions to be found in space and on many different worlds, and though the end product of each race's evolution had resulted in some difference, in essence they were similar. Neither of them, for example, required an atmosphere; and they could fuel their bodies with almost any chemical compound which would give off energy in the process of being broken down into its components parts. At a pinch, they could even get by on solar radiation, though this was an unsatisfying form of diet. Fleshed and muscled to meet fantastic gravities, pressures, and temperature extremes, they were at home just about anywhere.

These were the common points. In appearance each race had settled on a form of its own. The Snorap strongly resembled a very fat and sleepy lizard about ten feet in length—a sort of unterrifying, overstuffed dragon of the kind who would prefer a pleasant nap in a soft chair to eating maidens, any day in the week. His hide was heavy and dark and ridged like armor-plating.

The Lut, on the other hand, was built more on the model of an Earthly tiger, except that he was longer—being fully as long as the Snorap—and thicker, with an almost perfectly round body, rather like a big sewer main. He was tailless, his head was big and flat of face, and he possessed an enormous jaw which could crunch boulders like hard candy. His eyes had a fierce green glint to them and he was covered with very fine, but incredibly tough, small glassy scales which would have permitted him to take an acid shower every morning and never notice it at all. But in spite of his appearance, he was just as civilized, just as intelligent, and just as much a gentleman as the Snorap; which put them both, as a matter of fact, several notches above the two humans they were watching, in all those respects.

The two aliens were philosophical engineers, an occupation it is hard to explain in human terms. It might be attempted by saying that every living being, no matter how far down the intelligence scale it may be, has a sort of inherent philosophy of survival. When the philosophies of all life forms on one world balance nicely, there is no problem. When they fall out of balance with one another, the philosophical engineer moves in, hoping to correct the situation and incidentally, gain new knowledge.

These two, the Snorap and the Lut, had discovered this world they were on to be a new one, not heretofore checked, and they had just spent the last eighty years or so in going over it. Their own ship—which was more of a space-sled than a ship, being completely open, except for an energy shield for meteor protection—was clear on the other side of the planet, they having wandered away from it completely in the past half-century of philosophy-testing. Now they had just stumbled on a pair of human immigrants. These soft little bipeds were a new experience to the Snorap and the Lut, neither of their races having encountered the type before; and they sat in the obscurity of the vegetation that hemmed the little clearing where the human ship had landed, conversing in something that was not verbal speech, sign language, nor telepathy, but a mixture of all three—and they marveled.

"I do not understand it," repeated the Snorap. "I literally fail to comprehend. They will most certainly perish."

"Undoubtedly," replied the Lut, blinking his green eyes. "They believe in their machines, I think." He indicated the domed metal hut and the low hydroponics tank-building, like the top half a loaf of bread cut off and set close to the ground, and the small ship beyond, from which the two human figures were laboring to extract the motors for their power plant. The planet was at the hot end of its summer and the temperature was above a hundred and forty degrees Fahrenheit, a fact the Snorap and the Lut did not even notice. The humans sweated in conditioned clothing and face masks.

"I give them four months," said the Lut, snapping his heavy jaws closed.

"I'm afraid so," said the Snorap. "Their home world must be badly out of balance if they take the easy way of machines instead of trying to adapt. There can be no endurance, no philosophical strength in such creatures. Their original planet must be very badly off. I wonder where it is?"

"When the machines break down, they will have to leave," said the Lut. "We will follow."

And with entirely inhuman patience, the two settled
themselves in the shadow and shelter of the vegetation
to wait.

"What are they doing now?" asked the Lut.

He had been napping for the past two weeks; leaving
the Snorap to observe. The Snorap, who slept only
during the process of regrowing a lost limb, was quite
obviously fascinated.

"They've been getting ready for winter," he answered.

"Oh, winter," said the Lut, getting up and stretching
himself like the big cat he somewhat resembled. "That's
right."

The planet they were on did not tilt on its axis, but had
an orbit that carried it quite well out from its sun during
the shorter part of the year. The result was a brief, but
very severe winter. The temperature had, in fact, fallen
a good hundred degrees since they had first sighted the
human clearing; but neither the Snorap nor the Lut paid
any attention to this, a difference so minor hardly registered on their senses.

Under a heavy, gray sky, the humans were working feverishly to bank up the living dome, the hydroponics
tank-building and the ship. They had set up the ship's
motors in a little structure off to one side, with a thick
pipe-like affair running from it to the dome and off to
the hydroponics building. The Lut cocked his eyes at the
banks of earth.

"Why?" he asked.

"Insulation, I would imagine," replied the Snorap.

"It won't work," said the Lut. "The blizzards will blow
it away."

"Not if it freezes first," said the Snorap. "They are
ingenious."

"Now I suppose they'll go inside and hole up until the
warmth comes," said the Lut. "An underground sort of
existence." He looked across the chill earth to where the
two humans were laboring with hand shovels to pile the

crumbly brown soil of the planet against the side of the motor building. "How do you tell them apart?"

"They are almost identical, aren't they?" said the Snorap. "However, if you take the trouble to figure it out, you'll notice one has a slightly greater mass than the other. I call them the Greater Biped Colonist and the Lesser Biped Colonist. Great and Less for short. That's Great going around the corner of the motor building right now. And Less is still digging."

"I wonder why there are two of them?" said the Lut thoughtfully.

"There are two of us," said the Snorap.

"Of course," said the Lut, "but there's reason for that. We're different life forms. Our senses and abilities complement each other. But these two are exact duplicates. Doesn't make sense."

"Nonsense," retorted the Snorap. "There could be all sorts of possible explanations. For instance one might be a spare."

"A spare?"

"What's so fantastic about that?" said the Snorap. "Consider how fragile they are; and how far they are, undoubtedly, from their home world."

"All the same," said the Lut, snapping his big jaws shut, "I cannot agree with such a hypothesis. It is immoral in the extreme."

"I merely offered it as one possible explanation of why there were two of them," replied the Snorap, glancing at his friend and companion. "While you've been napping I've devoted a lot of time to close observation of them. Do you know what I deduce?"

"Don't ask rhetorical questions," grumbled the Lut.

"They haven't been civilized for more than eight or ten thousand years."

"What? Ridiculous!" snorted the Lut. "Obviously they're young; but eight to ten thousand is utterly fantastic."

"Not when you stop to consider this philosophical im-

balance that has driven them to the production of
machines for any and every possible use. That in itself is
the worst possible danger signal. Undoubtedly it has
sapped all of their moral fiber."

"I might point out," said the Lut, "that, to migrate to a
world like this when you are like that, takes a certain
amount of moral fiber."

"Ah, but there we come to another question," per-
sisted the Snorap, interlocking the big, blunt claws of
his forepaws together like a pedantic old man. "What
reason can they have for coming here? They show no intellectual interest in the planet. Their senses are
obviously very limited. They seem to have no purpose in
being here other than to exist."

"Under great difficulties," said the Lut.

"Granted," answered the Snorap, "under great difficulties. Which merely confirms my belief in their un-
balance."

The Lut was by nature a contrary creature; and in
addition he was always snappish after a nap.

"And I," he retorted, "prefer to assume that there may
be some good reason which you and I are too dull-witted
to understand."

"My dear fellow—" protested the Snorap, aghast.

"Why not?" The Lut sat down rather complacently.
"Simply because you and I know and understand the
philosophies of some hundreds of thousands of different
intelligent life forms, it does not necessarily follow that
we will be able to know and understand this one. Now
does it?"

"No, but—but—" the Snorap was actually floundering
in the sea of the Lut's sophistical argument.

"You will have to admit," said the Lut, "that there is
room for reasonable doubt. Let us clarify the argument.
You say that machines have sapped their moral fiber.
Therefore, it is clear that without their machines they
will show no instinct or capability for survival. Is this
not so?"

"Exactly," said the Snorap, sternly.

"And I," went on the Lut, "disagree. I do not understand, any more than you do, what they are doing here, why there are two of them, or what their philosophy of life is. But I claim that no members of a race which has made a migration to a world where conditions are so inhospitable to them, as this one, can be lacking in moral fiber. Now, I propose that we abandon our work on this planet temporarily, and observe these two instead—until we come to a conclusion."

"And if I should turn out to be right," countered the Snorap, stiffly, "do you agree to locating their home planet and doing a thorough job of philosophical rebalancing on this race?"

"I do," replied the Lut. "But what if I should turn out to be right? What concession will you make?"

"Concession?" said the Snorap, blinking.

"Certainly," said the Lut. "It's only fair that I should stand to gain something as well. If I am right, do you agree to introducing ourselves to them; and introducing them to the fact that many other intelligent races exist, of radically different philosophies?"

"I do," said the Snorap. He turned his heavy lizard-like muzzle to the sky. "And here comes the winter to seal the bargain and administer the first environmental test to our subjects."

From the dark sky, a first few snowflakes were falling. Around the buildings, Great and Less, the two odd little bipeds, tamped their last shovels-full of earth into place; and went inside the domed living quarters. The day wore on and darkness came swiftly. The ground was covered now with snow and the air was thick with swirling flakes.

Two weeks later, by the planet's local time, the snow ceased blowing, the distant winter sun came out, and the temperature dropped sharply to about eighty degrees below zero Fahrenheit. Behind the denuded branches of the vegetation surrounding the clearing, but almost as well shielded by their twisted tangle as they had been when leaves sprouted from the black limbs, the Snorap and the Lut sat in the snow, watching the dome.

"What are they doing in there?" the Lut kept asking. The Snorap's sense of hearing was more adaptable than that of the tigerish alien; and he had been keeping his companion posted on what went on out of their sight.

"They're talking," replied the Snorap.

"Still?" said the Lut, registering astonishment. "How can a strictly verbal language contain enough concepts to permit of prolonged discussion?"

"I don't understand it myself," answered the Snorap. He had been trying to learn the biped language from what he could overhear. "A lot of their talk doesn't make sense."

"Take a rest," suggested the Lut. "Forget about them for a while and let's have a talk about relative gravitic strains in a forty-body system."

Gravitic strains were the Snorap's hobby at the present and had been for the past two hundred years. Grumbling, he allowed himself to be persuaded. He and the Lut withdrew their attention from the clearing.

Great and Less grew sleepy and went to bed.

Unnoticed by human or alien, a pipe in the hydroponics building that was too close to the deadly cold of the outer wall, burst. Liquid sprayed from it onto the floor of the building; and gradually, but with an inexorable steadiness, the level of the nutrient fluid in the planting tanks began to go down.

"I blame myself," said the Snorap, miserably. "I blame myself."

"What for?" snapped the Lut. "We aren't here to protect them. We're waiting around to see if they have any moral fiber. I should think you'd be pleased by the whole thing."

They had just been watching Great and Less as they

struggled in temperatures that were now below the
hundred-below-zero mark, to transfer what could be
salvaged from the hydroponics building to their living-
dome. Helmeted and bundled in heavy suits, they had
been losing ground in their salvage effort. Finally, in
desperation they had cut down on clothing and had sub-
stituted improvised face masks. This permitted them to
carry more on each trip, but rendered them more vulnerable to the cold. Less had collapsed twice before
giving up; and Great had finished the job alone.
Apparently he had a touch of frostbite in his lungs,
though. Less was doing what their meager stock of
medical equipment permitted, to mend the condition.

"Are you convinced now?" asked the Lut.

The Snorap shook himself back into a less emotional
frame of mind.

"No," he said. "No. They didn't sit down and fold their
hands when their machine failed, true. But we—I—am
concerned with a matter of proper racial philosophy.
What strength have these creatures aside from the
strength of their machines and their own strength to
make more? What else have they? Here we have only
one machine that has failed. What if they all failed?
What if the *idea* of machines failed? They must prove
that it is more than their pride in their ability to build
that has given them reason to think that they can suc-
cessfully dare strange worlds."

"Humph!" said the Lut.

"But a race cannot *grow* without a proper philosophy,
you know that," said the Snorap, almost pleading with
him.

"Well—" growled the Lut. "I think I'll go for a walk.
Need some exercise." He turned and loped off into the
snow. When he reached a level spot out of sight of the
Snorap he turned on the speed, and the barren winter
plains were treated to the sight of him burning up his ill-
humor at the rate of better than a hundred miles an
hour. For the Lut was in a bad temper and did not quite

like to ask himself why.

The Snorap, left alone, looked doubtfully at the buildings in the clearing.

"I don't think I'm too hard on them," he said. "I don't *think* I am—"

The short winter wore itself out; and spring came in with a rush. The snow disappeared; and the ground around the buildings became brown mud. Great, fully recovered, and Less could be seen daily extending the clearing in the direction of a stream that ran from the hills west of their buildings down onto the plain below.

"Now, what's the point of that?" the Lut asked the Snorap.

"I'm not sure," answered the Snorap. "It has something to do with the hydroponics building."

They found out a few days later, when Great and Less began to plant in the muddy soil the seeds and shoots from the vegetable things they had saved. The soil itself they treated with chemicals and other necessary ingredients from the ruined building.

"Very clever," approved the Lut. He turned to the Snorap. "How do you like that?"

"Very good," said the Snorap. "But may I point out that if they are to prove themselves by doing without their machines, they'll have to do without all of them?"

"If the crops prosper, they can extend their planting," the Lut pointed out.

"That is true."

"—And with the long summer they have on this world they can probably get in two or three more crops before the next winter."

"The possibility," said the Snorap politely, "had not entirely escaped my notice."

The year warmed gradually. For a matter of weeks there was anxiousness in human and alien hearts alike, until the first shoots of the planted things began to show their heads above the brown soil.

"Beautiful," said the Snorap, one dark night, looking over the field with the Lut. He bent down to touch the soft firmness of a soft green spear-tip. His night vision, like the Lut's, was fully equal to the task of appreciating it in full color, although the humans would hardly have been able to see their hands before their faces. "Here indeed is beauty, and strength and purpose. In alien soil it fights as valiantly toward the light of a strange sun as ever it fought for light of its native star from the womb of its natural earth."

"It and the bipeds are probably sons of the same mother world," remarked the Lut.

"Almost undoubtedly," answered the Snorap, abandoning the plant and straightening up. "But there are good and bad on all worlds, as you well know, my friend."

The ice-green eyes of the Lut softened to turquoise.

"Except on Lut," he said.

"And Snorap," added the Snorap. "And some few others where the creatures have grown older and attained wisdom . . ." His words trailed off; and they stood together in silence for a moment, each thinking of the world that was his home.

They were feeling the weight of the universe as all thinking beings do, when they open their souls to the unknown. In their hearts they stood with bowed heads before the Mother of all Mysteries, the great and final *Why?* which is never answered, but merely moved back a step by those who win knowledge. The mood lasted for perhaps the space of five minutes; and then they had come back to their ordinary selves again.

"I gave them four months," said the Lut. "That time is up already."

"And I at least," said the Snorap, "am no closer to understanding their basic philosophy, if, truly, it is not that the machine is the answer to all problems."

"They have a strong will toward survival."

"I must admit it," replied the Snorap. "But that by itself is pure animal, non-thinking animal. And while we do not condemn the animal, we do not reach out our hands to him in friendship as you want us to do with these bipeds."

"I have a hunch," said the Lut.

"Real or wishful?" asked the Snorap. They were talking about a subconscious reasoning process that both knew to exist, but both instinctively distrusted.

"I don't know," said the Lut. "But their pattern of living is at odds with the conditions here. I foresee trouble."

Summer approached. The earth dried under a swelling sun and thrust forth the fruit of the biped's planting. Great and Less harvested feverishly under a cloudless sky, while the south winds that blew steadily now, grew stronger and warmer, day by day.

Finally the crops were all in and the ground re-planted. From the wreckage of the hydroponics building they had constructed a granary; and this was stocked with all that they had brought in. With the strenghtening winds and the heat came dust storms blown up over the empty plains and carried up the slopes into the shallow hills where Great and Less had built. Behind the screen of the new-grown vegetation behind the clearing, the Lut and the Snorap watched an area in which the humans were seldom seen. Heat as fierce in its own way as the cold of the winter past, held them virtual prisoners in the dome.

"It is not good for them," the Snorap informed the Lut.

"Why?" asked the Lut. An eighty-mile-an-hour gale was sand-blasting away at his scales, without apparently affecting them, beyond polishing them up so that they shone more brightly.

"The wind. The sound of the wind," said the Snorap.

"And the fact that they cannot go outside. They are often nervous and angry at one another without reason."

"The season will pass," said the Lut indifferently. "One day the winds will start to drop; and then it will be fall."

—And, of course, eventually it happened. The bipeds came forth at last into a temperature of a little over a hundred degrees. The wind had dropped steadily for nearly a week. Now it shifted suddenly to the north —and the rains came.

Gently at first; and then with increasing violence, they poured down on the dusty earth. The ground puffed, soaked, and steamed in the short intervals of sunshine. And after several weeks the two went out to examine the fields they had planted for the second growing season.

They found a muddy desert.

With time growing short before the winter, they had to break into the stored treasure of the granary and gamble that one more crop could be gotten in before the frost came.

"Do you think they'll have time?" the Lut asked Snorap.

"I don't know," replied the Snorap. "Theoretically they should. But will these crops grow as fast as those planted at the start of the summer?"

"Hum," said the Lut, thoughtfully. "Well, they've got an even chance, anyway."

Over the months, the Lut and the Snorap had grown sensitive to small changes in the two bipeds. But they were not perceptive enough to sense that the constant struggle for existence had strained the nerves of both humans to the breaking point. Indeed, they were living together now, through this second planting, like two caged animals, avoiding each other as much as possible for fear that a chance word would bring them into open conflict. This, the two aliens did not sense. Only the physical elements got through to them.

"Their mass has gone down," the Lut remarked critically to the Snorap one afternoon in late summer as the two sat watching the bowed figures readying the clearing for the approaching winter.

"Possibly they do not have enough food," answered the Snorap.

"I don't think that's it," said the Lut thoughtfully. "More likely it is overexertion. They are exercising themselves for long hours these last few weeks."

"They talk less," said the Snorap.

"And they do not laugh," added the Lut, who had finally gotten around to mastering the biped language and was able to grasp the difference between laughter and speech. "But maybe when the crop starts to show itself above ground they will cheer up."

"The visual emergence of new life into the world always has a stimulating effect," said the Snorap. "For those capable of understanding, it connotes the ever-fresh wonder of existence renewed."

"I was thinking more," said the Lut, "of what those crops mean to them in terms of food through the winter."

"That, of course, too," agreed the Snorap, a little miffed at being interrupted in his philosophizing.

But the first of the second crop pushing its way through the brown soil did have the good effect the Lut had anticipated. The two bipeds relaxed and fell once more into an easy, happy relationship between themselves. This second harvest came more slowly, indeed, but the growth was strong and hardy; and the yield, if anything, a shade heavier.

But now, with the ripening of the planted things, the native life of the planet came to prey upon the growing fields. Where they had been during the sterile winter, and through the fresh spring and the blasting heat of mid-summer, it was impossible to tell. It seemed vaguely to Great and Less that they had noticed some native life around before, but never paid a great deal of attention to it. The smallest came first—insects of all sizes and tiny animals; and the two bipeds, working late, dug a deep moat around their planted ground and filled it with water diverted from the stream beyond the fields. After these came larger animals; and for a few nights one or the other was always on duty all night long with a missile-hurling device that the Lut and the Snorap recognized as a weapon—for the larger animals came only in the hours of darkness when the bipeds were not visible in the fields.

This last fact finally struck home to the mind of Great, and the Lut and the Snorap saw him out in the fields one day, setting posts about their perimeters. On each post was a short, thick tube and from each post to the next ran what looked like heavy black rope. That night they went forth to investigate after dark.

"Cable," said the Snorap, picking up a section of it, "designed to conduct some form of energy. Come to think of it, I did notice Less working around the power-house; but I was so interested in what Great was doing out here, I didn't pay much attention. Now I wonder—"

At that moment, at the furthest end of the field, one of the tubes atop a post seemed suddenly to explode and throw out colored balls of fire at a great rate. It was, in fact, nothing more than a self-refueling roman candle, although that particular comparison did not occur to either the Snorap nor the Lut, in spite of the fact that they understood the nature of the thing almost instantly. Hardly had the pyrotechnics of the first ceased, when the next one up the border of the field burst out and lit up its own section. The Lut and the Snorap drew back into the darkness.

"There!" said the Lut in triumph. "You see the difference? The biped does not depend on the machine. It is a tool that he uses as he sees fit."

The Snorap turned his heavy head and looked at his companion.

"Well?" demanded the Lut. "You must admit that I'm right. Listen!" The sensitive hearing of the two ranged out into the darkness behind them. "The wild ones are frightened and drawing away."

"I admit it," said the Snorap ponderously. "But all through this business you have made it a practice to misunderstand me. It is not how the biped uses the tool that is important. It is whether he can lay aside the tool. It is whether he can attempt something where the tool will not aid him. It is his ability to conceive of meeting a problem without tools. When he shows evidence of that, and only then will I be willing and proud to face him and call him brother."

The Lut's eyes glowed with green anger.

"You are being unfair," he said. "The centuries past have taught me your nature. You mistrust your own softness of emotion which kindles an instinctive fellow feeling between you and the bipeds. In your efforts to be impartial you lean over backwards and place the benefit of the doubt against them."

There was enough truth in this to make the Snorap wince inwardly.

"After all those same centuries," he retorted bitterly, "must we descend to personal criticism?"

"Truth is truth!" said the Lut. And his great jaws rang shut together. "Your conclusions are your own."

"And I stand by them!" said the Snorap.

"And I by mine!"

For a moment they stood facing each other. Then the Snorap turned away and headed back to the shelter of their accustomed vegetation. The Lut stood watching him go for a minute; then he also turned and headed out away from the clearing, to run the plains and think himself back to reasonableness.

In the dome, the two exhausted humans slept their first good night of sleep in weeks.

Two days later they began their harvesting. By the end of the first day they had gathered in the produce of perhaps a fifth of their fields. And on the second day of harvesting, Less staggered suddenly and sat down. Watching in a mutual silence from which the old friendly warmth was still missing, the Lut and the Snorap saw Great break off his own work and run to the fallen biped.

"For God's sake, don't quit now!" they heard him say.

"One day—" Less forced the words through worn lips, "let's take one day off. I can't go any more, I tell you!"

"Something may go wrong—"

Less stirred and weakly rose; then turned toward the dome.

"The weather's good. The gadget you made will keep the beasts out. There's no point to killing ourselves. I've got to get some sleep."

For a long moment Great stood watching the other biped move slowly off toward the dome. Suddenly, he cursed. He threw down the tool he was holding and followed.

The Snorap and the Lut turned to look at each other.

"They are giving up," said the Snorap. "They are leaving the machine to guard the field."

The Lut faced him.

"I don't blame them," he said.

"To me," replied the Snorap, "they are failures."

They stood looking at each other.

"I think," said the Lut at last, "I think that we no longer possess the mutual understanding necessary to our partnership."

The Snorap bowed his head.

"I cannot disagree," he said.

"Our association in the past has been a long and good one," said the Lut. "I will remember it."

"Nor will I forget," said the Snorap. He paused. "I will wait here a little while yet to see the end of this."

"I will wait also, then," the Lut answered.

They stood facing each other. Suddenly, the Snorap raised his head and tilted it, listening to the southward. After a second the Lut's head followed suit.

—"And the end comes now," said the Snorap.

There are monsters on all young worlds. The creature that came northward over the plains, migrating with the seasons from tropics to temperate zone, was a proof of that statement. Vegetarian but vast, in size and strength beyond all natural enemies of his world, his body was all head, horns and stomach, balanced on four pillar-like legs; and he followed the comfortable temperatures of cool autumns northward, gleaning the land as he went.

From far out on the dark plains, he had scented the bipeds' crops. But because he stood at that time up to his tremendous midlegs in soft second growth grass, he had not turned immediately but had continued to feed where he was. When dawn came he had slept, standing with rock-like motionlessness upon his pillar legs. But when the midday breeze brought a scent of the ripe growing stuff once more to his flaring nostrils, he had stirred out of his sleep and methodically began to feed toward the clearing.

The beast came out toward the edge of the field, moving with inexorable ponderousness. Some fifty yards away impatience seemed to break through his normal calm, and abandoning his slow feeding pace, he lifted his head and broke into a sudden trot toward the orderly rows of cultivation.

In the dome, the vibration reached through the fogs of Great's sleep, and stirred him. He moved, groaned, and opened his eyes. He lay on his back, listening, with his eyes open.

The monster had reached the edge of the field. He slowed and halted, the burnt metal smell of the roman candle pots stirred his little brain to caution. Slowly he moved up the line of cable to the nearest one and sniffed at it, the sound of his heavy snuffling audible to the

Snorap and the Lut behind their screen of branches.

Suddenly he screamed—a fantastic sound that rolled and re-echoed between open earth and empty sky. And, lifting himself on his hind legs, he pounded with both forelegs on the post, driving it into the dusty ground. And, as if this action had set loose the fires of his rage, he began almost to dance on the remains of the heavy post, mashing it to matchstick wood.

From the dome, Great and Less came tumbling. Less, half-asleep and reeling with fatigue, Great cursing and trying to arm the weapon he carried—the gun the Snorap and the Lut had seen him use when he tried to drive away the night predators on the fields. Finally dropping on one knee he fired at the monster. A puff of dust rose from behind the creature's heavy shoulder, and it turned to charge the human.

Great fired again—this time for the head. And the missile richocheted from the heavy bone plates as from a granite boulder.

The second shot had caused the monster to hesitate. Now weaving its head back and forth, it caught sight of Less and turned after this new quarry. Less took one panic-stricken glance at the towering creature; and ran blindly into the open space that separated the clearing from the fields.

Great fired twice more before the gun jammed. By that time, the monster was upon Less. But, fantastically, because of its speed and huge bulk, it overran the fleeing biped, and Less stumbled and fell without being touched.

For perhaps two seconds, while the monster was slowing and turning, Great continued to wrestle with the weapon. Then seizing it by the barrel and swinging it like a club, he ran toward the creature.

"What is this?" cried the Snorap.

The monster had wheeled now and stood confronting them both. Great passed the fallen Less, shouting, "Get to the dome. Get to the dome! I'll hold him!"

The monster screamed his fury and turned to follow; and Great ran on, a living lure to give Less time to reach safety.

"No moral fiber, eh?" snarled the Lut, leaping to his feet. He started to spring from concealment, but the Snorap gripped him.

"I will go!" cried the Snorap. "I was wrong. It's my responsibility."

"But my pleasure!" growled the Lut. "You take care of the bipeds."

He crossed the distance separating himself from the monster like one long flash of glittering light. Reaching up with a forelimb as he passed he dealt it a blow that staggered it. For a second it stood dazed; then it raised its head and screamed.

The Lut stood looking at it, from a few feet before it. His ice-green eyes caught the wild black ones of the creature and held them.

The creature roared and shifted uncertainly, feeling an uneasiness that it could not understand. For a moment it fought for decision—then it charged.

The Lut shot from the ground like a projectile and met it head to head. There was a sound like a tree breaking in a high wind. The heavy bone that had warded off the missile from Great's gun, gave like cardboard before the fantastic stuff of which the Lut's body was constructed. The creature tumbled backwards, lay for a moment, then slowly struggled to its feet and reeled off. Its huge forehead was caved in and dark fluid dripped from it and dropped on the ground as it went.

"It will live," said the Lut, looking after it.

He turned to look at the bipeds. The Snorap had come up and Great, with Less shoved behind him, was frantically trying to unjam the gun and shoot at them.

"Put that thing away," said the Lut. "We're friends."

The man froze, his hands on the breech of his weapon. The Lut was forming the human words by swallowing air and forcing it back through his capable throat muscles; and the result was a deep, growling bass that did not at first identify itself with rational speech.

"I said we're friends," said the Lut. "We've been watching you for a year now. Besides, your weapon there can't hurt us." He turned to the Snorap. "Say something to reassure them that you're not a wild animal."

"I have been guilty of badly misjudging you," said the Snorap humbly to the humans. He was talking by the same process and the humans looked from him to the Lut as if they suspected the latter of being a ventriloquist.

"Who—who are you?" asked Great at last.

"We," said the Lut, "are individual members of two old and respected races, from elsewhere than this system. You might refer to me as a Lut and to my friend as a Snorap. And you call yourselves—?"

The man laughed a little wildly. Exchanging introductions with two nightmare beings after a hair-breadth escape from death, has a tendency to make anyone a bit hysterical.

"We're humans," he said. "I'm Jos Parner. This is my wife, Gela."

"What is a wife?" asked the Lut.

"Why—a wife—" answered the human in astonishment. "I'm a man, she's a woman. Male—female—"

"You mean," demanded the Lut, "that your race is bisexual?"

"Of course," answered the man. "Isn't everything? Aren't you—" He broke off and stared at them. "You mean it's not usual?"

The Lut turned his head slowly and looked at the Snorap, who sat down in the dust.

"I am an old fool," said the Snorap, penitently. "I am a senile old idiot who ought to have my brains examined. Sitting here engaged in high speculation about the source of their racial philosophy and questioning their moral basis, when all the time they were loving each other and complementing each other's character-traits right under my very nose. What else would be the basis of colonization in a bisexual race but the family unit? Where but in the urge to build a home would their drive lie? What would be their courage, but love transformed?" He sat with head hanging. "I am an old fool."

The Lut crossed over to him and hung his heavy head on the Snorap's shoulder.

"Friend of many years past and yet to come," he said. "We are old fools together."

IN THE BONE

Personally, his name was Harry Brennan.

Officially, he was the *John Paul Jones*, which consisted of four billion dollars worth of irresistible equipment—the latest and best of human science—designed to spread its four-thousand components out through some fifteen cubic meters of space under ordinary conditions—designed also to stretch across light-years under extraordinary conditions (such as sending an emergency messenger-component home) or to clump into a single magnetic unit in order to shift through space and explore the galaxy. Both officially and personally—but most of all personally—he represents a case in point.

The case is one having to do with the relative importance of the made thing and its maker.

It was, as we know, the armored horseman who dominated the early wars of the Middle Ages in Europe. But, knowing this, it is still wise to remember that it was not the iron shell that made the combination of man and metal terrible to the enemy—but rather the essentially naked man inside the shell. Later, French knights depending on their armor went down before the cloth-yard shafts of unarmored footmen with bows, at Crecy and Poitiers.

And what holds true for armor holds true for the latest developments of our science as well. It is not the spacecraft or the laser on which we will find ourselves depending when a time of ultimate decision comes, but the naked men within and behind these things. When that time comes, those who rank the made thing before its maker will die as the French knights died at Crecy and Poitiers. This is a law of nature as wide as the universe, which Harry Brennan, totally unsuspecting, was to discover once more for us, in his personal capacity.

Personally, he was in his mid-twenties, unremarkable except for two years of special training with the *John Paul Jones* and his superb physical condition. He was five-eleven, a hundred seventy-two pounds, with a round, cheerful face under his brown crew-cut hair. I was Public Relations Director of the Project that sent him out; and I was there with the rest to slap him on the back the day he left.

"Don't get lost, now," said someone. Harry grinned.

"The way you guys built this thing," he answered, "if I got lost the galaxy would just have to shift itself around to get me back on plot."

There was an unconscious arrogance hidden in that answer, but no one marked it at the time. It was not the hour of suspicions.

He climbed into the twelve-foot-tall control-suit that with his separate living tank were the main components of the *John Paul Jones* and took off. Up in orbit, he spent some thirty-two hours testing to make sure all the several thousand other component parts were responding properly. Then he left the solar system.

He clumped together his components, made his first

shift to orbit Procyon—and from there commenced his explorations of the stars. In the next nine weeks, he accumulated literally amazing amounts of new information about the nearby stars and their solar systems. And—this is an even better index of his success—located four new worlds on which men could step with never a spacesuit or even a water canteen to sustain them. Worlds so like Earth in gravity, atmosphere and even flora and fauna, that they could be colonized tomorrow.

Those were his first four worlds. On the fifth he encountered his fate—a fate for which he was unconsciously ripe.

The fact was the medical men and psychologists had overlooked a factor—a factor having to do with the effect of Harry's official *John Paul Jones* self upon his entirely human personal self. And over nine weeks this effect changed Harry without his ever having suspected it.

You see, nothing seemed barred to him. He could cross light-years by touching a few buttons. He could send a sensing element into the core of the hottest star, into the most poisonous planetary atmospheres or crushing gravities, to look around as if he were down there in person. From orbit, he could crack open a mountain, burn off a forest or vaporize a section of icecap in search of information just by tapping the energy of a nearby sun. And so, subtly, the unconscious arrogance born during two years of training, that should have been noted in him at take-off from Earth, emerged and took him over—until he felt that there was nothing he could not do; that all things must give way to him; that he was, in effect, master of the universe.

The day may come when a man like Harry Brennan may hold such a belief and be justified. But not yet. On the fifth Earthlike world he discovered—World 1242 in his records—Harry encountered the proof that his belief was unjustified.

The world was one which, from orbit, seemed to be the best of all the planets which he had discovered were suitable for human settlement; and he was about to go down to its surface personally in the control-suit, when his instruments picked out something already down there.

It was a squat, metallic pyramid about the size of a four-plex apartment building; and it was radiating on a number of interesting frequencies. Around its base there was mechanical movement and an area of cleared ground. Further out, in the native forest, were treaded vehicles taking samples of the soil, rock and vegetation.

Harry had been trained for all conceivable situations, including an encounter with other intelligent, space-going life. Automatically, he struck a specific button, and immediately a small torpedo-shape leaped away to shift through alternate space and back to Earth with the information so far obtained. And a pale, thin beam reached up and out from the pyramid below. Harry's emergency messenger component ceased to exist.

Shaken, but not yet really worried, Harry struck back instantly with all the power his official self could draw from the GO-type sun, nearby.

The power was funneled by some action below, directly into the pyramid itself; and it vanished there as indifferently as the single glance of a sunbeam upon a leaf.

Harry's mind woke suddenly to some understanding of what he had encountered. He reached for the controls to send the *John Paul Jones* shifting into the alternate universe and away.

His hands never touched the controls. From the pyramid below, a blue lance of light reached up to paralyze him, select the control-suit from among the other components and send it tumbling to the planetary surface below like a swatted insect.

But the suit had been designed to protect its occupant, whether he himself was operative or not. At fifteen hundred feet, the drag chute broke free, looking like a silver cloth candle-snuffer in the sunlight; and at five hundred feet the retro-rockets cut in. The suit tumbled to earth among some trees two kilometers from the pyramid, with Harry inside bruised, but released from his paralysis.

From the pyramid, a jagged arm of something like white lightning lashed the ground as far as the suit, and the suit's outer surface glowed cherry-red. Inside, the temperature suddenly shot up fifty degrees; instinctively Harry hit the panic button available to him inside the suit.

The suit split down the center like an overcooked frankfurter and spat Harry out; he rolled among the brush and fernlike ground cover, six or seven meters from the suit.

From the distant pyramid, the lightning lashed the suit, breaking it up. The headpiece rolled drunkenly aside, turning the dark gape of its interior toward Harry like the hollow of an empty skull. In the dimness of that hollow Harry saw the twinkle of his control buttons.

The lightning vanished. A yellow lightness filled the air about Harry and the dismembered suit. There was a strange quivering to the yellowness; and Harry half-smelled, half-tasted the sudden, flatbite of ozone. In the headpiece a button clicked without being touched; and the suit speaker, still radio-connected with the recording tank in orbit, spoke aloud in Harry's voice.

"Orbit . . ." it said. ". . . into . . . going . . ."

These were, in reverse order, the last three words Harry had recorded before sighting the pyramid. Now, swiftly gaining speed, the speaker began to recite backwards, word for word, everything Harry had said into it in nine weeks. Faster it went, and faster until it mounted to a chatter, a gabble, and finally a whine pushing against the upper limits of Harry's auditory register.

Suddenly, it stopped.

The little clearing about Harry was full of silence. Only the odd and distant creaking of something that might have been a rubbing branch or an alien insect, came to Harry's ears. Then the speaker spoke once more.

"Animal . . ." it said flatly in Harry's calm, recorded voice and went on to pick further words from the recordings, ". . . best. You . . . were an animal . . . wrapped in . . . made clothing. I have stripped you back to . . . animal again. Live, beast . . ."

Then the yellowness went out of the air and the taste of ozone with it. The headpiece of the dismembered suit grinned, empty as old bones in the sunlight. Harry scrambled to his feet and ran wildly away through the trees and brush. He ran in panic and utter fear, his lungs gasping, his feet pounding the alien earth, until the earth, the trees, the sky itself swam about him from exhaustion; and he fell tumbling to earth and away into the dark haven of unconsciousness.

When he woke, it was night, and he could not quite remember where he was or why. His thoughts seemed numb and unimportant. But he was cold, so he blundered about until he found the standing half-trunk of a lightning-blasted tree and crept into the burned hollow of its interior, raking frill-edged, alien leaves about him out of some half-forgotten instinct, until his own body-warmth in the leaves formed a cocoon of comfort about him; and he slept.

From then on began a period in which nothing was very clear. It was as if his mind had huddled itself away somehow like a wounded animal and refused to think. There was no past or future, only the endless now. If now was warm, it had always been warm; if dark—it had always been dark. He learned to smell water from a distance and go to it when he was thirsty. He put small things in his mouth to taste them. If they tasted good he ate them. If he got sick afterwards, he did not eat them again.

Gradually, blindly, the world about him began to take on a certain odor. He came to know where there were plants with portions he could eat, where there were small creatures he could catch and pull apart and eat and where there was water.

He did not know how lucky he was in the sheer chance of finding flora and fauna on an alien world that was edible—let alone nourishing. He did not realize that he had come down on a plateau in the tropical highlands, with little variation in day and night temperature and no large native predators which might have attacked him.

None of this, he knew. Nor would it have made any difference to him if he had, for the intellectual center of his brain had gone on vacation, so to speak, and refused to be called back. He was, in fact, a victim of severe psychological shock. The shock of someone who had come to feel himself absolute master of a universe and who then, in a few short seconds, had been cast down from that high estate by something or someone inconceivably greater, into the state of a beast of the field.

But still, he could not be a true beast of the field, in spite of the fact his intellectual processes had momentarily abdicated. His perceptive abilities still worked. His eyes could not help noting, even if incuriously, the progressive drying of the vegetation, the day-by-day shifting in the points of setting and rising of the sun. Slowly, instinctively, the eternal moment that held him stretched and lengthened until he began to perceive divisions within it—a difference between *now* and *was*, between *now* and *will be*.

The day came at last when he saw himself.

A hundred times he had crouched by the water to drink and, lowering his lips to its surface, seen color and shape rising to meet him. The hundredth and something time, he checked, a few inches above the liquid plane, staring at what he saw.

For several long seconds it made no sense to him. Then, at first slowly, then with a rush like pain flooding back on someone rousing from the anesthesia of unconsciousness, he recognized what he saw.

Those were eyes at which he stared, sunken and dark-circled under a dirty tangle of hair. That was a nose jutting between gaunt and sunken cheeks above a mouth, and there was a chin naked only because once an ultrafine laser had burned out the thousand and one roots of the beard that grew on it. That was a man he saw—*himself*.

He jerked back like someone who has come face-to-face with the devil. But he returned eventually, because he was thirsty, to drink and see himself again. And so, gradually, he got used to the sight of himself.

So it was that memory started to return to him. But it did not come back quickly or all at once. It returned instead by jerks and sudden, partial revelations—until finally the whole memory of what had happened was back in his conscious mind again.

But he was really not a man again.

He was still essentially what the operator of the pyramid had broken him down into. He was still an animal. Only the memory and imaginings of a man had returned to live like a prisoner in a body that went on reacting and surviving in the bestial way it had come to regard as natural.

But his animal peace was broken. For his imprisoned mind worked now. With the control-suit broken up—he had returned to the spot of its destruction many times, to gaze beastlike at the rusting parts—his mind knew he was a prisoner, alone on this alien world until he died. To know that was not so bad, but remembering this much meant remembering also the existence of the someone or something that made him a prisoner here.

The whoever it was who was in the pyramid.

That the pyramid might have been an automated,

mechanical device never entered his mind for a moment. There had been a personal, directed, living viciousness behind the announcement that had condemned him to live as a beast. No, in that blank-walled, metallic structure, whose treaded mechanical servants still prospected through the woods, there was something alive— something that could treat the awesome power of a solar tap as a human treated the attack of a mosquito— but something *living*. Some being. Some Other, who lived in the pyramid, moving, breathing, eating and gloating—or worse yet, entirely forgetful of what he had done to Harry Brennan.

And now that he knew that the Other was there, Harry began to dream of him nightly. At first, in his dreams, Harry whimpered with fear each time the dark shape he pursued seemed about to turn and show its face. But slowly, hatred came to grow inside and then outside his fear. Unbearable that Harry should never know the face of his destroyer. Lying curled in his nest of leaves under the moonless, star-brilliant sky, he snarled, thinking of his deprivation.

Then hate came to strengthen him in the daylight also. From the beginning he had avoided the pyramid, as a wild coyote avoids the farmyard where he was once shot by the farmer. But now, day after day, Harry circled closer to the alien shape. From the beginning he had run and hidden from the treaded prospecting machines. But now, slowly, he grew bolder, standing close enough at last to touch them as they passed. And he found that they paid no attention to him. No attention at all.

He came to ignore them in turn, and day by day he ventured closer to the pyramid. Until the morning came when he lay, silently snarling, behind a bush, looking out across the tread-trampled space that separated him from the nearest copper-colored face of the pyramid.

The space was roughly circular, thirty meters across, broken only by a small stream which had been diverted to loop inwards toward the pyramid before returning to its original channel. In the bight of the loop a machine like a stork straddled the artificial four-foot-wide channel, dipping a pair of long necks with tentacle-clustered heads into the water at intervals. Sometimes Harry could see nothing in the tentacles when they came up. Occasionally they carried some small water creature which they deposited in a tank.

Making a perfect circle about the tramped area, so that the storklike machine was guarded within them, was an open fence of slender wands set upright in the earth, far enough apart for any of the machines that came and went to the forest to pass between any two of them. There seemed to be nothing connecting the wands, and nothing happened to the prospecting machines as they passed through—but the very purposelessness of the wands filled Harry with uneasiness.

It was not until after several days of watching that he had a chance to see a small native animal, frightened by something in the woods behind it, attempt to bolt across a corner of the clearing.

As it passed between two of the wands there was a waveriness in the air between them. The small animal leaped high, came down and lay still. It did not move after that, and later in the day, Harry saw the indifferent treads of one of the prospecting machines bury it in the trampled earth in passing.

That evening, Harry brought several captive, small animals bound with grass up to the wand line and thrust them through, one by one at different spots. All died.

The next night he tried pushing a captive through a small trench scooped out so that the creature passed the killing line below ground level. But this one died also. For several days he was baffled. Then he tried running behind a slow-moving machine as it returned and tying a small animal to it with grass.

For a moment as the front of the machine passed

through, he thought the little animal would live. But then, as the back of the machine passed the line, it, too, died.

Snarling, Harry paced around outside the circle in the brush until the sun set and stars filled the moonless sky.

In the days that followed, he probed every gap in the wand-fence, but found no safe way through it. Finally, he came to concentrate on the two points at which the diverted stream entered and left the circle to flow beneath the storklike machine.

He studied this without really knowing what he was seeking. He did not even put his studying into words. Vaguely, he knew that the water went in and the water came out again unchanged; and he also wished to enter and come out safely. Then, one day, studying the stream and the machine, he noticed that a small creature plucked from the water by the storklike neck's mass of tentacles was still wriggling.

That evening, at twilight, while there was still light to see, he waded up the two-foot depth of the stream to the point where the killing line cut across its watery surface and pushed some more of his little animals toward the line underwater.

Two of the three surfaced immediately, twitched and floated on limply, to be plucked from the water and cast aside on the ground by the storklike machine. But the third swam on several strokes before surfacing and came up living to scramble ashore, race for the forest and be killed by wands further around the circle.

Harry investigated the channel below the killing line. There was water there up to his mid-thigh, plenty to cover him completely. He crouched down in the water and took a deep breath.

Ducking below the surface, he pulled himself along with his fingertips, holding himself close to the bottom. He moved in as far as the tentacled ends. These grabbed at him, but could not reach far enough back to touch him. He saw that they came within a few inches of the gravel bottom.

He began to need air. He backed carefully out and rose above the water, gasping. After a while his hard breathing stopped, and he sat staring at the water for a long while. When it was dark, he left.

The next day he came and crept underwater to the grabbing area of the storklike machine again. He scooped out several handfuls of the gravel from under the place where the arms grabbed, before he felt a desperate need for air and had to withdraw. But that day began his labors.

Four days later the bottom under the grasping tentacles was scooped out to an additional two feet of depth. And the fifth twilight after that, he pulled himself, dripping and triumphant, up out of the bend of the diverted stream inside the circle of the killing wands.

He rested and then went to the pyramid, approaching it cautiously and sidelong like a suspicious animal. There was a door in the side he approached through which he had seen the prospecting machines trundle in and out. In the dimness he could not see it; and when he touched the metallic side of the structure, his fingers, grimed and toughened from scrabbling in the dirt, told him little. But his nose, beast-sensitive now, located and traced the outline of the almost invisible crack around the door panel by its reek of earth and lubricant.

He settled down to wait. An hour later, one of the machines came back. He jumped up, ready to follow it in; but the door opened just before it and closed the minute it was inside—nor was there any room to squeeze in beside it. He hunkered down, disappointed, snarling a little to himself.

He stayed until dawn and watched several more machines enter and leave. But there was no room to squeeze inside, even with the smallest of them.

During the next week or so he watched the machines enter and leave nightly. He tied one of his small animals to an entering machine and saw it pass through the entrance alive and scamper out again with the next machine that left. And every night his rage increased. Then, wordlessly, one daytime after he had seen a machine deep in the woods lurch and tilt as its tread passed over a rock, inspiration took him.

That night he carried through the water with him several cantaloupe-sized stones. When the first machine came back to the pyramid, in the moment in which the door opened before it, he pushed one of the rocks before the right-hand tread. The machine, unable to stop, mounted the rock with its right tread, tilted to the left and struck against that side of the entrance.

It checked, backed off and put out an arm with the grasping end to remove the rock. Then it entered the opening. But Harry was already before it, having slipped through while the door was still up and the machine, busy pulling the stone aside.

He plunged into a corridor of darkness, full of clankings and smells. A little light from the opening behind him showed him a further, larger chamber where other machines stood parked. He ran toward them.

Long before he reached them, the door closed behind him, and he was in pitch darkness. But the clanking of the incoming machine was close behind him, and the adrenalinized memory of a wild beast did not fail him. He ran, hands outstretched, directly into the side of the parked machine at which he had aimed and clambered up on it. The machine entering behind him clanked harmlessly past him and stopped moving.

He climbed cautiously down in the impenetrable darkness. He could see nothing; but the new, animal sensitivity of his nose offered a substitute for vision. He moved like a hunting dog around the chamber, sniffing and touching; and slowly a clear picture of it and its treaded occupants built up in his mind.

He was still at this when suddenly a door he had not seen opened almost in his face. He had just time to leap backwards as a smaller machine with a boxlike body and a number of upward-thrusting arms entered, trundled to the machine that had just come back and began to relieve the prospecting machine of its sample box, replacing it with the one it carried itself.

This much, in the dim light from the open door, Harry was able to see. But then, the small machine turned back toward the doorway; and Harry, waking to his opportunity, ducked through ahead of it.

He found himself in a corridor dimly lit by a luminescent strip down the center of the ceiling. The corridor was wide enough for the box-collecting machine to pass him; and, in fact, it rolled out around him as he shrank back against one metal wall. It went on down the corridor, and he followed it into a larger room with a number of machines, some mobile, some not, under a ceiling lit as the corridor had been with a crossing of translucent strip.

In this area all the machines avoided each other—and him. They were busy with each other and at other incomprehensible duties. Hunched and tense, hair erect on the back of his neck and nostrils spread wide, Harry moved through them to explore other rooms and corridors that opened off this one. It took him some little time; but he discovered that they were all on a level, and there was nothing but machines in any of them. He found two more doors with shallow steps leading up to them, but these would not open for him; and though he watched by one for some time, no machine went up the steps and through it.

He began to be conscious of thirst and hunger. He made his way back to the door leading to the chamber where the prospecting machines were parked. To his surprise, it opened as he approached it. He slipped through into darkness.

Immediately, the door closed behind him; and sudden panic grabbed him, when he found he could not open it from this side. Then, self-possession returned to him.

By touch, smell and memory, he made his way among the parked machines and down the corridor to the outside door. To his gratification, this also opened when he came close. He slipped through into cool, fresh outer air and a sky already graying with dawn. A few moments later, wet but free, he was back in the woods again.

From then on, each night he returned. He found it was not necessary to do more than put any sizable object before the returning machine. It would stop to clear the path, and he could enter ahead of it. Then, shortly after he was inside, a box-collecting machine would open the inner door.

Gradually, his fear of the machines faded. He came to hold them in a certain contempt. They always did the same thing in the same situation, and it was easy to trick or out-maneuver them.

But the two inner doors of the machine area with the steps would not open to him; and he knew the upper parts of the pyramid were still unexplored by him. He sniffed at the cracks of these doors, and a scent came through—not of lubricating medium and metal alone, but of a different musky odor that raised the hairs on the back of his neck again. He snarled at the doors.

He went back to exploring minutely the machine level. The sample boxes from the prospecting machines, he found, were put on conveyorbelt-like strips that floated up on thin air through openings in the ceiling—but the openings were too small for him to pass through. But he discovered something else. One day he came upon one of the machines taking a grille off the face of one of the immobile devices. It carried the grille away, and he explored the opening that had been revealed. It was the entrance to a tunnel or duct leading upward; and it was large enough to let him enter it. Air blew silently from it;

and the air was heavy with the musky odor he had smelled around the doors that did not open.

The duct tempted him, but fear held him back. The machine came back and replaced the grille; and he noticed that it fitted into place with a little pressure from the outside, top and bottom. After the machine had left he pressed, and the grille fell out into his hands.

After a long wait, he ventured timorously into the tube—but a sudden sound like heavy breathing mixed with a wave of a strong, musky odor came at him. He backed out in panic, fled the pyramid and did not come back for two days.

When he came back, the grille was again neatly in place. He removed it and sat a long time getting his courage up. Finally, he put the grille up high out of reach of the machine which had originally removed it and crawled into the duct.

He crept up the tube at an angle into darkness. His eyes were useless, but the musky odor came strongly at him. Soon, he heard sounds.

There was an occasional ticking, then a thumping or shuffling sound. Finally, after he had crawled a long way up through the tube, there was a sound like a heavy puffing or hoarse breathing. It was the sound that had accompanied the strengthening of the musky odor once before; and this time the scent came strong again.

He lay, almost paralyzed with terror in the tube, as the odor grew in his nostrils. He could not move until sound and scent had retreated. As soon as they had, he wormed his way backward down to the lower level and freedom, replaced the grille and fled for the outside air, once again.

But once more, in time, he came back. Eventually he returned to explore the whole network of tubes to which the one he had entered connected. Many of the branching tubes were too small for him to enter, and the biggest tube he could find led to another grille from which the musky-smelling air was blasted with force.

Clearly it was the prime mover for the circulation of air through the exhaust half of the pyramid's ventilating system. Harry did not reason it out to himself in those intellectual terms, but he grasped the concept wordlessly and went back to exploring those smaller tubes that he could crawl into.

These, he found, terminated in grilles set in their floors through which he could look down and catch a glimpse of some chamber or other. What he saw was mainly incomprehensible. There were a number of corridors, a number of what could be rooms containing fixed or movable objects of various sizes and shapes. Some of them could be the equivalent of chairs or beds—but if so, they were scaled for a being plainly larger than himself. The lighting was invariably the low-key illumination he had encountered in the lower, machine level of the pyramid, supplied by the single translucent strip running across the ceiling.

Occasionally, from one grille or another, he heard in the distance the heavy sound of breathing, among other sounds, and smelled more strongly the musky odor. But for more than a week of surreptitious visits to the pyramid, he watched through various grilles without seeing anything living.

However, a day finally came when he was crouched, staring down into a circular room containing what might be a bed shape, several chair shapes and a number of other fixed shapes with variously spaced and depthed indentations in their surfaces. In a far edge of the circular room was a narrow alcove, the walls of which were filled with ranked indentations, among which several lights of different colors winked and glowed.

Suddenly, the dim illumination of the room began to brighten. The illumination increased rapidly, so that Harry cringed back from the grille, lifting a palm to protect his dimness-accustomed eyes. At the same moment, he heard approaching the sound of heavy

breathing and sniffed a sudden increase in the musky
odor.

He froze. Motionless above the grille, he stopped even
his breathing. He would have stopped his heart if he
could, but it raced, shaking his whole body and sounding its rapid beat in his ears until he felt the noise of it
must be booming through the pyramid like a drum. But
there was no sign from below that this was so.

Then, sliding into sight below him, came a massive
figure on a small platform that seemed to drift without
support into the room.

The aperture of the grille was small. Harry's view-
point was cramped and limited, looking down directly
from overhead. He found himself looking down onto
thick, hairless brown-skinned shoulders, a thick neck
with the skin creased at the back and a forward sloping,
hairless brown head, egg-shaped in outline from above,
with the point forward.

Foreshortened below the head and shoulders was a
bulging chinline with something like a tusk showing; it
had a squat, heavy, hairless, brown body and thick short
forearms with stubby claws at the end of four-fingered
hands. There was something walruslike about the tusks
and the hunching; and the musky odor rose sickeningly
into Harry's human nostrils.

The platform slid level with the alcove, which was too
narrow for it to enter. Breathing hoarsely, the heavy
figure on it heaved itself suddenly off the platform into
the alcove, and the stubby hands moved over the pattern
of indentations. Then, it turned and heaved itself out of
the alcove, onto the flat, bed surface adjoining. Just as
Harry's gaze began to get a full-length picture of it, the
illumination below went out.

Harry was left, staring dazzled into darkness, while
the heavy breathing and the sound of the figure read-
justing itself on the bed surface came up to his ears.
After a while, there was no noise but the breathing. But
Harry did not dare move. For a long time he held his

cramped posture, hardly breathing himself. Finally, cautiously, inch-by-inch, he retreated down the tube, which was too small to let him turn around. When he reached the larger tubes, he fled for the outside and the safety of the forest.

The next day, he did not go near the pyramid. Or the next. Every time he thought of the heavy, brown figure entering the room below the grille, he became soaked with the clammy sweat of a deep, emotional terror. He could understand how the Other had not heard him or seen him up behind the grille. But he could not understand how the alien had not *smelled* him.

Slowly, however, he came to accept the fact that the Other had not. Possibly the Other did not have a sense of smell. Possibly . . . there was no end to the possibilities. The fact was that the Other had not smelled Harry—or heard him—or seen him. Harry was like a rat in the walls—unknown because he was unsuspected.

At the end of the week, Harry was once more prowling around back by the pyramid. He had not intended to come back, but his hatred drew him like the need of a drug addict for the drug of his addiction. He had to see the Other again, to feed his hate more surely. He had to look at the Other, while hating the alien, and feel the wild black current of his emotions running toward the brown and hairless shape. At night, buried in his nest of leaves, Harry tossed and snarled in his sleep, dreaming of the small stream backing up to flood the interior of the pyramid, and the Other drowning—of lightning striking the pyramid and fire racing through it—of the Other burning. His dreams became so full of rage and so terrible that he woke, twisting and with the few rags of clothing that still managed to cling unnoticed to him, soaked with sweat.

In the end, he went back into the pyramid.

Daily he went back. And gradually, it came to the point where he was no longer fearful of seeing the Other.

Instead, he could barely endure the search and the waiting at the grilles until the Other came into sight. Meanwhile, outside the pyramid in the forest, the frill-edged leaves began to dry and wither and drop. The little stream sank in its bed—only a few inches, but enough so that Harry had to dig out the bottom of the streambed under the killing barrier in order to pass safely underwater into the pyramid area.

One day he noticed that there were hardly any of the treaded machines out taking samples in the woods any more.

He was on his way to the pyramid through the woods, when the realization struck him. He stopped dead, freezing in midstride like a hunting dog. Immediately, there flooded into his mind the memory of how the parking chamber for the treaded machines, inside the house of the pyramid, had been full of unmoving vehicles during his last few visits.

Immediately, also, he realized the significance of the drying leaves, the dropping of the water level of the stream. And something with the urgency of a great gong began to ring and ring inside him like the pealing of an alarm over a drowning city.

Time had been, when there had been no pyramid here. Time was now, with the year fading and the work of the collecting machines almost done. Time would be, when the pyramid might leave.

Taking with it the Other.

He began to run, instinctively, toward the pyramid. But, when he came within sight of it, he stopped. For a moment he was torn with indecision, an emotional maelstrom of fear and hatred all whirling together. Then, he went on.

He emerged a moment later, dripping, a fist-sized rock in each hand, to stand before the closed door that gave the machines entrance to the pyramid. He stood staring at it, in broad daylight, but his head now was full of madness. Fury seethed in him, but there was no machine to open the door for him. It was then that the fury and madness in him might have driven him to pound wildly on the door with his stones or to wrench off one of the necks of the storklike machine at the stream and try to pry the door open. Any of these insane things he might have done and so have attracted discovery and the awesome power of the machinery and killing weapons at the command of the Other. Any such thing he might have done if he was simply a man out of his head with rage—but he was no longer a man.

He was what the Other had made him, an animal, although with a man locked inside him. And like an animal, he did not rave or rant, any more than does the cat at the mousehole, or the wolf waiting for the shepherd to turn in the night. Instead, without further question, the human beast that had been Harry Brennan —that still called himself Harry Brennan, in a little, locked-away, back corner of its mind—dropped on his haunches beside the door and hunkered there, panting lightly in the sunlight and waiting.

Four hours later, as the sun was dropping close to the treetops, a single machine came trundling out of the woods. Harry tricked it with one of his stones and, still carrying the other, ran into the pyramid.

He waited patiently for the small collecting machine to come and empty out the machine returned from outside, then dodged ahead of it, when it came, into the interior, lower level of the pyramid. He made his way calmly to the grille that gave him entrance to the ventilating system, took out the grille and entered the tube. Once in the system, he crawled through the maze of ductwork, until he came at last to the grille overlooking the room with the alcove and the rows of indentations on the alcove walls.

When he looked down through the grille, it was completely dark below. He could hear the hoarse breathing and smell the musky odor of the Other, resting or perhaps asleep, on the bed surface. Harry lay there for a number of slow minutes, smelling and listening. Then he lifted the second rock and banged with it upon the grille.

For a second there was nothing but the echoing clang of the beaten metal in the darkness. Then the room suddenly blazed with light, and Harry, blinking his blinded eyes against the glare, finally made out the figure of the Other rising upright upon the bed surface. Great, round, yellow eyes in a puglike face with a thick upper lip wrinkled over two tusks stared up through the grille at Harry.

The lip lifted, and a bubbling roar burst from the heavy fat-looking shape of the Other. He heaved his round body off the bed surface and rolled, waddling across the floor to just below the grille.

Reaching up with one blunt-clawed hand, he touched the grille, and it fell to the floor at his feet. Left unguarded in the darkness of the ductwork, Harry shrank back. But the Other straightened up to his full near six-and-a-half feet of height and reached up into the ductwork. His blunt clawed hand fastened on Harry and jerked. Off balance, Harry came tumbling to the floor of the chamber.

A completely human man probably would have stiffened up and broken both arms, if not his neck, in such a fall. Harry, animal-like, attempted to cling to the shape of the Other as he fell, and so broke the impact of his landing. On the floor, he let go of the Other and huddled away from the heavy shape, whimpering.

The Other looked down, and his round, yellow eyes focused on the stone Harry had clung to even through his fall. The Other reached down and grasped it, and Harry gave it up like a child releasing something he has been told many times not to handle. The Other made another, lower-toned, bubbling roar deep in his chest, examining the rock. Then he laid it carefully aside on a low table surface and turned back to stare down at Harry.

Harry cringed away from the alien stare and huddled into himself, as the blunt fingers reached down to feel some of the rags of a shirt that still clung about his shoulders.

The Other rumbled interrogatively at Harry. Harry hid his head. When he looked up again, the Other had moved over to a wall at the right of the alcove and was feeling about in some indentations there. He bubbled at the wall, and a second later Harry's voice sounded eerily in the room.

"You . . . You are . . . the one I . . . made a beast . . ."

Harry whimpered, hiding his head again.

"You can't . . ." said Harry's voice, ". . . even speak now. Is . . . that so . . ."

Harry ventured to peek upward out of his folded arms, but ducked his head again at the sight of the cold, yellow eyes staring down at him.

". . . I thought . . . you would be . . . dead by now," said the disembodied voice of Harry, hanging in the air of the chamber. " . . . Amazing . . . survival completely without . . . equipment. Must keep you now . . ." The eyes, yellow as topaz, considered Harry, huddled abjectly on the floor. ". . . cage . . . collector's item . . ."

The alien revolved back to the indentations of the wall a little way from the alcove. The broad, fleshy back turned contemptuously on Harry, who stared up at it.

The pitiful expression of fear on Harry's face faded suddenly into a soundless snarl. Silently, he uncoiled, snatched up the rock the Other had so easily taken from him, and sprang with it onto the broad back.

As he caught and clung there, one arm wrapped around a thick neck, the stone striking down on the hairless skull, his silent snarl burst out at last into the sound of a scream of triumph.

The Other screamed too—a bubbling roar—as he clumsily turned, trying to reach around himself with his thick short arms and pluck Harry loose. His claws raked Harry's throat-encircling arm, and blood streamed from

the arm; but it might have been so much stage make-up
for the effect it had in loosening Harry's hold. Screaming, Harry continued to pound crushingly on the Other's
skull. With a furious spasm, the alien tore Harry loose,
and they both fell on the floor.

The Other was first up; and for a second he loomed
like a giant over Harry, as Harry was scrambling to his
own feet and retrieving the fallen rock. But instead of
attacking, the Other flung away, lunging for the alcove
and the control indentations there.

Harry reached the alcove entrance before him. The
alien dodged away from the striking rock. Roaring and
bubbling, he fled waddling from his human pursuer,
trying to circle around the room and get back to the
alcove. Half a head taller than Harry and twice Harry's
weight, he was refusing personal battle and putting all
his efforts into reaching the alcove with its rows of in-
dented controls. Twice Harry headed him off; and then
by sheer mass and desperation, the Other turned and
burst past into the alcove, thick hands outstretched and
grasping at its walls. Harry leaped in pursuit, landing
and clinging to the broad, fleshy back.

The Other stumbled under the added weight, and fell,
face down. Triumphantly yelling, Harry rode the heavy
body to the floor, striking at the hairless head . . . and
striking . . . and striking . . .

Sometime later, Harry came wearily to his senses and
dropped a rock he no longer had the strength to lift. He
blinked around himself like a man waking from a
dream, becoming aware of a brilliantly lit room full of
strange shapes—and of a small alcove, the walls of
which were covered with rows of indentations, in which
something large and dead lay with its head smashed into
ruin. A deep, clawing thirst rose to take Harry by the
throat, and he staggered to his feet.

He looked longingly up at the dark opening of the ventilator over his head; but he was too exhausted to jump

up, cling to its edge and pull himself back into the duct-work, from which he could return to the stream outside the pyramid and to the flowing water there. He turned and stumbled from the chamber into unfamiliar rooms and corridors.

A brilliant light illuminated everything around him as he went. He sniffed and thought he scented, through the musky reek that filled the air about him, the clear odor of water. Gradually, the scent grew stronger and led him at last to a room where a bright stream leaped from a wall into a basin where it pooled brightly before drain-ing away. He drank deeply and rested.

Finally, satiated, he turned away from the basin and came face-to-face with a wall that was all-reflecting sur-face; and he stopped dead, staring at himself, like Adam before the Fall.

It was only then, with the upwelling of his returning humanness, that he realized his condition. And words spoken aloud for the first time in months broke harshly and rustily from his lips like the sounds of a machine un-used for years.

"My God!" he said, croakingly. "I've got no clothes left!"

And he began to laugh. Cackling, cackling rasping more unnaturally even than his speech, his laughter lifted and echoed hideously through the silent, alien rooms. But it was laughter all the same—the one sound that distinguishes man from the animal.

He was six months after that learning to be a complete human being again and finding out how to control the pyramid. If it had not been for the highly sophisticated safety devices built into the alien machine, he would never have lived to complete that bit of self-education.

But finally he mastered the controls and got the pyramid into orbit, where he collected the rest of his official self and shifted back through the alternate universe to Earth.

He messaged ahead before he landed; and everybody who could be there was on hand to meet him as he landed the pyramid. Some of the hands that had slapped his back on leaving were raised to slap him again when at last he stepped forth among them.

But, not very surprisingly, when his gaunt figure in a spare coverall now too big for it, with shoulder-length hair and burning eyes, stepped into their midst, not one hand finished its gesture. No one in his right senses slaps an unchained wolf on the back; and no one, after one look, wished to risk slapping the man who seemed to have taken the place of Harry.

Of course, he was still the same man they had sent out—of *course* he was. But at the same time he was also the man who had returned from a world numbered 1242 and from a duel to the death there with a representative of a race a hundred times more advanced than his own. And in the process he had been pared down to something very basic in his human blood and bone, something dating back to before the first crude wheel or chipped flint knife.

And what was that? Go down into the valley of the shades and demand your answer of a dead alien with his head crushed in, who once treated the utmost powers of modern human science as a man treats the annoyance of a buzzing mosquito.

Or, if that once-mighty traveler in spacegoing pyramids is disinclined to talk, turn and inquire of other ghosts you will find there—those of the aurochs, the great cave bear and the woolly mammoth.

They, too, can testify to the effectiveness of naked men.

DANGER—HUMAN

The spaceboat came down in the silence of perfect working order—down through the cool, dark night of a New Hampshire late spring. There was hardly any moon and the path emerging from the clump of conifers and snaking its way across the dun pasture looked like a long strip of pale cloth, carelessly dropped and forgotten there.

The two aliens checked the boat and stopped it, hovering, some fifty feet above the pasture, and all but invisible against the low-lying clouds. Then they set themselves to wait, their woolly, bearlike forms settled on haunches, their uniform belts glinting a little in the shielded light from the instrument panel, talking now and then in desultory murmurs.

"It's not a bad place," said the one of junior rank, looking down at the earth below.

"Why should it be?" answered the senior.

The junior did not answer. He shifted on his haunches.

"The babies are due soon," he said. "I just got a message."

"How many?" asked the senior.

"Three—the doctor thinks. That's not bad for a first birthing."

"My wife only had two."

"I know. You told me."

They fell silent for a few seconds. The spaceboat rocked almost imperceptibly in the waters of night.

"Look—" said the junior, suddenly. "Here it comes, right on schedule."

The senior glanced overside. Down below, a tall, dark form had emerged from the trees and was coming out along the path. A little beam of light shone before him, terminating in a blob of illumination that danced along the path ahead, lighting his way. The senior stiffened.

"Take controls," he said. The casualness had gone out of his voice. It had become crisp, impersonal.

"Controls," answered the other, in the same emotionless voice.

"Take her down."

"Down it is."

The spaceboat dropped groundward. There was an odd sort of soundless, lightless explosion—it was as if concussive wave had passed, robbed of all effects but one. The figure dropped, the light rolling from its grasp and losing its glow in a tangle of short grass. The spaceboat landed and the two aliens got out.

In the dark night they loomed furrily above the still figure. It was that of a lean, dark man in his early thirties, dressed in clean, much-washed corduroy pants and checkered wool lumberjack shirt. He was unconscious, but breathing slowly, deeply and easily.

"I'll take it up by the head, here," said the senior. "You take the other end. Got it? Lift! Now, carry it into the boat."

The junior backed away, up through the spaceboat's

open lock, grunting a little with the awkwardness of his burden.

"It feels slimy," he said.

"Nonsense!" said the senior. "That's your imagination."

Eldridge Timothy Parker drifted in that dreamy limbo between awakeness and full sleep. He found himself contemplating his own name.

Eldridge Timothy Parker. Eldridgetimothyparker. Eldridge TIMOTHYparker. ELdrIDGEtiMOthyPARKer. . . .

There was a hardness under his back, the back on which he was lying—and a coolness. His flaccid right hand turned flat, feeling. It felt like steel beneath him. Metal? He tried to sit up and bumped his forehead against a ceiling a few inches overhead. He blinked his eyes in the darkness—

Darkness?

He flung out his hands, searching, feeling terror leap up inside him. His knuckles bruised against walls to right and left. Frantic, his groping fingers felt out, around and about him. He was walled in, he was surrounded, he was enclosed.

Completely.

Like in a coffin.

Buried—

He began to scream. . . .

Much later, when he awoke again, he was in a strange place that seemed to have no walls, but many instruments. He floated in the center of mechanisms that passed and repassed about him, touching, probing, turning. He felt touches of heat and cold. Strange hums and notes of various pitches came and went. He felt voices questioning him.

Who are you?

"Eldridge Parker—Eldridge Timothy Parker—"
What are you?
"I'm Eldridge Parker—"
Tell about yourself.
"Tell what? What?"
Tell about yourself.
"What? What do you want to know? What—"
Tell about. . . .
"But I—"
Tell. . . .

. . . well, i suppose i was pretty much like any of the
kids around our town . . . i was a pretty good shot and i
won the fifth grade seventy-five yard dash . . . i played
hockey, too . . . pretty cold weather up around our parts,
you know, the air used to smell strange it was so cold
winter mornings in january when you first stepped out
of doors . . . it is good, open country, new england, and
there were lots of smells . . . there were pine smells and
grass smells and i remember especially the kitchen
smells . . . and then, too, there was the way the oak
benches in church used to smell on sunday when you
knelt with your nose right next to the back of the pew
ahead. . . .
. . . the fishing up our parts is good too . . . i liked to
fish but i never wasted time on weekdays . . . we were
presbyterians, you know, and my father had the farm,
but he also had money invested in land around the country . . . we have never been badly off but i would have
liked a motor-scooter. . . .
. . . no i did not never hate the germans, at least i did
not think i ever did, of course though i was over in
europe i never really had it bad, combat, i mean . . . i
was in a motor pool with the raw smell of gasoline, i like
to work with my hands, and it was not like being in the
infantry. . . .
. . . i have as good a right to speak up to the town council
as any man . . . i do not believe in pushing but if they

push me i am going to push right back . . . nor it isn't any man's business what i voted last election no more than my bank balance . . . but i have got as good a right to a say in town doings as if i was the biggest landholder among them. . . .

. . . i did not go to college because it was not necessary . . . too much education can make a fool of any man, i told my father, and i know when i have had enough . . . i am a farmer and will always be a farmer and i will do my own studying as things come up without taking out a pure waste of four years to hang a piece of paper on the wall. . . .

. . . of course i know about the atom bomb, but i am no scientist and no need to be one, no more than i need to be a vetrinarian . . . i elect the men that hire the men that need to know those things and the men that i elect will hear from me johnny-quick if things do not go to my liking. . . .

. . . as to why i never married, that is none of your business though there were a couple of times, and i still may if jeanie lind. . . .

. . . i believe in god and the united states of america. . . .

He woke up gradually. He was in a room that might have been any office, except the furniture was different. That is, there was a box with doors on it and that might have been a filing cabinet and a table that looked like a desk in spite of the single thin rod underneath the center that supported it. However, there were no chairs—only small, flat cushions, on which three large woolly, bear-like creatures were sitting and watching him in silence.

He himself, he found, was in a chair, though.

As soon as they saw his eyes were open, they turned away from him and began to talk among themselves. Eldridge Parker shook his head and blinked his eyes, and would have blinked his ears if that had been possible. For the sounds the creatures were making were like nothing he had ever heard before; and yet he understood everything they were saying. It was an odd sensation, like a double-image earwise, for he heard the strange mouth-noises just as they came out and then something in his head twisted them around and made them into perfectly understandable English.

Nor was that all. For, as he sat listening to the creatures talk, he began to get the same double image in another way. That is, as he still saw the bearlike creature behind the desk as the weird sort of animal he was, out of the sound of his voice, or from something else, there gradually built up in Eldridge's mind a picture of a thin, rather harassed-looking gray-haired man in something resembling a uniform, but at the same time not quite a uniform. It was the sort of effect an army general might get if he wore his stars and a Sam Browne belt over a civilian suit. Similarly, the other creature sitting facing the one behind the desk, at the desk's side, was a young and black-haired man with something of the laboratory about him, and the creature further back, seated almost against the wall, was neither soldier nor scientist, but a heavy older man with a sort of book-won wisdom in him.

"You see, commander," the young one with the black-haired image was saying, "perfectly restored. At least on the physical and mental levels."

"Good, doctor, good," the outlandish syllables from the one behind the desk translated themselves in Eldridge's head. "And you say it . . . he, I should say . . . will be able to understand?"

"Certainly, sir," said the doctor-psychologist—whatever-he-was. "Identification is absolute—"

"But I mean comprehend—encompass—" The creature behind the desk moved one paw slightly. "Follow what we tell him—"

The doctor turned his ursinoid head toward the third member of the group. This one spoke slowly, in a deeper voice.

"The culture allows. Certainly."

The one behind the desk bowed slightly to the oldest one.

"Certainly, Academician, certainly."

They then fell silent, all looking back at Eldridge, who returned their gaze with equal interest. There was something unnatural about the whole proceeding. Both sides were regarding the other with the completely blunt and unshielded curiosity given to freaks.

The silence stretched out. It became tinged with a certain embarrassment. Gradually a mutual recognition arose that no one really wanted to be the first to address an alien being directly.

"It . . . he is comfortable?" asked the commander, turning once more to the doctor.

"I should say so," replied the doctor, slowly. "As far as we know. . . ."

Turning back to Eldridge, the commander said, "Eldridgetimothyparker, I suppose you wonder where you are?"

Caution and habit put a clamp on Eldridge's tongue. He hesitated about answering so long that the commander turned in distress to the doctor, who reassured him with a slight movement of the head.

"Well, speak up," said the commander, "we'll be able to understand you, just as you're able to understand us. Nothing's going to hurt you; and nothing you say will have the slightest effect on your . . . er . . . situation."

He paused again, looking at Eldridge for a comment. Eldridge still held his silence, but one of his hands unconsciously made a short, fumbling motion at his breast pocket.

"My pipe—" said Eldridge.

The three looked at each other. They looked back at Eldridge.

"We have it," said the doctor. "After a while we may give it back to you. For now . . . we cannot allow . . . it would not suit us."

"Smoke bother you?" said Eldridge, with a touch of his native canniness.

"It does not bother us. It is . . . merely . . . distasteful," said the commander. "Let's get on. I'm going to tell you where you are, first. You're on a world roughly similar to your own, but many . . ." he hesitated, looking at the academician.

"Light-years," supplemented the deep voice.

". . . Light-years in terms of what a year means to you," went on the commander, with growing briskness. "Many light-years distant from your home. We didn't bring you here because of any personal . . . dislike . . . or enmity for you; but for. . . ."

"Observation," supplied the doctor. The commander turned and bowed slightly to him, and was bowed back at in return.

". . . Observation," went on the commander. "Now, do you understand what I've told you so far?"

"I'm listening," said Eldridge.

"Very well," said the commander. "I will go on. There is something about your people that we are very anxious to discover. We have been, and intend to continue, studying you to find it out. So far—I will admit quite frankly and freely—we have not found it; and the concensus among our best minds is that you, yourself, do not know what it is. Accordingly, we have hopes of . . . causing . . . you to discover it for yourself. And for us."

"Hey. . . ." breathed Eldridge.

"Oh, you will be well treated. I assure you," said the commander, hurriedly. "You have been well treated. You have been . . . but you did not know . . . I mean you did not feel—"

"Can you remember any discomfort since we picked you up?" asked the doctor, leaning forward.

"Depends what you mean—"

"And you will feel none." The doctor turned to the commander. "Perhaps I'm getting ahead of myself?"

"Perhaps," said the commander. He bowed and turned back to Eldridge. "To explain—we hope you will discover our answer for us. We're only going to put you in a position to work on it. Therefore, we've decided to tell you everything. First—the problem. Academician?"

The oldest one bowed. His deep voice made the room ring oddly.

"If you will look this way," he said. Eldridge turned his head. The other raised one paw and the wall beside him dissolved into a maze of lines and points. "Do you know what this is?"

"No," said Eldridge.

"It is," rumbled the one called the academician, "a map of the known universe. You lack the training to read it in four dimensions, as it should be read. No matter. You will take my word for it . . . it is a map. A map covering hundreds of thousands of your light-years and millions of your years."

He looked at Eldridge, who said nothing.

"To go on, then. What we know of your race is based upon two sources of information. History. And Legend. The history is sketchy. It rests on archaeological discoveries for the most part. The legend is even sketchier and—fantastic."

He paused again. Still Eldridge guarded his tongue.

"Briefly, there is a race that has three times broken out to overrun this mapped area of our galaxy and dominate other civilized cultures—until some inherent lack or weakness in the individual caused the component parts of this advance to die out. The periods of these outbreaks has always been disastrous for the dominated cultures and uniformly without benefit to the race I am talking about. In the case of each outbreak, though the home planet was destroyed and all known remnants of the advancing race hunted out, unknown seed communities remained to furnish the material for a new advance some thousands of years later. That race," said the academician, and coughed—or at least made some kind of noise in his throat, "is your own."

Eldridge watched the other carefully and without moving.

"We see your race, therefore," went on the academician, and Eldridge received the mental impression of an elderly man putting the tips of his fingers together judiciously, "as one with great or overwhelming natural talents, but unfortunately also with one great natural flaw. This flaw seems to be a desire—almost a need—to acquire and possess things. To reach out, encompass, and absorb. It is not," shrugged the academician, "a unique trait. Other races have it—but not to such an extent that it makes them a threat to their co-existing cultures. Yet, this in itself is not the real problem. If it was a simple matter of rapacity, a combination of other races should be able to contain your people. There is a natural inevitable balance of that sort continually at work in the galaxy. No," said the academician, and paused, looking at the commander.

"Go on. Go on," said the commander. The academician bowed.

"No, it is not that simple. As a guide to what remains, we have only the legend, made anew and reinforced after each outward sweep of you people. We know that there must be something more than we have found—and we have studied you carefully, both your home world and now you, personally. There *must* be something more in you, some genius, some capability above the normal, to account for the fantastic nature of your race's previous successes. But the legend says only—*Danger, Human! High Explosive. Do not touch*—and we find nothing in you to justify the warning."

He sighed. Or at least Eldridge received a sudden, unexpected intimation of deep weariness.

"Because of a number of factors—too numerous to go into and most of them not understandable to you—it is our race which must deal with this problem for the rest of the galaxy. What can we do? We dare not leave you be until you grow strong and come out once more. And the legend expressly warns us against touching you in any way. So we have chosen to pick one—but I intrude upon your field, doctor."

The two of them exchanged bows. The doctor took up the talk speaking briskly and entirely to Eldridge.

"A joint meeting of those of us best suited to consider the situation recommended that we pick up one specimen for intensive observation. For reasons of availability, you were the one chosen. Following your return under drugs to this planet, you were thoroughly examined, by the best of medical techniques, both mentally and physically. I will not go into detail, since we have no wish to depress you unduly. I merely want to impress on you the fact that we found nothing. Nothing. No unusual power or ability of any sort, such as history shows you to have had and legend hints at. I mention this because of the further course of action we have decided to take. Commander?"

The being behind the desk got to his hind feet. The other two rose.

"You will come with us," said the commander.

Herded by them, Eldridge went out through the room's door into brilliant sunlight and across a small stretch of something like concrete to a stubby egg-shaped craft with ridiculous little wings.

"Inside," said the commander. They got in. The commander squatted before a bank of instruments, manipulated a simple sticklike control, and after a moment the ship took to the air. They flew for perhaps half an hour, with Eldridge wishing he was in a position to see out one of the high windows, then landed at a field apparently literally hacked out of a small forest of mountains.

Crossing this field on foot, Eldridge got a glimpse of some huge ships, as well as a number of smaller ones

such as the one in which he had arrived. Numbers of the
furry aliens moved about, none with any great air of
hurry, but all with purposefulness. There was a sudden,
single, thunderous sound that was gone almost before
the ear could register it; and Eldridge, who had ducked
instinctively, looked up again to see one of the huge
ships falling—there is no other word for it—skyward
with such unbelievable rapidity it was out of sight in
seconds.

The four of them came at last to a shallow, open
trench in the stuff which made the field surface. It was
less than a foot wide and they stepped across it with
ease. But once they had crossed it, Eldridge noticed a
difference. In the five hundred yard square enclosed by
the trench—for it turned at right angles off to his right
and to his left—there was an air of tightly-established
desertedness, as of some highly restricted area, and the
rectangular concrete-looking building that occupied the
square's very center glittered unoccupied in the clear
light.

They marched to the door of this building and it
opened without any of them touching it. Inside was
perhaps twenty feet of floor, stretching inward as a rim
inside the walls. Then a sort of moat—Eldridge could
not see its depth—filled with a dark fluid with a faint,
sharp odor. This was perhaps another twenty feet wide
and enclosed a small, flat island perhaps fifteen feet by
fifteen feet, almost wholly taken up by a cage whose
walls and ceiling appeared to be made of metal bars as
thick as a man's thumb and spaced about six inches
apart. Two more of the aliens, wearing a sort of harness
and holding a short, black tube apiece, stood on the
ledge of the outer rim. A temporary bridge had been laid
across the moat, protruding through the open door of
the cage.

They all went across the bridge and into the cage.

There, standing around rather like a board of directors viewing an addition to the company plant, they faced Eldridge; and the commander spoke.

"This will be your home from now on," he said. He indicated the cot, the human-type chair and the other items furnishing the cage. "It's as comfortable as we can make it."

"Why?" burst out Eldridge, suddenly. "Why're you locking me up here? Why—"

"In our attempt to solve the problem that still exists," interrupted the doctor, smoothly, "we can do nothing more than keep you under observation and hope that time will work with us. Also, we hope to influence you to search for the solution, yourself."

"And if I find it—what?" cried Eldridge.

"Then," said the commander, "we will deal with you in the kindest manner that the solution permits. It may be even possible to return you to your own world. At the very least, once you are no longer needed, we can see to it that you are quickly and painlessly destroyed."

Eldridge felt his insides twist within him.

"Kill me?" he choked. "You think that's going to make me help you? The hope of getting killed?"

They looked at him almost compassionately.

"You may find," said the doctor, "that death may be something you will want very much, only for the purpose of putting a close to a life you've become weary of. Look,"—he gestured around him—"you are locked up beyond any chance of ever escaping. This cage will be illuminated night and day; and you will be locked in it. When we leave, the bridge will be withdrawn, and the only thing crossing that moat—which is filled with acid—will be a mechanical arm which will extend across and through a small opening to bring you food twice a day. Beyond the moat, there will be two armed guards on duty at all times, but even they cannot open the door to this building. That is opened by remote control from outside, only after the operator has check-ed on his vision screen to make sure all is as it should be inside here."

He gestured through the bar, across the moat and through a window in the outer wall.

"Look out there," he said.

Eldridge looked. Out beyond, and surrounding the building, the shallow trench no longer lay still and empty under the sun. It now spouted a vertical wall of flickering, weaving distortion, like a barrier of heat waves.

"That is our final defense, the ultimate in destructive-ness that our science provides us—it would literally burn you to nothingness, if you touched it, though of course we would then reconstitute you. It will be turned off only for seconds, and with elaborate precautions, to let guards in, or out."

Eldridge looked back in, to see them all watching him.

"We do this," said the doctor, "not only because we may discover you to be more dangerous than you seem, but to impress you with your helplessness so that you may be more ready to help *us*. Here you are, and here you will stay."

"And you think," demanded Eldridge hoarsely, "that this's all going to make me want to help you?"

"Yes," said the doctor, "because there's one thing more that enters into the situation. You were literally taken apart physically, after your capture; and as literally put back together again. We are advanced in the organic field, and certain things are true of all life forms. I supervised the work on you, myself. You will find that you are, for all practical purposes immortal and irretrievably sane. This will be your home forever, and you will find that neither death nor insanity will provide you a way of escape."

They turned and filed out. From some remote control, the cage door was swung shut. He heard it click and lock. The bridge was withdrawn from the moat. A screen lit up and a woolly face surveyed the building's interior.

The building's door opened. They went out; and the guards took up their patrol, around the rim in opposite directions, keeping their eyes on Eldridge and their weapons ready in their hands. The building's door closed again. Outside, the flickering wall blinked out for a second and then returned again.

The silence of a warm, summer, mountain afternoon descended upon the building. The footsteps of the guards made shuffling noises on their path around the rim. The bars enclosed him.

Eldridge stood still, holding the bars in both hands and looking out.

He could not believe it.

He could not believe it as the days piled up into weeks, and the weeks into months. But as the seasons shifted and the year came around to a new year, the realities of his situation began to soak into him like water into a length of dock piling. For outside, Time could be seen at its visible and regular motion; but in his prison, there was no Time.

Always, the lights burned overhead, always the guards paced about him. Always the barrier burned beyond the building, the meals came swinging in on the end of a long metal arm extended over the moat and through a small hatchway which opened automatically as the arm approached; regularly, twice weekly, the doctor came and checked him over, briefly, impersonally—and went out again with the changing of the guard.

He felt the unbearableness of his situation, like a hand winding tighter and tighter day by day the spring of tension within him. He took to pacing feverishly up and down the cage. He went back and forth, back and forth, until the room swam. He lay awake nights, staring at the endless glow of illumination from the ceiling. He rose to pace again.

The doctor came and examined him. He talked to Eldridge, but Eldridge would not answer. Finally there came a day when everything split wide open and he began to howl and bang on the bars. The guards were frightened and called the doctor. The doctor came, and with two others, entered the cage and strapped him down. They did something odd that hurt at the back of his neck and he passed out.

When he opened his eyes again, the first thing he saw was the doctor's woolly face, looking down at him—he had learned to recognize that countenance in the same way a sheep-herder eventually comes to recognize individual sheep in his flock. Eldridge felt very weak, but calm.

"You tried hard—" said the doctor. "But you see, you didn't make it. There's no way out *that* way for you."

Eldridge smiled.

"Stop that!" said the doctor sharply. "You aren't fooling us. We know you're perfectly rational."

Eldridge continued to smile.

"What do you think you're doing?" demanded the doctor. Eldridge looked happily up at him.

"I'm going home," he said.

"I'm sorry," said the doctor. "You don't convince me."
He turned and left. Eldridge turned over on his side and dropped off into the first good sleep he'd had in months.

In spite of himself, however, the doctor was worried. He had the guards doubled, but nothing happened. The days slipped into weeks again and nothing happened. Eldridge was apparently fully recovered. He still spent a great deal of time walking up and down his cage and grasping the bars as if to pull them out of the way before him—but the frenzy of his earlier pacing was gone. He had also moved his cot over next to the small, two-foot square hatch that opened to admit the mechanical arm bearing his meals, and would lie there, with his face pressed against it, waiting for the food to be delivered.

The doctor felt uneasy, and spoke to the commander privately about it.

"Well," said the commander, "just what is it you suspect?"

"I don't know," confessed the doctor. "It's just that I see him more frequently than any of us. Perhaps I've become sensitized—but he bothers me."

"Bothers you?"

"Frightens me, perhaps. I wonder if we've taken the right way with him."

"We took the only way." The commander made the little gesture and sound that was his race's equivalent of a sigh. "We must have data. What do you do when you run across a possibly dangerous virus, doctor? You isolate it—for study, until you know. It is not possible, and too risky to try to study his race at close hand, so we study him. That's all we're doing. You lose objectivity, doctor. Would you like to take a short vacation?"

"No," said the doctor, slowly. "No. But he frightens me."

Still, time went on and nothing happened. Eldridge paced his cage and lay on his cot, face pressed to the bars of the hatch, and staring at the outside world. Another year passed; and another. The double guards were withdrawn. The doctor came reluctantly to the conclusion that the human had at last accepted the fact of his confinement and felt growing within him that normal sort of sympathy that feeds on familiarity. He tried to talk to Eldridge on his regularly scheduled visits, but Eldridge showed little interest in conversation. He lay on the cot watching the doctor as the doctor examined him, with something in his eyes as if he looked on from some distant place in which all decisions were already made and finished.

"You're as healthy as ever," said the doctor, concluding his examination. He regarded Eldridge. "I wish you would, though. . . ." He broke off. "We aren't a cruel people, you know. We don't like the necessity that makes us do this."

He paused. Eldridge considered him without stirring.

"If you'd accept that fact," said the doctor, "I'm sure you'd make it easier on yourself. Possibly our figures of speech have given you a false impression. We said you are immortal. Well, of course, that's not true. Only practically speaking, are you immortal. You are now capable of living a very, very, very long time. That's all."

He paused again. After a moment of waiting, he went on.

"Just the same way, this business isn't really intended to go on for eternity. By its very nature, of course, it can't. Even races have a finite lifetime. But even that would be too long. No, it's just a matter of a long time as you might live it. Eventually, everything must come to a conclusion—that's inevitable."

Eldridge still did not speak. The doctor sighed.

"Is there anything you'd like?" he said. "We'd like to make this as little unpleasant as possible. Anything we can give you?"

Eldridge opened his mouth.

"Give me a boat," he said. "I want a fishing rod. I want a bottle of applejack."

The doctor shook his head sadly. He turned and signaled the guards. The cage door opened. He went out.

"Get me some pumpkin pie," cried Eldridge after him, sitting up on the cot and grasping the bars as the door closed. "Give me some green grass in here."

The doctor crossed the bridge. The bridge was lifted up and the monitor screen lit up. A woolly face looked out and saw that all was well. Slowly the outer door swung open.

"Get me some pine trees!" yelled Eldridge at the doctor's retreating back. "Get me some plowed fields! Get me some earth, some dirt, some plain, earth dirt! *Get me that!*"

The door shut behind the doctor; and Eldridge burst

into laughter, clinging to the bars, hanging there with glowing eyes.

"I would like to be relieved of this job," said the doctor to the commander, appearing formally in the latter's office.

"I'm sorry," said the commander. "I'm very sorry. But it was our tactical team that initiated this action; and no one has the experience with the prisoner you have. I'm sorry."

The doctor bowed his head; and went out.

Certain mild but emotion-deadening drugs were also known to the woolly, bearlike race. The doctor went out and began to indulge in them. Meanwhile, Eldridge lay on his cot, occasionally smiling to himself. His position was such that he could see out the window and over the weaving curtain of the barrier that ringed his building, to the landing field. After a while one of the large ships landed and when he saw the three members of its crew disembark from it and move, antlike off across the field toward the buildings at its far end, he smiled again.

He settled back and closed his eyes. He seemed to doze for a couple of hours and then the sound of the door opening to admit the extra single guard bearing the food for his three o'clock mid-afternoon feeding. He sat up, pushed the cot down a ways, and sat on the end of it, waiting for the meal.

The bridge was not extended—that happened only when someone physically was to enter his cage. The monitor screen lit up and a woolly face watched as the tray of food was loaded on the mechanical arm. It swung out across the acid-filled moat, stretched itself toward the cage, and under the vigilance of the face in the monitor, the two-foot square hatch opened just before it to let it extend into the cage.

Smiling, Eldridge took the tray. The arm withdrew, as it cleared the cage, the hatch swung shut and locked.

Outside the cage, guards, food carrier and face in the monitor relaxed. The food carrier turned toward the door, the face in the monitor looked down at some invisible control board before it and the outer door swung open.

In that moment, Eldridge moved.

In one swift second he was on his feet and his hands had closed around the bars of the hatch. There was a single screech of metal, as—incredibly—he tore it loose and threw it aside. Then he was diving through the hatch opening.

He rolled head over heels like a gymnast and came up with his feet standing on the inner edge of the moat. The acrid scent of the acid faintly burnt at his nostrils. He sprang forward in a standing jump, arms outstretched—and his clutching fingers closed on the end of the food arm, now halfway in the process of its leisurely mechanical retraction across the moat.

The metal creaked and bent, dipping downward toward the acid, but Eldridge was already swinging onward under the powerful impetus of his arms from which the sleeves had fallen back to reveal bulging ropes of smooth, powerful muscle. He flew forward through the air, feet first, and his boots took the nearest guard in the face, so that they crashed to the ground together.

For a second they rolled entangled, then the guard flopped and Eldridge came up on one knee, holding the black tube of the guard's weapon. It spat a single tongue of flame and the other guard dropped. Eldridge thrust to his feet, turning to the still-open door.

The door was closing. But the panicked food-carrier, unarmed, had turned to run. A bolt from Eldridge's weapon took him in the back. He fell forward and the door jammed on his body. Leaping after him, Eldridge squeezed through the remaining opening.

Then he was out under the free sky. The sounds of

alarm screechers were splitting the air. He began to run—

The doctor was already drugged—but not so badly that he could not make it to the field when the news came. Driven by a strange perversity of spirit, he went first to the prison to inspect the broken hatch and the bent food arm. He traced Eldridge's outward path and it led him to the landing field where he found the commander and the academician by a bare, darkened area of concrete. They acknowledged his presence by little bows.

"He took a ship here?" said the doctor.

"He took a ship here," said the commander.

There was a little silence between them.

"Well," said the academician, "we have been answered."

"Have we?" the commander looked at them almost appealingly. "There's no chance—that it was just chance? No chance that the hatch just happened to fail—and he acted without thinking, and was lucky?"

The doctor shook his head. He felt a little dizzy and unnatural from the drug, but the ordinary processes of his thinking were unimpaired.

"The hinges of the hatch," he said, "were rotten—eaten away by acid."

"Acid?" the commander stared at him. "Where would he get acid?"

"From his own digestive processes—regurgitated and spat directly into the hinges. He secreted hydrochloric acid among other things. Not too powerful—but over a period of time. . . ."

"Still—" said the commander, desperately, "I think it must have been more luck than otherwise."

"Can you believe that?" asked the academician. "Consider the timing of it all, the choosing of a moment when the food arm was in the proper position, the door open at the proper angle, the guard in a vulnerable situation. Consider his unhesitating and sure use of a weapon—

which could only be the fruits of hours of observation, his choice of a moment when a fully supplied ship, its drive unit not yet cooled down, was waiting for him on the field. No," he shook his woolly head, "we have been answered. We put him in an escape-proof prison and he escaped."

"But none of this was possible!" cried the commander.

The doctor laughed, a fuzzy, drug-blurred laugh. He opened his mouth but the academician was before him.

"It's not what he did," said the academician, "but the fact that he did it. No member of another culture that we know would have even entertained the possibility in their minds. Don't you see—he disregarded, he *denied* the fact that escape was impossible. *That* is what makes his kind so fearful, so dangerous. The fact that something is impossible presents no barrier to their seeking minds. That, alone, places them above us on a plane we can never reach."

"But it's a false premise!" protested the commander. "They cannot contravene natural laws. They are still bound by the physical order of the universe."

The doctor laughed again. His laugh had a wild quality. The commander looked at him.

"You're drugged," he said.

"Yes," choked the doctor. "And I'll be more drugged. I toast the end of our race, our culture, and our order."

"Hysteria!" said the commander.

"Hysteria?" echoed the doctor. "No—*guilt*! Didn't we do it, we three? The legend told us not to touch them, not to set a spark to the explosive mixture of their kind. And we went ahead and did it, you, and you, and I. And now we've sent forth an enemy—safely into the safe hiding place of space, in a ship that can take him across the galaxy, supplied with food to keep him for years, rebuilt into a body that will not die, with star charts and all the keys to understand our culture and locate his home again, using the ability to learn we have encouraged in him."

"I say," said the commander, doggedly, "he is not that dangerous—yet. So far he has done nothing one of us could not do, had we entertained the notion. He's shown nothing, nothing supernormal."

"Hasn't he?" said the doctor thickly. "What about the defensive screen—our most dangerous most terrible weapon—that could burn him to nothingness if he touched it?"

The commander stared at him.

"But—" said the commander. "The screen was shut off, of course, to let the food carrier out, at the same time the door was opened. I assumed—"

"I checked," said the doctor, his eyes burning on the commander. "They turned it on again before he could get out."

"But he *did* get out! You don't mean . . ." the commander's voice faltered and dropped. The three stood caught in a sudden silence like stone. Slowly, as if drawn by strings controlled by an invisible hand, they turned as one to stare up into the empty sky and space beyond.

"You mean—" the commander's voice tried again, and died.

"Exactly!" whispered the doctor.

Halfway across the galaxy, a child of a sensitive race cried out in its sleep and clutched at its mother.

"I had a bad dream," it whimpered.

"Hush," said its mother. "Hush." But she lay still, staring at the ceiling. She, too, had dreamed.

Somewhere, Eldridge was smiling at the stars.

TIGER GREEN

A man with hallucinations he cannot stand trying to strangle himself in a home-made straitjacket is not a pretty sight. But after a while, grimly thought Jerry McWhin, the *Star Scout*'s navigator, the ugly and terrible seem to backfire in effect, filling you with fury instead of harrowing you further. Men in crowds and packs could be stampeded briefly, but after a while the individual among them would turn, get his back up, and slash back.

At least—the hyper-stubborn individual in himself had finally so reacted.

Determinedly, with fingers that fumbled from lack of sleep, he got the strangling man—Wally Blake, an assistant ecologist—untangled and into a position where it would be difficult for him to try to choke out his own life, again. Then Jerry went out of the sickbay storeroom, leaving Wally and the other seven men out of the *Star Scout*'s complement of twelve who were in total restraint. He was lightheaded from exhaustion; but a berserk something in him snarled like a cornered tiger and refused to break like Wally and the others.

When all's said and done, he thought half-crazily, there's worse ways to come to the end of it than a last charge, win or lose, alone into the midst of all your enemies.

Going down the corridor, the sight of another figure jolted him a little back toward common sense. Ben Akham, the drive engineer, came trudging back from the air-lock corridor with a flame thrower on his back. Soot etched darkly the lines on his once-round face.

"Get the hull cleared?" asked Jerry. Ben nodded exhaustedly.

"There's more jungle on her every morning," he grunted. "Now those big thistles are starting to drip a corrosive liquid. The hull needs an anti-acid washing. I can't do it. I'm worn out."

"We all are," said Jerry. His own five-eleven frame was down to a hundred and thirty-eight pounds. There was plenty of food—it was just that the four men left on their feet had no time to prepare it; and little enough time to eat it, prepared or not.

Exploration Team Five-Twenty-Nine, thought Jerry, had finally bitten off more than it could chew, here on the second planet of Star 83476. It was nobody's fault. It had been a gamble for Milt Johnson, the Team Captain, either way—to land or not to land. He had landed; and it had turned out bad.

By such small things was the scale toward tragedy tipped. A communication problem with the natives, a native jungle evidently determined to digest the spaceship, and eight of twelve men down with something like suicidal delirium tremens—any two of these things the Team could probably have handled.

But not all three at once.

Jerry and Ben reached the entrance of the Control Room together and peered in, looking for Milt Johnson.

"Must be ootside, talking to that native again," said Jerry.

"Ootside?—*Oot*-side!" exploded Ben, with a sudden snapping of frayed nerves. "Can't you say " 'out-side' ?—'*Out*-side.' like everybody else?"

The berserk something in Jerry lunged to be free, but he caught it and hauled it back.

"Get hold of yourself!" he snapped.

"Well . . . I wouldn't mind you sounding like a blasted Scotchman all the time!" growled Ben, getting himself, nevertheless, somewhat under control. "It's just you always do it when I don't expect it!"

"If the Lord wanted us all to sound alike, he'd have propped up the Tower of Babel," said Jerry wickedly. He was not particularly religious himself, but he knew Ben to be a table-thumping atheist. He had the satisfaction now of watching the other man bite his lips and control himself in his turn.

Academically, however, Jerry thought as they both headed out through the ship to find Milt, he could not really blame Ben. For Jerry, like many Scot-Canadians, appeared to speak a very middle-western American sort of English most of the time. But only as long as he avoided such vocabulary items as "house" and "out"; which popped off Jerry's tongue as "hoose" and "oot." However, every man aboard had his personal peculiarities. You had to get used to them. That was part of spaceship—in fact, part of human—life.

They emerged from the lock, rounded the nose of the spaceship, and found themselves in the neat little clearing on one side of the ship where the jungle paradoxically refused to grow. In this clearing stood the broad-shouldered figure of Milt Johnson, his whitish-blond hair glinting in the yellow-white sunlight.

Facing Milt was the thin, naked, and saddle-colored, humanoid figure of one of the natives from the village, or whatever it was, about twenty minutes away by jungle trail. Between Milt and the native was the glittering metal console of the translator machine.

". . . Let's try it once more," they heard Milt saying as they came up and stopped behind him.

The native gabbled agreeably.

"Yes, yes. Try it again," translated the voice of the console.

"I am Captain Milton Johnson. I am in authority over the crew of the ship you see before me."

"Gladly would not see it," replied the console on translation of the native's gabblings. "However—I am Communicator, messenger to you sick ones."

"I will call you Communicator, then," began Milt.

"Of course. What else could you call me?"

"Please," said Milt, wearily. "To get back to it—I also am a Communicator."

"No, no," said the native. "You are not a Communicator. It is the sickness that makes you talk this way."

"But," said Milt, and Jerry saw the big, white-haired captain swallow in an attempt to keep his temper. "You will notice, I am communicating with you."

"No, no."

"I see," said Milt patiently. "You mean, we aren't communicating in the sense that we aren't understanding each other. We're talking, but you don't understand me—"

"No, no. I understand you perfectly."

"Well," said Milt, exhaustedly. "I don't understand you."

"That is because you are sick."

Milt blew out a deep breath and wiped his brow.

"Forget that part of it, then," he said. "Many of my crew are upset by nightmares we all have been having. They *are* sick. But there are still four of us who are well—"

"No, no. You are all sick," said the Communicator

earnestly. "But you should love what you call nightmares. All people love them."

"Including you and your people?"

"Of course. Love your nightmares. They will make you
well. They will make the little bit of proper life in you
grow, and heal you."

Ben snorted beside Jerry. Jerry could sympathize
with the other man. The nightmares he had been having
during his scant hours of sleep, the past two weeks,
came back to his mind, with the indescribably alien,
terrifying sensation of drifting in a sort of environmental soup with identifiable things changing shape
and identity constantly around him. Even pumped full
of tranquilizers, he thought—which reminded Jerry.

He had not taken his tranquilizers lately.

When had he taken some last? Not since he woke up,
in any case. Not since . . . yesterday, sometime. Though
that was now hard to believe.

"Let's forget that, too, then," Milt was saying. "Now,
the jungle is growing all over our ship, in spite of all we
can do. You tell me your people can make the jungle do
anything you want."

"Yes, yes," said Communicator, agreeably.

"Then, will you please stop it from growing all over
our spaceship?"

"We understand. It is your sickness, the poison that
makes you say this. Do not fear. We will never abandon
you." Communicator looked almost ready to pat Milt
consolingly on the head. "You are people, who are more
important than any cost. Soon you will grow and cast off
your poisoned part and come to us."

"But we can come to you right now!" said Milt, between his teeth. "In fact—we've come to your village a
dozen times."

"No, no." Communicator sounded distressed. "You
approach, but you do not come. You have never come to

us."

Milt wiped his forehead with the back of a wide hand. "I will come back to your village now, with you," he said. "Would you like that?" he asked.

"I would be so happy!" said Communicator. "But—you will not come. You say it, but you do not come."

"All right. Wait—" about to take a hand transceiver from the console, Milt saw the other two men. "Jerry," he said, "you go this time. Maybe he'll believe it if it's you who goes to the village with him."

"I've been there before. With you, the second time you went," objected Jerry. "And I've got to feed the men in restraint, pretty soon," he added.

"Try going again. That's all we can do—try things. Ben and I'll feed the men," said Milt. Jerry, about to argue further, felt the pressure of a sudden wordless, exhausted appeal from Milt. Milt's basic berserkedness must be just about ready to break loose, too, he realized.

"All right," said Jerry.

"Good," said Milt, looking grateful. "We have to keep trying. I should have lifted ship while I still had five well men to lift it with. Come on, Ben—you and I better go feed those men now, before we fall asleep on our feet."

They went away around the nose of the ship. Jerry unhooked the little black-and-white transceiver, that would radio-relay his conversations with Communicator back to the console of the translator for sense-making during the trip.

"Come on," he said to Communicator, and led off down the pleasantly wide jungle trail toward the native village.

They passed from under the little patch of open sky above the clearing and into green-roofed stillness. All about them, massive limbs, branches, ferns and vines intertwined in a majestic maze of growing things. Small flying creatures, looking half-animal and half-insect, flittered among the branches overhead. Some larger, more animal-like, creatures sat on the heavier limbs and moaned off-key like abandoned puppies. Jerry's head spun with his weariness, and the green over his head seemed to close down on him like a net flung by some giant, crazy fisherman, to take him captive.

He was suddenly and bitterly reminded of the Team's high hopes, the day they had set down on this world. No other Team or Group had yet to turn up any kind of alien life much more intelligent than an anthropoid ape. Now they, Team 529, had not only uncovered an intelligent, evidently semi-cultured alien people, but an alien people eager to establish relations with the humans and communicate. Here, two weeks later, the natives were still apparently just as eager to communicate, but what they said made no sense.

Nor did it help that, with the greatest of patience and kindness, Communicator and his kind seemed to consider that it was the humans who were irrational and uncommunicative.

Nor that meanwhile, that the jungle seemed to be mounting a specifically directed attack on the human spaceship.

Nor that the nightmares afflicting the humans had already laid low eight of the twelve crew and were grinding the four left on their feet down to a choice between suicidal delirium or collapse from exhaustion.

It was a miracle, thought Jerry, lightheadedly trudging through the jungle, that the four of them had been able to survive as long as they had. A miracle based probably on some individual chance peculiarity of strength that the other eight men in straitjackets lacked. Although, thought Jerry now, that strength that was had so far defied analysis. Dizzily, like a man in a high fever, he considered their four surviving personalities in his

mind's eye. They were, he thought, the four men of the
team with what you might call the biggest mental
crotchets.

—Or ornery streaks.

Take the fourth member of the group—the Medician,
Arthyr Loy, who had barely stuck his nose out of the sick
bay lab in the last forty-eight hours. Not only because he
was the closest thing to an M.D. aboard the ship, was Art
still determined to put the eight restrained men back on
their feet again. It just happened, in addition, that Art
considered himself the only true professional man
aboard, and was not the kind to admit any inability to
the lesser mortals about him.   •

And Milt Johnson—Milt made an excellent captain. He
was a tower of strength, a great man for making decisions. The only thing was, that having decided, Milt
could hardly be brought to consider the remote possibility that anyone else might have wanted to decide dif-
ferently.

Ben Akham was another matter. Ben hated religion
and loved machinery—and the jungle surrounding was
attacking *his* spaceship. In fact, Jerry was willing to bet
that by the time he got back, Ben would be washing the
hull with an acid-counteractant in spite of what he had
told Jerry earlier.

And himself? Jerry? Jerry shook his head woozily. It
was hard to be self-analytical after ten days of three and
four hours sleep per twenty. He had what his grand-
mother had once described as the curse of the Gael—
black stubbornness and red rages.

All of these traits, in all four of them, had normally
been buried safely below the surfaces of their personalities and had only colored them as individuals. But
now, the last two weeks had worn those surfaces down
to basic personality bedrock. Jerry shoved the thought
out of his mind.

"Well," he said, turning to Communicator, "we're al-

most to your village now . . . You can't say someone
didn't come with you, this time."

Communicator gabbled. The transceiver in Jerry's
hand translated.

"Alas," the native said, "but you are not with me."

"Cut it out!" said Jerry wearily. "I'm right here beside
you."

"No," said the Communicator. "You accompany me,
but you are not here. You are back with your dead
things."

"You mean the ship and the rest of it?" asked Jerry.

"There is no ship," said Communicator. "A ship must
have grown and been alive. Your thing has always been
dead. But we will save you."

They came out of the path at last into a clearing dotted
with whitish, pumpkin-like shells some ten feet in height
above the brown earth in which they were half-buried.
Wide cracks in the out-curving sides gave view of
tangled roots and plants inside, among which other
natives could be seen moving about, scratching, tasting
and making holes in the vegetable surfaces.

"Well," said Jerry, making an effort to speak cheerfully, "here I am."

"You are not here."

The berserk tigerishness in Jerry leaped up unawares
and took him by the inner throat. For a long second he
looked at Communicator through a red haze. Communicator gazed back patiently, evidently unaware how close
he was to having his neck broken by a pair of human
hands.

"Look—" said Jerry, slowly, between his teeth, getting
himself under control, "if you will just tell me what to
do to join you and your people, here, I will do it."

"That is good!"

"Then," said Jerry, still with both hands on the inner
fury that fought to tear loose inside him, "what do I do?"

"But you know—" The enthusiasm that had come into Communicator a moment before, wavered visibly. "You must get rid of the dead things, and set yourself free to grow, inside. Then, after you have grown, your unsick self will bring you here to join us!"

Jerry stared back. Patience, he said harshly to himself.

"Grow? How? In what way?"

"But you have a little bit of proper life in you," explained Communicator. "Not much, of course . . . but if you will rid yourself of dead things and concentrate on what you call nightmares, it will grow and force out the poison of the dead life in you. The proper life and the nightmares are the hope for you—"

"Wait a minute!" Jerry's exhaustion-fogged brain cleared suddenly and nearly miraculously at the sudden surge of excitement into his bloodstream. "This proper life you talk about—does it have something to do with the nightmares?"

"Of course. How could you have what you call nightmares without a little proper life in you to give them to you? As the proper life grows, you will cease to fight so against the 'nightmares' . . ."

Communicator continued to talk earnestly. But Jerry's spinning brain was flying off on a new tangent. What was it he had been thinking earlier about tranquilizers—that he had not taken any himself for some time? Then, what about the nightmares in his last four hours of sleep?

He must have had them—he remembered now that he *had* had them. But evidently they had not bothered him as much as before—at least, not enough to send him scrambling for tranquilizers to dull the dreams' weird impact on him.

"Communicator!" Jerry grabbed at the thin, leathery-skinned arm of the native. "Have I been chang—growing?"

"I do not know, of course," said the native, courteously. "I profoundly hope so. Have you?"

"Excuse me—" gulped Jerry. "I've got to get oot of here—back to th' ship!"

He turned, and raced back up the trail. Some twenty minutes later, he burst into the clearing before the ship to find an ominous silence hanging over everything. Only the faint rustle and hissing from the ever-growing jungle swallowing up the ship sounded on his eardrums.

"Milt—Ben!" he shouted, plunging into the ship. "Art!"

A hail from farther down the main corridor reassured him, and he followed it up to find all three unrestrained members of the crew in the sickbay. But—Jerry brought himself up short, his throat closing on him—there was a figure on the table.

"Who . . ." began Jerry. Milt Johnson turned around to face him. The captain's big body mercifully hid most of the silent form on the table.

"Wally Blake," said Milt emptily. "He managed to strangle himself after all. Got twisted up in his restraint jacket. Ben and I heard him thumping around in there, but by the time we got to him, it was too late. Art's doing an autopsy."

"Not exactly an autopsy," came the soft, Virginia voice of the Medician from beyond Milt. "Just looking for something I suspected . . . and here it is!"

Milt spun about and Jerry pushed between the big captain and Ben. He found himself looking at the back of a human head from which a portion of the skull had been removed. What he saw before him was a small expanse of whitish, soft, inner tissue that was the brainstem; and fastened to it almost like a grape growing there, was a small, purplish mass.

Art indicated the purple shape with the tip of a sharp, surgical instrument.

"There," he said. "And I bet we've each got one."

"What is it?" asked Ben's voice, hushed and a little nauseated.

"I don't know," said Art harshly. "How the devil would I be able to tell? But I found organisms in the bloodstreams of those of us I've taken blood samples from—organisms like spores, that look like this, only smaller, microscopic in size."

"You didn't tell me that!" said Milt, turning quickly to face him.

"What was the point?" Art turned toward the Team Captain. Jerry saw that the Medician's long face was almost bloodless. "I didn't know what they were. I thought if I kept looking, I might know more. Then I could have something positive to tell you, as well as the bad news. But—it's no use now."

"Why do you say that?" snapped Milt.

"Because it's the truth." Art's face seemed to slide apart, go loose and waxy with defeat. "As long as it was something non-physical we were fighting, there was some hope we could throw it off. But—you see what's going on inside us. We're being changed physically. That's where the nightmares come from. You can't overcome a physical change with an effort of will!"

"What about the Grotto at Lourdes?" asked Jerry. His head was whirling strangely with a mass of ideas. His own great-grandfather—the family story came back to mind—had been judged by his physician in eighteen ninety-six to have advanced pulmonary tuberculosis. Going home from the doctor's office, Simon Fraser McWhin had decided that he could not afford to have tuberculosis at this time. That he would not, therefore, have tuberculosis at all. And he had dismissed the matter fully from his mind.

One year later, examined by the same physician, he had no signs of tuberculosis whatsoever.

But in this present moment, Art, curling up in his chair at the end of the table, seemed not to have heard

Jerry's question. And Jerry was suddenly reminded of the question that had brought him pelting back from the native village.

"Is it growing—I mean was it growing when Wally strangled himself—that growth on his brain?" he asked.

Art roused himself.

"Growing?" he repeated fully. He climbed to his feet and picked up an instrument. He investigated the purple mass for a moment.

"No," he said, dropping the instrument wearily and falling back into his chair. "Looks like its outer layer has died and started to be reabsorbed—I think." He put his head in his hands. "I'm not qualified to answer such questions. I'm not trained . . ."

"Who is?" demanded Milt, grimly, looking over the table and the rest of them. "And we're reaching the limit of our strength as well as the limits of what we know—"

"We're done for," muttered Ben. His eyes were glazed, looking at the dissected body on the table. "It's not my fault—"

"Catch him! Catch Art!" shouted Jerry, leaping forward.

But he was too late. The Medician had been gradually curling up in his chair since he had sat down in it again. Now, he slipped out of it to the floor, rolled in a ball, and lay still.

"Leave him alone." Milt's large hand caught Jerry and held him back. "He may as well lie there as someplace else." He got to his feet. "Ben's right. We're done for."

"Done for?" Jerry stared at the big man. The words he had just heard were words he would never have imagined hearing from Milt.

"Yes," said Milt. He seemed somehow to be speaking from a long distance off.

"Listen—" said Jerry. The tigerishness inside him had woken at Milt's words. It tugged and snarled against the words of defeat from the captain's lips. "We're winning.

We aren't losing!"

"Quit it, Jerry," said Ben dully, from the far end of the room.

"Quit it—?" Jerry swung on the engineer. "You lost your temper with me before I went down to the village, about the way I said '*oot*'! How could you lose your temper if you were full of tranquilizers? I haven't been taking any myself, and I feel better because of it. Don't tell me you've been taking yours!—And that means we're getting stronger than the nightmares."

"The tranquilizers've been making me sick, if you must know! That's why I haven't been taking them—" Ben broke off, his face graying. He pointed a shaking finger at the purplish mass. "I'm being changed, that's why they made me sick! I'm changing already!" His voice rose toward a scream. "Don't you see, it's changing me—" He broke off, suddenly screaming and leaping at Milt with clawing fingers. "We're all changing! And it's your fault for bringing the ship down here. You did it—"

Milt's huge fist slammed into the side of the smaller man's jaw, driving him to the floor beside the still shape of the Medician, where he lay quivering and sobbing.

Slowly Milt lifted his gaze from the fallen man and faced Jerry. It was the standard seventy-two degrees in the room, but Jerry saw perspiration standing out on Milt's calm face as if he had just stepped out of a steam bath.

"But he may be right," said Milt, emotionlessly. His voice seemed to come from the far end of some lightless tunnel. "We may be changing under the influence of those growths right now—each of us."

"Milt!" said Jerry, sharply. But Milt's face never changed. It was large, and calm, and pale—and drenched with sweat. "Now's the last time we ought to give up! We're starting to understand it now. I tell you, the thing is to meet Communicator and the other natives head on! Head to head we can crack them wide open. One of us has to go down to that village."

"No. I'm the captain," said Milt, his voice unchanged. "I'm responsible, and I'll decide. We can't lift ship with less than five men and there's only two of us—you and I—actually left. I can't risk one of us coming under the influence of the growth in him, and going over to the alien side."

"Going over?" Jerry stared at him.

"That's what all this has been for—the jungle, the natives, the nightmare. They want to take us over." Sweat ran down Milt's cheeks and dropped off his chin, while he continued to talk tonelessly and gaze straight ahead. "They'll send us—what's left of us—back against our own people. I can't let that happen. We'll have to destroy ourselves so there's nothing for them to use."

"Milt—" said Jerry.

"No." Milt swayed faintly on his feet like a tall tree under a wind too high to be felt on the ground at its base. "We can't risk leaving ship or crew. We'll blow the ship up with ourselves in it—"

"*Blow up my ship!*"

It was a wild-animal scream from the floor at their feet; and Ben Akham rose from almost under the table like a demented wildcat, aiming for Milt's jugular vein. So unexpected and powerful was the attack that the big captain tottered and fell. With a noise like worrying dogs, they rolled together under the table.

The chained tiger inside Jerry broke his bonds and flung free.

He turned and ducked through the door into the corridor. It was a heavy pressure door with a wheel lock, activating metal dogs to seal it shut in case of a hull blowout and sudden loss of air. Jerry slammed the door shut, and spun the wheel.

The dogs snicked home. Snatching down the portable fire extinguisher hanging on the wall alongside, Jerry dropped the foam container on the floor and jammed the metal nozzle of its hose between a spoke of the locking wheel and the unlocking stop on the door beneath it.

He paused. There was silence inside the sickbay lab. Then the wheel jerked against the nozzle and the door tried to open.

"What's going on?" demanded the voice of Milt. There was a pause. "Jerry, what's going on out there? Open up!"

A wild, crazy impulse to hysterical laughter rose inside Jerry without warning. It took all his will power to choke it back.

"You're locked in, Milt," he said.

"Jerry!" The wheel spoke clicked against the jamming metal nozzle, in a futile effort to turn. "Open up! That's an order!"

"Sorry, Milt," said Jerry softly and lightheadedly. "I'm not ready yet to burn the hoose about my ears. This business of you wanting to blow up the ship's the same sort of impulse to suicide that got Wally and the rest. I'm off to face the natives now and let them have their way with me. I'll be back later, to let you oot."

"Jerry!"

Jerry heard Milt's voice behind him as he went off down the corridor.

"*Jerry!*" There was a fusillade of pounding fists against the door, growing fainter as Jerry moved away. "Don't you see?—That growth in you is finally getting you! Jerry, come back! Don't let them take over one of us! Jerry . . ."

Jerry left the noise and the ship together behind him as he stepped out of the airlock. The jungle, he saw, was covering the ship's hull again, already hiding it for the most part. He went on out to the translator console and began taking off his clothes. When he was completely undressed, he unhooked the transceiver he had brought back from the native village, slung it on a loop of his belt, and hung the belt around his neck.

He headed off down the trail toward the village,

wincing a little as the soles of his shoeless feet came into contact with pebbles along the way.

When he got to the village clearing, a naked shape he recognized as that of Communicator tossed up its arms in joy and came running to him.

"Well," said Jerry. "I've grown. I've got rid of the poison of dead things and the sickness. Here I am to join you!"

"At last!" gabbled Communicator. Other natives were running up. "Throw away the dead thing around your neck!"

"I still need it to understand you," said Jerry. "I guess I need a little help to join you all the way."

"Help? We will help!" cried Communicator. "But you must throw that away. You have rid yourself of the dead things that you kept wrapped around your limbs and body," gabbled Communicator. "Now rid yourself of the dead thing hanging about your neck."

"But I tell you, if I do that," objected Jerry, "I won't be able to understand you when you talk, or make you understand me!"

"Throw it away. It is poisoning you! Throw it away!" said Communicator. By this time three or four more natives had come up and others were headed for the gathering. "Shortly you will understand all, and all will understand you. Throw it away!"

"Throw it away!" chorused the other natives.

"Well . . ." said Jerry. Reluctantly, he took off the belt with the transceiver, and dropped it. Communicator gabbled unintelligibly.

". . . come with me . . ." translated the transceiver like a faint and tinny echo from the ground where it landed.

Communicator took hold of Jerry's hand and drew him toward the nearest whitish structure. Jerry swallowed unobtrusively. It was one thing to make up his mind to do this; it was something else again to actually do it. But he let himself be led to and in through a crack in the structure.

Inside, the place smelled rather like a mixture of a root cellar and a bayloft—earthy and fragrant at the same time. Communicator drew him in among the waist high tangle of roots rising and reentering the packed earth floor. The other natives swarmed after them. Close to the center of the floor they reached a point where the roots were too thick to allow them to pick their way any further. The roots rose and tangled into a mat, the irregular surface of which was about three feet off the ground. Communicator patted the roof surface and gabbled agreeably.

"You want me to get up there?" Jerry swallowed again, then gritted his teeth as the chained fury in him turned suddenly upon himself. There was nothing worse, he snarled at himself, than a man who was long on planning a course of action, but short on carrying it out.

Awkwardly, he clambered up on to the matted surface of the roots. They gave irregularly under him and their rough surfaces scraped his knees and hands. The natives gabbled, and he felt leather hands urging him to stretch out and lie down on his back.

He did so. The roots scored and poked the tender skin of his back. It was exquisitely uncomfortable.

"Now what—?" he gasped. He turned his head to look at the natives and saw that green tendrils, growing rapidly from the root mass, were winding about and garlanding the arms and legs of Communicator and several other of the natives standing by. A sudden pricking at his left wrist made him look down.

Green garlands were twining around his own wrists and ankles, sending wire-thin tendrils into his skin. In unconscious reflex of panic he tried to heave upward, but the green bonds held him fast.

"*Gabble-gabble-gabble* . . ." warbled Communicator, reassuringly.

With sudden alarm, Jerry realized that the green

tendrils were growing right into the arms and legs of the natives as well. He was abruptly conscious of further prickings in his own arms and legs.

"What's going on—" he started to say, but found his tongue had gone unnaturally thick and unmanageable. A wave of dizziness swept over him as if a powerful general anesthetic was taking hold. The interior of the structure seemed to darken; and he felt as if he was swooping away toward its ceiling on the long swing of some monster pendulum . . .

It swung him on into darkness. And nightmare.

It was the same old nightmare, but more so. It was nightmare experienced *awake* instead of asleep; and the difference was that he had no doubt about the fact that he was experiencing what he was experiencing, nor any tucked-away certainty that waking would bring him out of it.

Once more he floated through a changing soup of uncertainty, himself a changing part of it. It was not painful, it was not even terrifying. But it was hideous—it was an affront of nature. He was not himself. He was a thing, a part of the whole—and he must reconcile himself to being so. He must accept it.

Reconcile himself to it—no! It was not possible for the unbending, solitary, individualistic part that was *him* to do so. But accept it—maybe.

Jerry set a jaw that was no longer a jaw and felt the determination in him to blast through, to comprehend this incomprehensible thing, become hard and undeniable as a sword-point of tungsten steel. He drove through—

And abruptly the soup fell into order. It slid into focus like a blurred scene before the gaze of a badly myopic man who finally gets his spectacles before his eyes. Suddenly, Jerry was aware that what he observed was a scene not just before his eyes, but before his total awareness. And it was not the interior of the structure where he lay on a bed of roots, but the whole planet.

It was a landscape of factories. Countless factories, interconnected, intersupplying, integrated. It lacked only that he find his own working place among them.

Now, said this scene. *This is the sane universe, the way it really is. Reconcile yourself to it.*

The hell I will!

It was the furious unbending, solitary, individualistic part that was essentially *him*, speaking again. Not just speaking. Roaring—snarling its defiance, like a tiger on a hillside.

And the scene went—*pop.*

Jerry opened his eyes. He sat up. The green shoots around and in his wrists and ankles pulled prickingly at him. But they were already dying and not able to hold him. He swung his legs over the edge of the mat of roots and stood down. Communicator and the others, who were standing there, backed fearfully away from him, gabbling.

He understood their gabbling no better than before, but now he could read the emotional overtones in it. And those overtones were now of horror and disgust, overlying a wild, atavistic panic and terror. He walked forward. They scuttled away before him, gabbling, and he walked through the nearest crack in the wall of the structure and out into the sunlight, toward the transceiver and the belt where he had dropped them.

"Monster!" screamed the transceiver tinnily, faithfully translating the gabbling of the Communicator, who was following a few steps behind like a small dog barking behind a larger. "Brute! Savage! Unclean . . ." it kept up a steady denunciation.

Jerry turned to face Communicator, and the native tensed for flight.

"You know what I'm waiting for," said Jerry, almost smiling, hearing the transceiver translate his words into gabbling—though it was not necessary. As he had said,

Communicator knew what he was waiting for.

Communicator cursed a little longer in his own tongue, then went off into one of the structures, and returned with a handful of what looked like lengths of green vine. He dropped them on the ground before Jerry and backed away, cautiously, gabbling.

"Now will you go? And never come back! Never . . ."

"We'll see," said Jerry. He picked up the lengths of green vine and turned away up the path to the ship.

The natives he passed on his way out of the clearing huddled away from him and gabbled as he went.

When he stepped back into the clearing before the ship, he saw that most of the vegetation touching or close to the ship was already brown and dying. He went on into the ship, carefully avoiding the locked sickbay door, and wound lengths of the green vine around the wrists of each of the men in restraints.

Then he sat down to await results. He had never been so tired in his life. The minute he touched the chair, his eyes started to close. He struggled to his feet and forced himself to pace the floor until the green vines, which had already sent hair-thin tendrils into the ulnar arteries of the arms around which they were wrapped, pumped certain inhibitory chemicals into the bloodstreams of the seven men.

When the men started to blink their eyes and look about sensibly, he went to work to unfasten the home-made straitjackets that had held them prisoner. When he had released the last one, he managed to get out his final message before collapsing.

"Take the ship up," croaked Jerry. "Then, let yourself into the sickbay and wrap a vine piece around the wrists of Milt, and Art, and Ben. Ship up first—then when you're safely in space, take care of them, in the sickbay. Do it the other way and you'll never see Earth again."

They crowded around him with questions. He waved them off, slumping into one of the abandoned bunks.

"Ship up—" he croaked. "Then release and fix the

others. Ask me later. Later—"

. . . And that was all he remembered, then.

At some indefinite time later, not quite sure whether he had woken by himself, or whether someone else had wakened him, Jerry swam back up to consciousness. He was vaguely aware that he had been sleeping a long time; and his body felt sane again, but weak as the body of a man after a long illness.

He blinked and saw the large face of Milt Johnson, partly obscured by a cup of something. Milt was seated in a chair by the side of the bunk Jerry lay in, and the Team Captain was offering the cup of steaming black liquid to Jerry. Slowly, Jerry understood that this was coffee and he struggled up on one elbow to take the cup.

He drank from it slowly for a little while, while Milt watched and waited.

"Do you realize," said Milt at last, when Jerry finally put down the three-quarters empty cup on the night-stand by the bunk, "that what you did in locking me in the sickbay was mutiny?"

Jerry swallowed. Even his vocal chords seemed drained of strength and limp.

"You realize," he croaked, "what would have happened if I hadn't?"

"You took a chance. You followed a wild hunch—"

"No hunch," said Jerry. He cleared his throat. "Art found that growth on Wally's brain had quit growing before Wally killed himself. And I'd been getting along without tranquilizers—handling the nightmares better than I had with them."

"It could have been the growth in your own brain," said Milt, "taking over and running you—working better on you than it had on Wally."

"Working better—talk sense!" said Jerry, weakly, too pared down by the past two weeks to care whether school kept or not, in the matter of service courtesy to a superior. "The nightmares had broken Wally down to where we had to wrap him in a straitjacket. They hadn't even knocked me off my feet. If Wally's physiological processes had fought the alien invasion to a standstill, then I, you, Art, and Ben—all of us—had to be doing even better. Besides—I'd figured out what the aliens were after."

"What were they after?" Milt looked strangely at him.

"Curing us—of something we didn't have when we landed, but they thought we had."

"And what was that?"

"Insanity," said Jerry, grimly.

Milt's blond eyebrows went up. He opened his mouth as if to say something disbelieving—then closed it again. When he did speak, it was quite calmly and humbly.

"They thought," he asked, "Communicator's people thought that we were insane, and they could cure us?"

Jerry laughed; not cheerfully, but grimly.

"You saw that jungle around us back there?" he asked. "That was a factory complex—an infinitely complex factory complex. You saw their village with those tangles of roots inside the big whitish shells?— That was a highly diversified laboratory."

Milt's blue eyes slowly widened, as Jerry watched.

"That's right." Jerry drained the cup and set it aside. "Their technology is based on organic chemistry, the way ours is on the physical sciences. By our standards, they're chemical wizards. How'd you like to try changing the mind of an alien organism by managing to grow an extra part on to his brain—the way they tried to do to us humans? To them, it was the simplest way of convincing us."

Milt stared again. Finally, he shook his head.

"Why?" he said. "Why would they want to change our minds?"

"Because their philosophy, their picture of life and the universe around them grew out of a chemically oriented science," answered Jerry. "The result is, they see all life as part of a closed, intra-acting chemical circuit with no loose ends; with every living thing, intelligent or not, a part of the whole. Well, you saw it for yourself in your nightmare. That's the cosmos as they see it—and to them it's beautiful."

"But why did they want us to see it the way they did?"

"Out of sheer kindness," said Jerry and laughed barkingly. "According to their cosmology, there's no such thing as an alien. Therefore we weren't alien—just sick in the head. Poisoned by the lumps of metal like the ship and the translator, we claimed were so important. And our clothes and everything else we had. The kind thing was to cure and rescue us."

"Now, wait a minute," said Milt. "They saw those things of ours *work*—"

"What's the fact they worked got to do with it? What you don't understand, Milt," said Jerry, lying back gratefully on the bunk, "is that Communicator's peoples' minds were *closed*. Not just unconvinced, not just refusing to see—but *closed*! Sealed, and welded shut from prehistoric beginnings right down to the present. The fact our translator worked meant nothing to them. According to their cosmology, it shouldn't work, so it didn't. Any stray phenomena tending to prove it did were simply the product of diseased minds."

Jerry paused to emphasize the statement and his eyes drifted shut. The next thing he knew Milt was shaking him.

". . . Wake up!" Milt was shouting at him. "You can dope off after you've explained. I'm not going to have any crew back in straitjackets again, just because you were too sleepy to warn me they'd revert!"

". . . Won't revert," said Jerry, thickly. He roused himself. "Those lengths of vine released chemicals into their bloodstreams to destroy what was left of the growths. I wouldn't leave until I got them from Communicator." Jerry struggled up on one elbow again.

"And after a short walk in a human brain—mine—he and his people couldn't get us out of sight and forgotten fast enough."

"Why?" Milt shook him again as Jerry's eyelids sagged. "Why should getting their minds hooked in with yours shake them up so?"

". . . Bust—bust their cosmology open. Quit shaking . . . I'm awake."

"*Why* did it bust them wide open?"

"Remember—how it was for you with the nightmares?" said Jerry. "The other way around? Think back, about when you slept. There you were, a lone atom of humanity, caught up in a nightmare like one piece of stew meat in a vat stewing all life together—just one single chemical bit with no independent existence, and no existence at all except as part of the whole. Remember?"

He saw Milt shiver slightly.

"It was like being swallowed up by a soft machine," said the Team Captain in a small voice. "I remember."

"All right," said Jerry. "That's how it was for you in Communicator's cosmos. But remember something about the cosmos? It was warm, and safe. It was all-embracing, all-settling, like a great, big, soft, woolly comforter."

"It was too much like a woolly comforter," said Milt, shuddering. "It was unbearable."

"To you. Right," said Jerry. "But to Communicator, it was ideal. And if that was ideal, think what it was like when he had to step into a human mind—mine."

Milt stared at him.

"Why?" Milt asked.

"Because," said Jerry. "He found himself *alone* there!"

Milt's eyes widened.

"Think about it, Milt," said Jerry. "From the time we're born, we're individuals. From the moment we open our eyes on the world, inside we're alone in the universe. All the emotional and intellectual resources that Communicator draws from his identity with the stewing vat of his cosmos, each one of us has to dig up for and out of himself!"

Jerry stopped to give Milt a chance to say something. But Milt was evidently not in possession of something to say at the moment.

"That's why Communicator and the others couldn't take it, when they hooked into my human mind," Jerry went on. "And that's why, when they found out what we were like inside, they couldn't wait to get rid of us. So they gave me the vines and kicked us out. That's the whole story." He lay back on the bunk.

Milt cleared his throat.

"All right," he said.

Jerry's heavy eyes closed. Then the other man's voice spoke, still close by his ear.

"But," said Milt, "I still think you took a chance, going down to butt heads with the natives that way. What if Communicator and the rest had been able to stand exposure to your mind? You'd locked me in and the other men were in restraint. Our whole team would have been part of that stewing vat."

"Not a chance," said Jerry.

"You can't be sure of that."

"Yes I can." Jerry heard his own voice sounding harshly beyond the darkness of his closed eyelids. "It wasn't just that I knew my cosmological view was too tough for them. It was the fact that their minds were closed—in the vat they had no freedom to change and adapt themselves to anything new."

"What's that got to do with it?" demanded the voice of Milt.

"Everything," said Jerry. "Their point of view only made us more uncomfortable—but our point of view, being individually adaptable, and open, threatened to destroy the very laws of existence as they saw them. An open mind can always stand a closed one, if it has to—by making room for it in the general picture. But a closed mind can't stand it near an open one without risking immediate and complete destruction in its own terms. In a closed mind, there's no more room."

He stopped speaking and slowly exhaled a weary breath.

"Now," he said, without opening his eyes, "will you finally get oot of here and let me sleep?"

For a long second more, there was silence. Then, he heard a chair scrape softly, and the muted steps of Milt tiptoeing away.

With another sigh, at last Jerry relaxed and let consciousness slip from him.

He slept.

—As sleep the boar upon the plain, the hawk upon the crag, and the tiger on the hill . . .

THE MAN FROM EARTH

The Director of the crossroads world of Duhnbar had no other name, nor needed any, and his handsomeness and majesty were not necessarily according to the standards of the human race. But then, he had never heard of the human race.

He sat in his equivalent of a throne room day by day, while the representatives of a thousand passing races conducted their business below and before the dais on which his great throne chair sat. He enjoyed the feeling of life around him, so he permitted them to be there. He did not like to be directly involved in that life. Therefore none of them looked or spoke in his direction.

Before him, he saw their numbers spread out through a lofty hall. At the far end of the hall, above the lofty portal, was a balcony pierced through to the outside, so that it overlooked not only the hall but the armed guards on the wide steps that approached the buiding. On this balcony, more members of different races talked and stood.

133

Next to the Director's chair, on his left, was a shimmering mirror surface suspended in midair, so that by turning his head only slightly he could see himself reflected at full length. Sometimes he looked and saw himself.

But at this moment, now, he looked outward. In his mind's eye, he looked beyond the throne room and the balcony and the steps without. He saw in his imagination all the planetwide city surrounding, and the five other worlds of this solar system, which were the machine shops and granaries of this crown-world of Duhnbar. This world and system he . . . *ruled* is too mild a word. This world he owned, and wore like a ring on his finger.

All of it, seen in his mind's eye, had the dull tinge of familiarity and sameness.

He moved slightly the index one of his four-jointed fingers, of which he had three, with an opposed thumb on each hand. The male adult of his own race who currently filled a role something like that of chamberlain stepped forward from behind the throne chair. The Director did not look at the Chamberlain, knowing he would be there. The Director's thin lips barely moved in his expressionless, pale green face.

"It has been some moments," he said. "Is there still nothing new?"

"Director of All," said the low voice of the Chamberlain at his ear. "Since you last asked, there has been nothing on the six worlds which has not happened before. Only the landing here at the throne city of a single alien of a new race. He has passed into the city now, omitting to sacrifice at a purple shrine but otherwise behaving as all behave on your worlds."

"Is there anything new," said the Director, "about his failure to sacrifice?"

"The failure is a common one," said the Chamberlain. "It has been many generations since anyone seriously worshiped at a purple shrine. The sacrifice is a mere custom of our port. Strangers not knowing of it invariably fail to light incense on the cube before the purple."

The Director said nothing immediately. The Chamberlain stood waiting. If he had been left to wait until he collapsed another would have taken his place.

"Is there a penalty for this?" said the Director at last.

"The penalty," said the Chamberlain, "by ancient rule is death. But for hundreds of years it has been remitted on payment of a small fine."

The Director turned these words over in his mind.

"There is a value in old customs," he said after a while. "Old customs long fallen into disuse seem almost like something new when they are revived. Let the ancient penalty be reestablished."

"For this transgressor," asked the Chamberlain, "as well as all others after?"

The Director moved his index finger in silent assent and dismissal. The Chamberlain stepped backward and spoke to the under-officers who were always waiting.

The Director, sated with looking out over the hall, turned his gaze slightly to his own seated image in the mirror surface at his left. He saw there an individual a trifle over seven feet in height, seated in a tall, carven chair with ornate armrests. The arms, the legs, the body was covered in a slim, simple garment of sky blue. From the neck of the garment emerged a tall and narrow head with lean features, a straight, almost lipless mouth, narrow nose and a greenish, hairless skull. The eyes were golden, enormous and beautiful.

But neither the eyes nor the face showed any expression. The faces of the Chamberlain and the guards and others of the race sometimes showed expressions. But the Director's face, never. He was several hundreds of years old and would live until he became weary of life.

He had never known what it was to be sick. He had

never known cold, hunger or any discomfort. He had
never known fear, hatred, loneliness or love. He
watched himself now in the mirror; for he posed an un-
ending enigma to himself—an enigma that alone relieved the boredom of his existence. He did not attempt
to investigate the enigma. He only savored it as a con-
noisseur might savor a fine wine.

The image in the mirror he gazed upon was the image
of a being who could find no alternative but to consider
himself as a God.

Will Mauston was broken-knuckled and wrinkled
about the eyes. The knuckles he had broken on human
and alien bones, fighting for what belonged to him. The
wrinkles about the eyes had come from the frowning
harshness of expression evolved from endless bargains
driven. On the infrequent occasions that he got back to
Earth to see his wife and two young children, the
wrinkles almost disappeared . . . for a while. But Earth
was overcrowded and the cost of living there was high.
He always had to leave again, and the wrinkles always
came back. He was twenty-six years old.

He had heard of Duhnbar through a race of inter-
stellar traders called the Kjaka, heavy-bodied, lion-
featured and honest. He had assumed there must be
such a world, as on Earth in the past there had been
ancient cities like Samarkand under Tamerlane, where
the great trade routes crossed. He had searched and in-
quired and the Kjakas had told him. Duhnbar was the
Samarkand of the stars. One mighty stream of trade
flowed out from the highly developed worlds of the
galaxy's center and met here with several peripheral
routes among the outlying, scattered stars.

Will had come alone and he was the first from Earth
to reach it. From this one trip, he could well make
enough to retire and not have to leave his family on
Earth again. The Kjakas were honest and had taught
him the customs of the Duhnbar port. They had sent him

to Khal Dohn, one of their own people on Duhnbar, who would act as Will's agent there. They had forgotten the small matter of the purple shrine. The custom was all but obsolete, the fine was nominal. They had talked of larger transactions and values.

Passing through the terminal building of the port, Will saw a cube of metal, a purple cloth hanging on the wall above it and small purple slivers that fumed and reeked. He passed at a good distance. Experience had taught him not to involve himself with the religions and customs of peoples he did not know.

Riding across the city in an automated vehicle set for the address of his agent, Will passed a square in which there was what seemed to be a sort of forty-foot high clothespole. What was hung on it, however, were not clothes, but bodies. The bodies were not all the native race, and he was glad to leave it behind.

He reached the home of the Kjakan agent. It was a pleasant, two story, four-sided structure surrounding an interior courtyard rich with vegetation unknown to Will. He and his host sat on an interior balcony of the second floor overlooking the courtyard, and talked. The agent's name was Khal Dohn. He ate a narcotic candy particular to his own race and saw that Will was supplied with a pure mixture of distilled water and ethyl alcohol—to which Will added a scotch flavor from one of the small vials he carried at his belt. Will had set up a balance of credit on several Kjakan worlds. Khal Dohn would buy for him on Duhnbar against that credit.

They were beginning a discussion of what was available on Duhnbar that would be best for Will to purchase, speaking in the stellar lingua franca, the trading language among the stars. Abruptly, they were interrupted by a voice from one of the walls, speaking in a tongue Will did not understand. Khal Dohn listened, answered and turned his heavy, leonine face on Will.

"We must go downstairs," he said.

He led Will back down to the room which led to the

street before his home. Waiting there were two of the native race in black, short robes, belted at the waist with silver belts. A black rod showed in a sort of silver pencil-case attached to the belt of each native.

As Will and Khal came down a curving ramp to them, the golden eyes of both natives fastened on Will with mild curiosity.

"Stranger and alien," said one of them in the trade tongue, "you are informed that you are under arrest."

Will looked at them, and opened his mouth. But Khal Dohn was already speaking the native tongue; and after a little while the natives bowed shortly and went out. Khal Dohn turned back to Will.

"Did you see in the terminal—" Khal Dohn described the Purple Shrine. Will nodded. "Did you go near it?"

"No," said Will. "I always steer clear of such things, unless I know about them."

Khal Dohn stared at him for a long moment. Below the heavy, rather oriental fold of flesh, his eyes were sad, dark and unreadable to Will.

"I don't understand," he said at last. "But you are my guest, and my duty is to protect you. We'd better go see an acquaintance of mine—one who has more influence here in the throne city than I do."

He led Will out to one of the automated vehicles. On their way to the home of the acquaintance he answered Will's questions by describing the custom of the Purple Shrine.

"—I don't understand," the Kjaka said. "I should have been able to pay your fine to the police and settle it. But they had specific orders to arrest you and take you in."

"Why didn't they, then?" asked Will.

The dark eyes swung and met his own.

"You're my guest," said Khal Dohn. "I've taken on the responsibility of your surrender at the proper time, while they fulfill my request for the verification of the order to arrest you."

Outside the little vehicle, as they turned into the shadow of a taller building, a coolness seemed to gather about them and reach inside to darken and slow Will's spirits.

"Do you think it's something really important?" he said.

"No," answered Khal Dohn. "No. I'm sure it's all a mistake."

They stopped before a building very like the home of Khal Dohn. Khal led Will up a ramp to a room filled with oversized furniture. From one large chair rose a narrow-bodied, long-handed alien with six fingers to a hand. His face was narrow and horselike. He stood better than seven and a half feet, in jacket and trousers of a dark red color. A dagger hung at his belt.

"You are my guest as always, Khal Dohn!" he cried. His voice was strident and high-pitched. He spoke the trade tongue, but he pronounced the Kjakan name of Khal Dohn with a skill Will had not been able to master. "And welcome as the guest of my guest is—" he turned to Will, speaking to Khal—"what is its name—?"

"*His* name," said Khal, "is Will Mau—" his own, Kjakan tongue failed the English *st* sound—"Will Mauzzon."

"Welcome," said the tall alien. "I am Avoa. What is it?"

"Something I don't understand." Khal switched to the native tongue of Duhnbar and Will was left out of the conversation. They talked some little while.

"I will check," cried Avoa, finally, breaking back into the trade tongue. "Come tomorrow early, Khal Dohn. Bring it with you."

"Him," said Khal. "I will bring him."

"Of course. Of course. Come together. I'll have news for you then. It can be nothing serious."

Khal and Will left and came back to the balcony above the courtyard of Khal's home. They sat talking. The sunset of the planet spread across the western skyline of the throne city, its light staining the white ceiling above them with a wash of red.

"You're sure it's nothing to worry about?" Will asked the Kjaka.

"I'm sure." Khal Dohn fingered one of his narcotic candies in thick fingers. "They have a strict but fair legal code here. And if there is any misunderstanding, Avoa can resolve it. He has considerable influence. Shall we return to talk of business?"

So they talked as the interior lights came on. Later they ate their different meals together—Will's from supplies he had brought from his ship—and parted for the night.

It was a comfortable couch in a pleasant, open-balconied room giving on the courtyard below, that Khal assigned Will. But Will found sleep standing off some distance from him. He was a man of action, but here there was no action to be taken. He walked to the balcony and looked down into the courtyard.

Below, the strange plants were dim shapes in the light of a full moon too weak and pale to be the moon of Earth. He wondered how his wife and the two children were. He wondered if, across the light-years of distance, they were thinking of him at this moment, perhaps worrying about him.

He breathed the unfamiliar, tasteless night air and it seemed heavy in his lungs. At his belt was a container of barbiturates, four capsules of seconal. He had never found the need to take one before in all these years between the stars. He took one now, washing it down with the flat, distilled water they had left in this room for him.

He slept soundly after that, without dreams.

When he woke in the morning, he felt better. Khal Dohn seemed to him to be quite sensible and undisturbed. They rode over to the home of Avoa together;

and Will took the opportunity he had neglected before to pump Khal about the city as they rode through it.

When they entered the room where they had met Avoa the day before, the tall alien was dressed in clothing of a lighter, harsher red but seemed the same in all other ways.

"Well," said Will to him, smiling, after they had greeted each other in the trade tongue. "What did you find out the situation is?"

Avoa stared back at him for a moment, then turned and began to speak rapidly to Khal in the native tongue. Khal answered. After a moment they both stopped and looked at Will without speaking.

"What's happened?" said Will. "What is it?"

"I'm sorry," said Khal slowly, in the trade tongue. "It seems that nothing can be done."

Will stared at him. The words he had heard made no sense.

"Nothing can be done?" he said. "About what? What do you mean?"

"I'm sorry," said Khal. "I mean, Avoa can do nothing."

"Nothing?" said Will.

Neither of the aliens answered. They continued to watch him. Suddenly, Avoa shifted his weight slightly on his long feet, and half-turned toward the doorway of the room.

"I am sorry!" he cried sharply. "Very sorry. But it is a situation out of my control. I can do nothing."

"Why?" burst out Will. He turned to Khal. "What's wrong? You told me their legal system was fair. I didn't know about the shrine!"

"Yes," said Khal. "But this isn't a matter for their law. Their Director has given an order."

"Director?" The word buzzed as deadly and foolishly as a tropical mosquito in Will's ears. "The one on the throne? What's he got to do with it?"

"It was his command," said Avoa suddenly in his strident voice. "The ancient penalty was to be enforced.

After he heard about your omission. From now on, new-comers will be warned. They are fair here."

"Fair!" the word broke from between Will's teeth. "What about me? Doesn't this Director know about me? What is he, anyway?"

Khal and Avoa looked at each other, then back at Will.

"These people here," said Khal slowly, "control trade for light-years in every direction. Not because of any virtue in themselves, but because of the accident of their position here among the stars. They know this—so they need something. A symbol, something to set up, to reassure themselves of their right position."

"In all else, they are reasonable," said Avoa.

"Their symbol," said Khal, "is the Director. They identify with him as being all-powerful, over things in the universe. His slightest whim is obeyed without hesitation. He could order them all to cut their own throats and they would do it, without thinking. But of course he will not. He is not in the least irresponsible. He is sane and of the highest intelligence. But the only law he knows is his own."

Cried Avoa, "He is all but impotent. Ordinarily he does nothing. We interest and amuse him, and he is bored, so he lets us trade here with impunity. But if he does act, there is no appeal. It is a risk we all take. You are not the only one."

"But I've got a wife—" Will broke off suddenly. He had shouted out without thinking in English. They were gazing back at him now without understanding. For a moment a watery film blurred them before his eyes.

The desert-dry wind of a despair blew through him, shriveling his hopes. What did they know of wives and children, or Earth? He saw their faces clearly now, both alien, one heavy and leonine, one patrician and equine. He thought of his wife again, and the children. Without his income they would be forced to emigrate. A remembrance of the bitter, crude and barren livings of the frontier planets came to his mind like strangling smoke.

"Wait," he said, as Avoa turned to go. Will brought his voice down to a reasonable tone. "There must be someone I can appeal to. Khal Dohn." He turned to the Kjaka. "I'm your guest."

"You are my guest," said Khal. "But I can't protect you against this. It's like a natural, physical force—a great wind, an earthquake against which I would be helpless to protect any guest, or even myself."

He looked at Will with his dark, alien eyes, like the eyes of an intelligent beast.

"Pure chance—the chance of the Director hearing about you and the shrine when he did," said Khal, "has selected you. All those who face the risk of trading among the stars know the chance of death. You must have figured the risk, as a good trader should."

"Not like this—" said Will between his teeth, but Avoa interrupted, turning to leave.

"I must go," he said. "I have appointments on the throne room balcony. Khal Dohn, give it anything that will make these last hours comfortable and my house will supply. You must surrender it before midday to the police."

"No!" Will called after the tall alien. "If nobody else can save me, then I want to see him!"

"Him?" said Khal. Avoa suddenly checked, and slowly turned back.

"The Director." Will looked at both of them. "I'll appeal to him."

Khal and Avoa looked at each other. There was a silence.

"No," said Avoa, finally. "It is never done. No one speaks to him." He seemed about to turn again.

"Wait." It was Khal who spoke this time. Avoa looked sharply at him. Khal met the taller alien's eyes. "Will Mauzzon is my guest."

"It is not *my* guest," said Avoa.

"*I* am your guest," said Khal, without emotion.

Avoa stared now at the shorter, heavier-bodied alien.

Abruptly he said something sharply in the native tongue.

Khal did not answer. He stood looking at Avoa without moving.

"It is already dead," Avoa said at last slowly, in the trade tongue, glancing at Will, "and being dead can have no further effect upon the rest of us. You waste your credit with me."

Still Khal neither spoke nor moved. Avoa turned and went out.

"My guest," said Khal, sitting down heavily in one of the oversize chairs of the room, "you have little cause for hope."

After that he sat silent. Will paced the room. Occasionally he glanced at the chronometer on his wrist, adjusted to local time. It showed the equivalent of two and three-quarters hours to noon when the wall chimed and spoke in Avoa's voice.

"You have your audience," said Khal, rising. "I would still advise against hope." He looked with his heavy face and dark eyes at Will. "Worlds can't afford to war against worlds to protect their people, and there is no reason for a Director to change his mind."

He took Will in one of the small automated vehicles to the throne room. Inside the portal, at the steps leading up to the balcony, he left Will.

"I'll wait for you above," Khal said. "Good luck, my guest."

Will turned. At the far end of the room he saw the dais and the Director. He went toward it through the crowd, that at first had hardly noticed him but grew silent and parted before him as he proceeded, until he could hear in the great and echoing silence of the hall the sound of his own footsteps as he approached the dais, the seated figure and the throne, behind which stood natives with the silver pencil cases and black rods at their silver belts.

He came at last to the edge of the dais and stopped,

looking up. Above him, the high greenish skull, the narrow mouth, the golden eyes leaned forward to look down at him; and he saw them profiled in the mirror surface alongside. The profile was no more remote than the living face it mirrored.

Will opened his mouth to speak, but one of the natives behind the throne, wearing the Chamberlain's silver badge, stepped forward as the finger of the Director gestured.

"Wait," said the Chamberlain in the trade tongue. He turned and spoke behind him. Will waited, and the silence stretched out long in the hall. After a while there was movement and two natives appeared, one with a small chair, one with a tube-shaped container of liquid.

"Sit," said the Chamberlain. "Drink. The Director has said it."

Will found himself seated and with the tube in his hand. An odor of alcohol diluted with water came to his nostrils; and for a moment a burst of wild laughter trembled inside him. Then he controlled it and sipped from the tube.

"What do you say?" said the Chamberlain.

Will lifted his face to the unchanging face of the Director. Like the unreachable stare of an insect's eyes the great golden orbs regarded him.

"I haven't intentionally committed any crime," said Will.

"The Director," said the Chamberlain, "knows this."

His voice was flat, uninflected. But he seemed to wait. The golden eyes of the throned figure seemed to wait, also watching. Irrationally, Will felt the first small flame of a hope flicker to life within him. His trader's instinct stirred. If they would listen, there must always be a chance.

"I came here on business," he said, "the same sort of business that brings so many. Certainly this world and the trading done on it are tied together. Without Duhnbar there could be no trading place here. And without the trading would Duhnbar and its other sister worlds still be the same?"

He paused, looking upward for some reaction.

"The Director," said the Chamberlain, "is aware of this."

"Certainly, then," said Will, "if the traders here respect the laws and customs of Duhnbar, shouldn't Duhnbar respect the lives of those who come to trade?" He stared at the golden eyes hanging above him, but he could read no difference in them, no response. They seemed to wait still. He took a deep breath. "Death is—"

He stopped. The Director had moved on his throne. He leaned slowly forward until his face hung only a few feet above Will's. He spoke in the trade tongue, in a slow, deep, unexpectedly resonant voice.

"Death," he said, "is the final new experience."

He sat slowly back in his chair. The Chamberlain spoke.

"You will go now," he said.

Will sat staring at him, the tube of alcohol and water still in his grasp.

"You will go," repeated the Chamberlain. "You are free until midday and the moment of your arrest."

Will's head jerked up. He snapped to his feet from the chair.

"Are you all insane?" he shouted at the Chamberlain. "You can't do this sort of thing without an excuse! My people take care of their own—"

He broke off at the sight of the Chamberlain's unmoved face. He felt suddenly dizzy and nauseated at the pit of his stomach.

Said the Chamberlain, "It is understandable that you do not want to die. You will go now or I will have you taken away."

Something broke inside Will.

It was like the last effort of a man in a race who feels the running man beside him pulling away and tries, but cannot match the pace. Dazedly, dully, he turned. Blindly he walked the first few steps back toward the distant portal.

"*Wait.*"

The Chamberlain's voice turned him around.

"Come back," said the Chamberlain. "The Director will speak."

Numbly he came back. The Director leaned forward once more, until when Will halted their faces were only a few feet apart.

"You will not die," said the Director.

Will stared up at the alien face without understanding. The words rang and reechoed like strange, incomprehensible sounds in his ears.

"You will live," said the Director. "And when I send for you, from time to time, you will come again and talk to me."

Will continued to stare. He felt the smooth, flexible tube of liquid in his right hand, and he felt it bulge between his fingers as his fingers contracted spasmodically. He opened his lips but no words worked their way past his tight muscles of his throat.

"It is interesting," said the deep and thrilling voice of the Director, as his great, golden eyes looked down at Will, "that you do not understand me. It is interesting to explain myself to you. You give me reasons why you should not die."

"—Reasons?" Between Will's dry lips, the little word slipped huskily out. Miraculously, out of the ashes of his despair, he felt the tiny warmth of a new hope.

"Reasons," said the Director. "You give me reasons. And there are no reasons. There is only me."

The hope flickered and stumbled in its reach for life.

"I will make you understand now," said the deep and measured voice of the Director. "It is I who am responsible for all things that happen here. It is my whim that moves them. There is nothing else."

The golden eyes looked into Will's.

"It was my whim," said the Director, "that the penalty of the shrine's neglect should be imposed once more. Since I had decided so, it was unavoidable that you should die. For when I decide, all things follow inexorably. There is no other way or thing."

Will stared, the muscles of his neck stiff as an iron brace.

"But then," said the deep voice beneath the glorious eyes, "as you were leaving another desire crossed my mind. That you might interest me again on future occasions."

He paused.

"Once more," he said, "all things followed. If you were to interest me in the future, you could not die. And so you are not to." His eyes held Will's. "And now you understand."

A faint thoughtfulness clouded his golden eyes.

"I have done something with you this day," he said almost to himself, "that I have never done before. It is quite new. I have made you know what you are, in respect to what I am. I have taken a creature not even of my own people and made it understand it has no life or death or reasons of its own, except those my desires desire."

He stopped speaking. But Will still stood, rooted.

"Do not be afraid," said the Director. "I killed you. But I have brought another creature who understands to life in your body. One who will walk this world of mine for many years before he dies."

A sudden brilliance like a sheet of summer lightning flared in Will's head, blinding him. He heard his own voice shouting, in a sound that was rage without meaning. He flung his right arm forward and up as his sight cleared, and saw the liquid in the tube he had held splash itself against the downward-gazing, expressionless face above him, and the container bounce harmlessly from the sky-blue robe below the face.

There was a soundless jerk through all the natives behind the throne. A soundless gasp as if the air had changed. Native hands had flown to the black rods. But there they hung.

The Director had not moved. The watered alcohol dripped slowly from his nose and chin. But his features were unchanged, his hands were still, no finger on either hand stirred.

He continued to gaze at Will. After a long second, Will turned. He was not quite sure what he had done, but something sullen and brave burned redly in him.

He began to walk up the long aisle through the crowd, toward the distant portal. In that whole hall he was the only thing moving. The thousand different traders followed him with their eyes, but otherwise none moved, and no one made a sound. From the crowd there was silence. From the balcony overlooking, and the steps beyond the entrance, there was silence.

Step by echoing step he walked the long length of the hall and passed through the towering archway into the bright day outside. He made it as far as halfway down the steps before, inside the hall, the Director's finger lifted, the message of that finger was flashed to the ranked guards outside, and the black rods shot him down with flame in the sunlight.

On the balcony above, overlooking those steps, Avoa stirred at last, turning his eyes from what was left of Will and looking down at Khal Dohn beside him.

"What was . . ." Avoa's voice fumbled and failed. He added, almost humbly. "I am sorry. I do not even know the proper pronoun."

"He," said Khal Dohn, still looking down at the steps.

"He. What did he call himself?" Avoa said. "You told me, but I do not remember. I should have listened, but I did not. What did you say—what was he?"

Khal Dohn lifted his heavy head and looked up at last.

"He was a man," said Khal Dohn.

ANCIENT, MY ENEMY ·

They stopped at the edge of the mountains eight hours after they had left the hotel. The day was only a dim paling of the sky above the rugged skyline of rock to the east when they set up their shelter in a little level spot—a sort of nest among the granitic cliffs, ranging from fifty to three hundred meters high, surrounding them.

With the approach of dawn the Udbahr natives trailing them had already begun to seek their own shelters, those cracks in the rock into which they would retreat until the relentless day had come and gone again and the light of the nearer moon called them out. Already holed up high among the rocks, some of the males had begun to sing.

"What's he saying? What do the words mean?" demanded the girl graduate student, fascinated. Her name was Willy Fairchild and in the fading light of the nearer moon she showed tall and slim, with short whitish-blond hair around a thin-boned face.

Kiev Archad shrugged. He listened a moment.

He translated:

> You desert me now, female,
> Because I am crippled,
> And yet all my fault was
> That I did not lack courage.
> Therefore I will go now to the
> high rocks to die,
> And another will take you.
> For what good is a warrior
> Whose female forsakes him?

Kiev stopped translating.

"Go on," said Willy. The song was still mournfully falling upon them from the rocks above.

"There isn't any more," said Kiev. "He just keeps singing it over and over again. He'll go on singing until it's time to seal his hole and keep the heat from drying him up."

"Oh," said Willy. "Is he really crippled, do you think?"

Kiev shrugged again.

"I doubt it," he said. "If he were really hurt he'd be keeping quiet, so none of the other males could find him. As it is, he's probably just hoping to lure another one of them close—so that he can kill himself a full meal before the sun rises."

She gasped.

He looked at her. "Sorry," he said. "If you weren't printed with the language, maybe you weren't printed with the general info—"

"Like the fact they're cannibals? Of course I was," she said. "It doesn't disturb me at all. Cannibalism is perfectly reasonable in an environment like this where the only other protein available is rock rats—and everything else, except humans, is carbohydrates."

She glanced at one of the several moonplants growing like outsize mushrooms from the rocky rubble of the surface beside the shelter's silver walls. They had already pulled their petals into the protection of horny overhoods. But they had not yet retreated into the ground.

"After all," she said into his silence, "my field's anthropopathic history. People who disturb easily just don't take that up for a study. There were a number of protein-poor areas back on Earth and so-called primitive local people became cannibals out of necessity."

"Oh," said Kiev. He wriggled his wide shoulders briefly against the short pre-dawn chill. "We'd better be getting inside and settled. You'll need as much rest as you can get. We'll have to strike the shelter so as to start our drive at sunset."

"Sunset?" She frowned. "It'll still be terribly hot, won't it? What drive?"

He turned sharply to look at her.

"I thought—if you knew about their eating habits—"

"No," she said, interested. "No one said anything to me about drives."

"We've been picking up a gang of them ever since we left the hotel," he said. "And we're protein, too, just as you say. Or at least, enough like their native protein for them to hope to eat us. Sooner or later, if there get to be enough of them, they'll attack—if we don't drive them first."

"Oh, I see. You scare them off before they can start something."

"Something like that—yes." He turned, ran his finger down the closure of the shelter and threw back the flap. "That's why Wadjik and Shant came this far with us—so we could have four men for the drive. Come on, we've got to get inside."

She went past him into the shelter.

Inside, Johnson and the other prospecting team of Wadjik and Shant—who would split with them next evening—were already cozy. Johnson was hunched in his thermal sleeping bag, reading. Wadjik and Shant were at a card table playing bluet. Johnson turned his dark face to Kiev and Willy as they came in.

He said, "I laid your bags out for you—beyond the stores."

"Regular nursemaid," said Wadjik without looking up from his cards.

"Wad," said Johnson, quietly. "You and Shanny can shelter up separately if you want." His bare arms and chest swelled with muscle above the partly open slit of his thermal bag. He was not as big as Wadjik or Kiev but he was the oldest and knew the mountains better than any of them.

"Two more cards," said Wadjik looking to Shant.

The gray-headed man dealt.

Kiev led the way around the card table. Two unrolled thermal bags occupied the floor space next to the entrance to the lavatory partition that gave privacy to the shelter's built-in chemical toilet. Kiev gave the one nearest to the partition to Willy and unrolled the other next to the pile of stores.

The pile was really not much as a shelter divider. By merely lifting himself on one elbow, once he was in his bag, Kiev was able to see the other three bags and Johnson, reading. The card players, sitting up at their table, could look down on both Kiev and Willy—but, of course, once it really started to heat up, they would be in their sacks too.

Kiev undressed within his thermal bag, handing his clothes out as he took them off and keeping his back turned to the girl. When at last he turned to her he saw that, while she was also in her bag, she still wore a sort of light blouse or skivvy shirt—he had no idea what the proper name for it was.

"That's all right for now," he said, nodding at the blouse. "But later on you'll be wanting to get completely down into the bag for coolness, anyhow, so it won't matter for looks. And any kind of cloth between you and the bag's inner surface cuts its efficiency almost in half."

"I don't see why," she answered stiffly.

"They didn't tell you that either?" he asked. "Part of the main idea behind using the thermal bag is that we don't have to carry too heavy an air-conditioning unit. If you take heat from anything, even a human body, you've got to pump it somewhere else. That's what an air-conditioning unit does. But these bags are stuffed between the walls with a chemical heat-absorbent—"

He went on, trying to explain to her that the bag could soak up the heat from her naked body over a fourteen-hour period without getting so full of heat it lost its cooling powers. But the lining of the bag was built to operate in direct contact with the human skin. Anything like cloth in between caused a build-up of stored heat that would overload the bag before the fourteen hours until cool-off was over. It was not just a matter of comfort—she would be risking heat prostration and even death.

She listened stiffly. He did not know if he had convinced her or not. But he got the feeling that when the time finally came she would get rid of the garment. He lay back in his own bag, closed his eyes and tried to get some sleep. In another four hours sleep would be almost impossible even in the bags.

Wadjik and Shant were fools with their cards. A man could tough out a drive with only a couple of hours of sleep; but what if some accident during the next shelter stop kept him from getting any sleep at all? He could be half-dead with heat and exhaustion by the following

cool-off, his judgment gone and his reflexes shot. One
little bit of bad luck could finish him off. Characters like
Johnson had survived in the mountains all these years
by always keeping in shape. After four trips into the
grounds Kiev had made up his mind to do the same
thing.

He slept. The heat woke him.
He found he had instinctively slid down into his bag
and sealed it up to the neck without coming fully awake.
Opening his eyes now, feeling the blasting dryness and
quivering heat of the air against his already parched
face, he first pulled his head down completely into the
bag and took a deep breath. The hot air from above,
pulled momentarily into the bag, cooled on his dust-dry
throat and mouth. He worked some saliva into existence, swallowed several times and then, sitting up, pushed his head and one arm out of the bag. He found his
salve and began to grease his face and neck.

He glanced over at Willy as he worked. She was lying
muffled in her thermal bag, watching him, her features
shining with salve.

"You take that shirt off?" he asked.

She nodded briefly. He looked over past the deserted
card table at the three other thermal bags. Johnson,
encased to his nose, slept with the ease of an old prospector, his upper face placidly shining with salve. Shant
was out of sight in his bag—all but his close-cut cap of
gray hair. Wadjik was propped up against a case from
the stores, his heavy-boned face under its uncombed
black hair absent-eyed, staring at and through Kiev.

"Wad," said Kiev, "better get Shanny up out of that.
He'll overload his sack in five hours if he goes to sleep
breathing down there like that."

Wadjik's eyes focused. He grinned unpleasantly and
rolled over on his side. He bent in the middle and kicked
the foot of his thermal bag hard against the side of
Shant's. Shant's head popped into sight.

"You go to sleep down there," Wad snarled, "and you won't live until sunset."

"Oh—sure, Wad. Sorry," Shant said, quickly.

A short silence fell. Wadjik had gone back to staring through unfocused eyes. Johnson woke but the only sign he gave was the raising of his eyelids. He did not move in his bag. Around them all, now, the heat was becoming a living thing—an invisible but sentient presence, a demon inside the shelter who could be felt growing stronger almost by the second. The shelter's little air-conditioner· hummed, keeping the air about them moving and just below unbreathable temperature.

"Kiev," said Wadjik, suddenly. "Was that old Hehog you and Willy were listening to out there, just before dawn?"

"Yes," said Kiev.

"This time we'll get him."

"Maybe," said Kiev.

"No maybe. I mean it, man." "

"We'll see," said Kiev.

A movement came beside Kiev. Willy sat up in her bag.

"Mr. Wadjik—"

"Joe. I told you—Joe."

Wadjik grinned at her.

"All right. Joe. Do you mean you don't know which Udbahr male that was—the one who was singing? Don't you know why I'm going to these prospecting grounds of yours? Don't you know about the remains of a city there built by these same Udbahrs?"

"Sure, I've seen it. What of it?"

"I'm telling you what of it! They had a high level of civilization once—or at least a higher level than now. But that doesn't mean anything to you—"

"They degenerated. That's what it means to me. They're cannibal degenerates. And you want me to treat them like human beings—"

"I want you to treat them like intelligent beings—

which they are. Even an uneducated, brutal, stupid man like you ought to understand—"

"Listen to who's talking. The kid historian speaks. I thought you were still in school, writing a thesis. You didn't tell me you'd been at this for years—"

"I may be only a graduate student but I've learned a few things you never did—"

Looking past Wadjik's heat-reddened face, flaming under its salve, Kiev saw the upper part of Johnson's countenance beyond. Johnson seemed to be calmly listening. There was nothing to do, Kiev knew, but listen. It was the heat—the sickening intoxication of the deadly heat in the shelter—that was making the argument. When the heat reached its most relentless intensity only the instinct keeping men in their thermal bags stopped them from killing each other.

Wadjik finally broke off the argument by drawing down into his bag and rolling across the floor of the shelter to the lavatory door. He pressed the bottom latch through his bag, opened the door, rolled inside and shut himself off from the rest of the room. Willy fell silent.

Kiev looked sideways at her.

"It's no use," he whispered to her. "Save your energy."

She turned and glared at him.

"And I thought you were different!" she spat and slid down, head and all, into her bag.

Kiev backed into his own cocoon. Fueled by the feverishness induced by the heat, his mind ran on. They were all a little crazy, he thought, all who had taken up prospecting. Crazy or they had something to hide in their pasts that would keep them from ever leaving this planet.

But a man who was clean elsewhere could become rich in five years if he kept his head—and kept his health —both on the trips and back in civilization. On Kiev's first trip into the mountains, two years ago, he had not known what he was after. Just a lot of money, he had thought, to blow back at the hotels. But now he knew better. He was going to take it cool and calm, like Johnson—who could never leave the planet.

Kiev meant to keep his own backtrail clear. And he would leave when the time came with enough to buy him citizenship and a good business franchise back on one of the Old Worlds. He had his picture of the future clear in his mind. A modern home on a settled world, a steady, good income. Status. A family.

He had seen enough of the wild edges of civilization. Leave the rest of it to the new kids coming out. He was still young but he could look ahead and see thirty up there waiting for him.

His thoughts rambled on through the deadly hours as his body temperature was driven slowly upward by the heat. In the end his mind rambled and staggered. He awoke suddenly.

He had passed from near-delirium into sleep without realizing it. The deadly heat of mid-afternoon had broken toward cool-off and with the first few degrees of relief within the shelter he, like all the rest, had dropped immediately into exhausted slumber. By now—he glanced at the wristwatch on the left sleeve of his outer-gear—the hour was nearly sunset.

He looked about the shelter. Willy, Shant, Wadjik, Johnson were still sleeping.

"Hey," he croaked at them, speaking above a whisper for the first time in hours. "Time for the drive. Up and at 'em."

In forty-five minutes they were all dressed, fed and outside, with the shelter folded and packed, along with the outer equipment, on grav-sleds ready to travel. Wadjik and Shant took off to the north, towing their own grav-sled. Kiev and Johnson were left with their sled and the girl. They looked at her thoughtfully. The sun was already down below the peaks to the west. But three-quarters of the sky above them was still white with a glare too bright to look at directly and the heat, even with outersuit and helmet sealed, made every movement a new cause for perspiration. The climate units of the suits whined with their effort to keep the occupants dry and cool.

"I'm not going to join you," Willy snapped. "I won't be a party to any killing of the natives."

"We can't leave you behind," Kiev answered. "Unless you can handle a gun—and will use it. If any of the males break away from the drive they'll double back and you'd make an easy meal."

Inside the transparent helmet her face was pale even in the heat.

"You can stick with the grav-sled," said Kiev. "You don't have to join the drive. Just keep up."

She did not look at him or speak. She was not going to give him the satisfaction of an answer, he thought.

"Move out, then," said Johnson.

They began to climb the cliffs toward the brightness in the sky, the grav-sled trailing behind them on slave circuit, its load piled high. Willy, looking small in her suit, trudged behind it. Under the crown of the cliffs they turned about, deployed to cover both sides of the clearing below and began their drive.

They worked forward, each man firing into every rock niche or cranny that might have an Udbahr sealed up within it. Deep, booming sounds—made by the air and moisture within each cranny exploding outward—began to echo between the cliffs. Soon a shout came over Kiev's suit intercom in Johnson's deep voice.

"One running! One running! Eleven o'clock, sixty meters, down in the cleft there."

Kiev jerked his gaze ahead and caught a glimpse of an adult-sized, humanlike, brown figure with a greenishly naked, round skull and large tarsierlike eyes, vanishing up a narrow cut.

"No clothing," called Kiev over the intercom. "Must be a female, or a young male."

"Or maybe old Hehog playing it incognito—" Johnson began but was interrupted.

"One running! One running!" bellowed Wadjik's voice distantly over the intercom. "Two o'clock, near clifftop."

"One running! Deep in the pass there at three o'clock!" chimed in Johnson, again. "Keep them moving!"

The sounds of the blasting attack were now routing out Udbahrs who had denned up for the day. Most were females or young, innocent of either clothing or weapons. But here and there was a heavier, male figure, running with spear or throwing-stick in hand and wearing anything from a rope of twisted rock vines or rat furs around his waist to some tattered article of clothing, stolen, scavenged—or just possibly taken as a war prize—from the dead body of a human prospector.

The males were slowed by their insistence on herding the females and the young ahead of them. They always did this, even though nearly all prospectors made it a point to kill only the grown males—the warriors who were liable to attack if left alive. The pattern was old, familiar—one of the things that made most prospectors swear the Udbahrs had to be animal rather than intelligent. The females and young were gathering into a herd as they ran, joining up beyond the screen of the males following them. When the herd was complete—when all who should be in it had been accounted for—the males would choose their ground, stop and turn to fight and hold up the pursuers while the females and young escaped.

They always reacted the same way, no matter whether the tactic were favorable or not in the terrain where they being driven, Kiev thought suddenly. Everything the Udbahrs did was by rote. And strange to creatures who reasoned like men. No matter what Willy said, it was hard to think of them as any kind of

people—let alone people with whom you could become
involved. For example, if he, Johnson, Shant and Wadjik
quit driving the natives now and pulled back, the
Udbahr males would immediately turn around and start
trying to kill each other. It was only when they were
being driven or were joining for an attack on prospectors that the males had ever been known to cooper-
ate.

So, as it always went, it went this sunset hour on the
Udbahr Planet. By the time the last light of the day star
was beginning to evaporate from the western sky and
the great ghostly circle of the nearer moon was beginning to be visible against a more reasonably lighted
sky, some half dozen of the Udbahr males disappeared
suddenly among the boulders and rocks at the mouth of
a pass down which the herd of females and young were
vanishing.

"Hold up," Johnson gasped over the intercom. "Hold
it up. They've forted. Stop and breathe."

Kiev checked his weary legs and collapsed into sitting
position on a boulder, panting. His body was damp all
over in spite of the efforts of his suit to keep him dry.
His head rang with a headache induced by exhaustion
and the heat.

The Udbahr males hidden among the rocks near the
mouth of the pass began to sing their individual songs of
defiance.

Kiev's breathing eased. His headache receded to a dull
ache and finally disappeared. The last of the daylight
was all but gone from the sky behind them. The nearer
moon, twice as large as the single moon of Earth by
which all moons were measured, was sharply outlined,
bright in the sky, illuminating the scene with a sort of
continuing twilight.

"What're you waiting for?" Willy's voice said dully in
his earphones. "Why don't you go and kill them?"

He turned to look for her and was astonished to find
her, with the grav-sled, almost beside him. She had sat

down on the ground, her back bowed as if in deep discouragement, her face turned away and hidden from him within the transparent helmet.

"They'll come to us," he muttered without thinking.

Suddenly she curled up completely into a huddled ball of silver outerwear suit and crystalline helmet. The sheer, unutterable anguish of her pose squeezed at his throat.

He dropped down to his knees beside her and put his arms around her. She did not respond.

"You don't understand—" he said. And then he had the sense to tongue off the interphone and speak to her directly and privately through the closeness of their helmets, alone. "You don't understand."

"I do understand. You like to do this. You like it."

Her voice was muffled, dead.

His heart turned over at the sound of it and suddenly, unexpectedly, he realized that he had somehow managed to fall in love with her. He felt sick inside. It was all wrong—all messed up. He had meant to go looking for a woman—but eventually, after he'd made his stake and gone back to some civilized world. He had not planned anything like this involvement with a girl he had known only five days and who had all sorts of wild notions about how things should be. He did not know what to do except kneel there, holding her.

"If you don't like it why do you do it?" her voice said. "If you really don't like it—then don't do it. Now. Let these go."

"I can't," he said.

The singing broke off suddenly in a concerted howl from the Udbahr males, mingled with a triumphant cry over the intercom from Wadjik.

"Got one." And then: "Look out. Stones."

Kiev jerked into the shelter of a boulder, dragging Willy with him. Two rocks, each about half the size of his fist, dug up the ground where they had crouched together.

"You see?"

He pushed her roughly from him and drew his side-arm. Leaning around the boulder, he searched the rocks of the slope below the pass, watching the vernier needle of the heat-indicator slide back and forth on the weapon's barrel. It jumped suddenly and he stopped moving.

He peered into the gun's rear sights, thumbing the near lens to telescopic. He held his aim on the warm location, studying the small area framed in the sight screen. Suddenly he made it out—a tiny patch of brown between a larger boulder and a bit of upright, broken rock.

He aimed carefully.

"Don't do it."

He jerked involuntarily, sending his beam wide of the mark at the sound of her voice. A patch of bare gravel boomed and flew. The bit of brown color disappeared from between the rocks. He leaned the front of his helmet wearily against the near side of the boulder before him.

"Damn you," he said helplessly. "What are you doing to me?"

"I'm trying to save you," she said fiercely, "from being a murderer."

Another stone hit the top of the boulder behind which they hid and caromed off their heads.

"How about saving me from that?" he said emptily. "Don't you understand? If we don't kill them they'll try to kill us—"

"I don't believe it." She, too, had shut off her inter-com. Her voice came to him distantly through two thick-nesses of transparent material. "Have you ever tried? Has anyone ever tried?"

Another sudden volley of stones was followed by more dull explosives as the heat of the human weapons found and destroyed live targets. Shant and Wadjik were howling in triumph and shooting steadily.

"We got five—they're on the run." Shant whooped.
"Kiev! Johnson! They're on the run."

The explosions ceased. Kiev peered cautiously around
his boulder, stood up slowly. Wadjik, Shant, and Johnson had risen from positions in a semicircle facing the
distant pass.

"Any get away?" Johnson was asking.

"One, maybe two—" Shant cut himself short. "Look
out—duck. Twelve o'clock, fifty meters."

At once Kiev was again down behind his boulder. He
dragged down Willy, tongued on his intercom.

"What is it?"

"That chunk of feldspar about a meter high—"

Kiev looked down the slope until his eyes found the
rock. A glint that came and went behind and above it,
winking in the waxing light of the nearer moon that now
seemed as bright as a dull, cloudy day back on Earth.
The flash came and went, came and went.

Kiev recognized it presently as a reflection from the
top curve of a transparent helmet bobbing back and
forth like the head of someone dancing just behind the
boulder. A male Udbahr's voice began to sing behind the
rock.

> Man with a head-and-a-half,
> come and get your half-head.
> Man with a head-and-a-half
> Come so I can kill you.
> Ancient, my enemy.
> Ancient, my enemy—

"Hehog," snapped Johnson's voice over the helmet
intercom.

Silence held for a minute. Then Wadjik's voice came
thinly through the phones.

"What are you waiting for, Kiev?"

Kiev said nothing. The transparent curve of the

helmet top rose again, bobbed and danced behind the boulder. It danced higher. Within it now was a bald, round, greenish skull with reddish, staring tarsier eyes and—finally revealed—the lipless gash of a fixedly grinning mouth.

"What is it? What's Wadjik mean?" Willy asked.

Her voice rang loud in Kiev's helmet phones. She had reactivated her intercom.

"It's Hehog down there," Kiev said between stiff jaws. "That's my helmet he's wearing. He's had it ever since he first took it off me my first trip into the mountains."

"Took it off you?"

"I was new. I'd never been on a drive before," muttered Kiev. "I got hit in the chest by a stone, had the wind knocked out of me. Next thing I knew Hehog was lifting off my helmet. My partners came up shooting and drove him off."

"What about it, Kiev?" The voice was Johnson's. "Do you want us to spread out and get behind him? Or you want to go down and get the helmet by yourself?"

Kiev grunted under his breath, took his sidearm into his left hand and flexed the cramped fingers of his right. They had been squeezing the gunbutt as if to mash it out of all recognizable shape.

"I'm going alone," he said over the intercom. "Stay back."

He got his heels under him and was ready to rise when he was unexpectedly yanked backward to the gravel. Willy had pulled him down.

"You're not going."

He tongued off his intercom, turned and jerked her hand loose from his suit.

"You don't understand," he shouted at her through his helmet. "That's the trouble with you. You don't understand a damn thing."

He pushed her from him, rose and dived for the protection of a boulder four meters down the slope in front of him and a couple of meters to his right.

A flicker of movement came from below as he moved —the upward leap of a throwing-stick behind the rock where Hehog hid. Kiev glimpsed something dark racing through the air toward him. A rock fragment struck and burst on the boulder-face, spraying him with stone chips and splinters.

Reckless now, he threw himself toward the next bit of rock cover farther down the slope. His foot caught on a stony outcropping in the shale. He tripped and rolled, tumbling helplessly to a stop beside the very boulder behind which Hehog crouched, throwing-stick in one hand, stone-tipped spear in the other.

Kiev sprawled on his back. He stared helplessly up into the great eyes and humorlessly grinning mouth looming over him inside the other helmet less than an arm's length away. The spear twitched in the brown hand—but that was all.

Hehog stared into Kiev's eyes. Kiev was aware of Willy and the others shouting through his helmet phones. A couple of shots blasted grooves into the boulder-top above his head. And with a sudden, wordless cry Hehog bounded to his feet and dodged away among the boulders toward the pass.

The bright beams of shots from the human guns followed him but lost him. He vanished into the pass.

Kiev climbed to his feet, shaking inside. He awoke to the fact that he was still holding his sidearm. A bitter understanding broke upon him with the hard, unsparing clarity of an Udbahr Planet dawn.

He could have shot Hehog at pointblank range during the moment he had spent staring frozenly at the spear in Hehog's hand and at the great-eyed, grinning head within the helmet. Hehog had to have seen the gun. And that would have been why he had not tried to throw the spear.

Kiev cursed blackly. He was still cursing when the others slid down the loose rock of the slope to surround him.

"What happened?" demanded Shant.

"He—" Kiev discovered that his intercom was still off. He tongued it on. "He got away."

"We know he got away," said Wadjik. "What we want to know is how come?"

"You saw," Kiev snapped. "I fell. He had me. You scared him off."

"He had you? I thought you had *him*, damn it!"

"All right, he's gone," Johnson said. "That's the main thing. Leave the other bodies for whoever wants to eat them. We've had a good drive. We'll split up, now." He looked at Wadjik and Shant. "See you back in civilization."

Wadjik cursed cheerfully.

"Team with the heaviest load buys the drinks," he said. "Come on, Shanny."

The two of them turned away, dragging their loaded grav-sled through the air behind them.

Kiev, Willy and Johnson reached Dead City a good two hours before dawn. They had time to pick out one of the empty, windowless houses, half-cave, half-building, to use as permanent headquarters. Tomorrow night they would cut stone to fill the open doorway but for today the shelter, fitted double-thick into the opening, would do well enough.

No singing came from the surrounding cliffs. Johnson crawled in. Kiev lingered to speak to Willy.

"You don't have to worry." The words were not what he had planned to say. "The Udbahrs are scared of this place."

"I know." She did not look at him. "Of course. I know more about this city and the Udbahrs than even Mr. Johnson does. There's a taboo on this place for them."

"Yes." Kiev looked down at his gloved right hand and spread the fingers, still feeling the hard butt of his sidearm clamped inside them. "About earlier tonight, with Hehog—"

"It's all right," she said softly, looking unexpectedly up at him. Her intercom was off and her voice came to him through her helmet. In the combination of the low-angled moonlight and the first horizon glow of the dawn, her face seemed luminescent. "I know you did it for me—after all."

He stared at her.

"Did what?"

She still spoke softly: "I know why you let that Udbahr male live. It was because of what I'd said, wasn't it? But you need to be ashamed of nothing. You simply haven't gone bad inside, like the others. Don't worry—I won't tell anyone."

She took his arm gently with both hands and lifted her head as if—had they been unhelmeted—she might have kissed his cheek. Then she turned and disappeared into the cave.

He followed her after some moments. A small filter panel in the shelter had let a little of the terrible daylight through for illumination. Here artificial lighting had to be on. Kiev saw by it that she had piled stores and opened some of her own gear to set up a four-foot wall that gave her individual privacy.

He laid out his own thermal bag. The heat was quite bearable behind the insulation of the thick-walled building as the day began. Kiev fell into a deep, exhausted sleep that seemed completely dreamless.

He awoke without warning. Instantly alert, he rose to an elbow.

The light was turned down. He heard no sound from Willy. Johnson snored.

Kiev remained stiffly propped on one elbow. A feeling of danger prickled his skin. He found his ears were straining for some noise that did not belong here.

He listened.

For a long moment he heard only the snoring and be-yond it silence. Then he heard what had awakened him. It came again, like the voice of some imprisoned spirit—not from beyond the wall but from under the stone floor on which he lay.

> *Man with a head-and-a-half,*
> *come and get your half-head.*
> *Man with a head-and-a-half,*
> *Come, so I can kill you.*
> *Ancient, my enemy.*
> *Ancient, my enemy.*

The singing broke off suddenly. Kiev jerked bolt up-right and the thermal bag fell down around his waist. Suddenly more loudly through the rock, and nearer, the voice echoed in the dim interior of the stone building:

> *Only for ourselves is the killing*
> *of each other!*
> *Man with a head-and-a-half,*
> *come and get your half-head.*
> *Man with a head-and-a-half . . .*

The singing continued. Fury uprushed like vomit in Kiev. He swore, tearing off his thermal bag and pawing through his piled outerwear. His fingers closed on the butt of the weapon. He jerked it clear, aimed it at the section of the floor from which the singing was coming and pressed the trigger.

Light, heat and thunder shredded the sleeping quiet of the dimly lit room. Kiev held the beam steady, a hotter rage inside him than he could express with the rock-rending gun. He felt his arm seized. The sidearm was torn from his grip. He whirled to find Johnson holding the weapon out of reach.

"Give me that," Kiev said thickly.

"Wake up," Johnson said, low-voiced. "What's got into you?"

"Didn't you hear?" Kiev shouted at him. "That was Hehog—Hehog! Down there!"

He pointed at the hole with its melted sides, half a meter deep into the floor of the building.

"I heard," said Johnson. "It was Hehog, all right. There must be tunnels under some of these buildings."

Willy chimed in.

"But Udbahrs don't—"

Kiev and Johnson turned to see her staring at them over the top of her barricade. Kiev became suddenly conscious that, like Johnson, he was completely without clothes.

Willy's face disappeared abruptly. Kiev turned back to look at the hole his gun had burned in the stone. It showed no breakthrough into further darkness at the bottom.

"All right," he said shakily. "I'm sorry. I woke up hearing him and just jumped—that's all. We can shift to another building tomorrow. And sound for tunnels before we move in."

Johnson turned and returned to his thermal bag. Kiev resumed his cocoon. He lay on his back, hands behind his head, staring up at the shadowy ceiling.

. . . *Ancient, my enemy . . . ancient, my enemy . . .*

The memory of Hehog's chant continued to run through his head.

You and me, Hehog. I'll show you, Udbahr . . .

After some time he fell asleep.

They moved camp the next night, as soon as the sun was down. Kiev and Johnson quarried large chunks of rock from the wall of an adjoining building, melted them into place to fill up the new door opening, except for the entrance unit, which was set up double as a heat lock and fitted into place.

Now the shelter air-conditioner could keep the whole interior of the new building comfortable all day long. The night was half over by the time they finished.

Kiev and Johnson had some four hours left to trek to their prospecting area. The gold ore deposits in the neighborhood of Dead City were almost always in pipes and easily worked out in a few days by men with the proper equipment.

Kiev hesitated.

"I'll stay," he said. "With Hehog around, someone's got to stay with Miss Fairchild."

Johnson regarded him thoughtfully.

"You're right. If we leave her here alone Hehog's sure to get her. And who would sell us gear for our next trip if word got out about how we left her to be killed?" He hesitated. "Tell you what—we'll draw straws."

Kiev said, "I'll stay. Drop back in a week. I'll tell you then if I need you to take over."

Johnson nodded. He turned away and began his packing—food, weapons, equipment, a water drill for tapping the moonflower root systems. Also, a breathing membrane for sealing the caves they would be denning up in by day. Kiev, squatting, making a final check of the seal around the entrance, saw a shadow fall across a seam he was examining.

He stood up, turned and saw Willy down the street, taking solidographs of one of the buildings. Johnson stood just behind him, equipment already on his backpack.

"We haven't had a chance to talk," Johnson said.

"No."

"Let me say now what I've wanted to say. Why don't you pack up and go back—and take the girl with you?"

"I've got my stake to make out here—like everybody else."

"You know there's more to the situation. Hehog's changed everything. Also, there's the girl—we both know what I mean. And there's something else—something I don't think you're aware of."

"What?"

"You've heard how sometimes the males—if they've just fed so they aren't hungry and there's only one of them around—will come into your camp and sit down to talk?"

Kiev frowned at him.

"I've heard of it," he said. "It's never happened to me."

"It's happened to me," said Johnson. "They ask you things that'd surprise you. Surprise you what they tell you, too. You know why Hehog's broken taboo and come right into Dead City?"

"Do you?"

Johnson nodded.

"There's a thing the Udbahrs believe in," Johnson said. "They figure that when they eat someone they eat his soul, too."

"Sure," said Kiev. "And that soul stays inside them until they're killed. Then, when they die, if no one else eats them right away, all the souls of all the bodies they've eaten in their lives fly loose and take over the bodies of pups too young to have strong souls of their own."

Johnson nodded. He tilted his head at the distant figure of Willy.

"You've been learning from her," he said.

"Her? As a matter of fact, I have," said Kiev. "But you were the one told me about Udbahr cannibalism—a year or more ago."

"Did I?" Johnson looked at him. "Did I tell you about Ancient Enemies?"

Kiev shook his head.

"Once in a while a couple of males get a real feud going. It's not an ordinary hate. It's almost a noble thing—if you follow me. And from then on the feud never stops, no matter how many times they both die. Every time one is killed and born again—when he grows up it's his turn to kill the other one. The next time the roles are reversed. You follow me?"

Kiev frowned.

"No."

"Figure both souls live forever through any number of bodies. They take turns killing each other physically." Johnson looked strangely at Kiev. "The only thing is that no soul ever remembers from one body to the next—they never know whose turn it is to be killed and which one's to be the killer. So they just keep running into each other until the soul of one of them tells him, 'Go!' Then he kills the other and goes off to wait to die."

Johnson stopped speaking. Kiev stared.

"You mean Hehog thinks he and I—he thinks we're these Ancient Enemies?"

"Night before last," said Johnson, "you and he were face to face, both armed—and neither one of you killed the other. Yesterday—while we were denned up—he showed up here in the Dead City where it's taboo for him to be. Being Ancient Enemies is the only thing that'd set him free of a taboo like that. What do you think?"

Kiev turned for a second look down the street at Willy.

"Hehog's not going to leave you alone if I'm right," said Johnson. "And he's smart. He might even get away with killing one of us so he could stay close to you. And the easiest one for him to kill would be that girl. And it's true what I said. We lose a human woman out here and no supplier's going to touch us with a ten-foot pole."

"Yeah," said Kiev.

"I'm not afraid of Hehog, myself. But I've got no place else to go. I plan to die out here some day—but not yet for a few trips. Take the girl and head back. Give up the mountains while you still can. Kiev—I mean it."

"You can't make us leave," Kiev said slowly.

"No," said Johnson. His face looked old and dark as weather-stained oak. "But you keep that girl here and

Hehog'll get her. She doesn't know anything but books and she doesn't understand someone like Hehog. She doesn't even understand us." He took a step back. "So long, partner," he said. "See you in three nights—maybe."

He turned and walked away slowly, leaning forward against the weight of the pack, until he was lost among the rocks of the western cliffs.

Kiev turned and saw the small shape of Willy even farther down the street, still taking pictures.

He continued to think for the next two days and nights, which were quiet. He spent most of his time studying the aerial maps of areas near Dead City he had planned to work during this trip. Actually he was getting his ideas in order for explanation to Willy, who seemed to be having the time of her life. She was measuring and photographing Dead City inch by inch, as excited over it as if it were one large Christmas present. She had changed toward him, too, teasing him and doing for him, by turns.

Hehog did not sing from underground in the new building.

On the third night Kiev invited himself along on her work with the City.

He realized now that what Johnson had told him was true. Johnson's words had been the final shove he had needed to make up his mind. The fact that he and Willy had met less than a week ago meant nothing. Out here things were different.

He had worried about how he would bring up the subject of his future—and hers. But it turned out that he had no need to bring it up. It was already there. Almost before he knew it they were talking as if certain things were understood and taken for granted.

He said, "I've got at least five more trips to make to get the stake I need for a move back to the Old Worlds. You'd have to wait."

"But you don't need to keep coming back here," she said. "I know how you can make the rest of the money you need without even one more trip. I know because a publishing company talked to me about doing something like it. There's a steady market for information about humanoids like the Udbahrs. Books, lectures. Acting as industrial and economic consultant—"

He stared at her.

"I couldn't do anything like that," he said. "I'm no good with words and theories—"

"You don't have to be. All you have to do is tell what you've seen and done on these trips of yours. You'll collect enough on advance bookings alone for us to go back to any Old World you want—after I get my doctorate, of course—and settle down there. Don't forget I've got my work, too. I'll be teaching." She stared at him eagerly. "And think of what you'll be achieving. Intelligent natives are being killed off or exploited on new worlds like this one simply because there's no local concern over them and because our civilization hasn't understood them enough to make the necessary concessions for them to accept it. You could be the one to get the ball rolling that could save the Udbahrs from being hunted down and killed off—"

"By people like me, you mean," he said, a little sourly.

"Not you. You haven't yet been infected with the sort of killing lust Wadjik and Shant—and even Johnson— have."

"It isn't a lust. Out here you have to kill the Udbahrs to keep them from killing you."

She looked at him sharply.

"Yes—if you're a savage," she said. "As the Udbahrs are savages. I couldn't love an Udbahr. I could only love a man who was civilized—able to keep the savage part inside him chained up. That Ancient Enemy business Hehog sang at you—that's the way a savage thinks. I don't expect you not to have the psychological capacity to lust for killing—but if you're a healthy-minded man you can keep that sort of Ancient Enemy locked up inside you. You don't have to let him take you over."

He opened his mouth to make one more stubborn effort to explain himself to her, then closed it again rather helplessly. He found a certain uncomfortable rightness in part of what she was saying. Although from that rightness she went off into left field somewhere to an area where he was sure she was wrong. While he groped for words to express himself the still air around him was suddenly torn by the sound of a gun-bolt explosion.

He found himself running toward the building they had set up as their headquarters, sidearm in his hand, the sound of Willy's voice and footsteps following him. The distance was not great and he did not slow down for her. Better if he made it first—or if she did not come at all until he knew what had happened.

He rounded the corner of the building and saw the shelter entrance hanging in blackened tatters. He dove past it. By some miracle the light was still burning against the ceiling but the interior it illuminated was a scene of wreckage. Concussion and heat from the bolt had torn apart or scorched everything in the place.

With a wild coldness inside him, he pawed swiftly through the rubble for whatever was usable. Two thermal sleeping bags were still in working condition, though their outer covering was charred in spots and stinking of burned plastic. Food containers were ripped open and their contents destroyed. The water drill was workable and most of one air membrane was untouched.

"What happened? Who did it? Kiev—"

He awoke to the fact that Willy was with him again, literally pulling at him to get his attention. He came erect wearily.

"I don't know," he said, dully. "Maybe some prospector has gone out of his head entirely. Or—"

He hesitated.

"Or what?"

He looked at her.

"Or an Udbahr male has gotten hold of the gun of a dead prospector."

Her face thinned and whitened under the light of the overhead lamp.

"A dead—"

She did not finish.

"That's right," he said. "One of our people, it could be—Wadjik, Shant, or Johnson."

"How could a savage who knows only sticks and stones kill an experienced, armed man?"

Willy sounded outraged.

"All sorts of animals kill people." He felt sick inside, hating himself for not having set up at least a trigger wire to guard the building area. "We've got to get out of here. We can't spend another night in a building, anyway, without a shelter entrance."

"Where'll we go?"

"We'll head toward Johnson," Kiev said. "He isn't digging so far away that we shouldn't be able to make it before dawn—if he isn't dead."

They started out on the bearing Johnson had taken and soon left the city behind them. Fully risen moon-flowers—some of them giants over three meters high—surrounded them.They were lost in a forest of strange, pale beauty, where by day there would only be the bare, heat-blasted mountainside.

"Aren't we likely to pass him and not even see him?" asked Willy.

"No," Kiev said absently. "He'll be following contours at a constant elevation. So are we. When he gets close enough, we'll hear static in our earphones."

He did not again mention the possibility of Johnson's being dead—partly because he wanted to be easy on himself.

They tramped on in silence. Kiev's mind was busy among the number of problems opened up by their present situation. After about an hour he heard the hiss of interference in his helmet phones that signaled the approach of another transmitting unit.

He stopped so suddenly that Willy bumped into him. He rotated his helmet slowly, listening for the maximum noise. When he found it, he spoke.

"Johnson? Johnson, can you hear me?"

"Thought it was you, Kiev." Johnson's voice came distorted and weakened by rock distance. "The girl with you? What's up?"

"Somebody fired a gun into our building," said Kiev. "I scraped together a sort of maintenance kit out of what was left—but I'm carrying all the salvage."

"I see." Johnson did not waste breath on speculation. "Stop where you are and wait for me. We better head back toward Wad's and Shanny's diggings as soon as we're together. No point your burning energy trying to meet me halfway."

"Right."

Kiev loosened his pack and sat down with his back to the trunk of a moonflower. Willy sat beside him. She said nothing and, busy with his own thoughts still, he hardly noticed her silence.

By the time Johnson found them Kiev had already worked out the new compass heading from their present location to the diggings where Wadjik and Shant had planned to work. A little over three hours of the night remained.

"Do you think we can make it before dawn?" Kiev asked as the three of them started out on the new heading. "You've been through that area before, haven't you?"

Johnson nodded.

"I don't know," he said. "It'll be faster going once the moonflowers are down." He looked at Willy. "We'll be pushing on as fast as we can. Think you can keep up?"

"Yes," she said without looking at him. Her voice was dull.

"Good. If you start really to give out, though, speak up. Don't overdo it to the point where we have to carry you. All right?"

"Yes."

They continued their march. Soon the moonflowers had drawn in their petals until they were hardly visible under the hoods and began their retreat into the ground. The men were now able to see, across the tops of the hoods, the general shape of the terrain and pick the most direct route from contour point to contour point. Willy walked between them. The moonflower hoods still stood above her head—tall as she was for a woman—but did not seem to bother her. She looked at nothing.

Johnson glanced at Kiev across the top of her helmet, and tongued off his helmet phones. He let her walk slightly ahead, then leaned toward Kiev until their helmets touched.

"I told you," Johnson said softly through the helmet contact. "She didn't understand or believe. We were something out of books to her—so were the Udbahrs. Now she's trying hard to keep on not believing. You see why I told you yesterday to get her out of here?"

Kiev said nothing.

Johnson pulled back his helmet, tongued his intercom back on, kept walking.

After a while the sky began to whiten ominously. The nearer moon was low and paling on the horizon behind. Johnson halted. Kiev and Willy also stopped.

"It's no good," said Johnson, over the intercom to Kiev. "We're going to have to take time to find a hole to crawl into before day. We're going to have to quit now and wait for night."

Kiev nodded.

"A hole?" echoed Willy.

Kiev looked at Johnson. Johnson shrugged. The message of the shrug was clear—there were no caves in this area. But they hunted until Johnson called a halt.

"This will have to do."

He pointed to a crack in a rock face. He and Kiev attacked the crack with mining tools and their guns.

Twenty minutes' work hollowed out a burrow three meters in circular diameter, with an entrance two feet square. Above the entrance the crack had been sealed with melted rock. The trio crawled inside and fitted the breathing membrane in place against the opening.

Kiev waited until all were undressed and in their thermal bags before setting the light he had saved from the building in place against the rocky ceiling. The cramped closeness of their enclosure came to solid life around them. The den was beginning to heat up.

The place had no air-conditioning unit—the shelter had been a palace by comparison. Even Kiev had to struggle against the intoxicating effect of the heat and the claustrophobic panic of the enclosed space. Willy went out of her head before noon. Kiev and Johnson had to hold her in her thermal bag. Shortly after that she went into syncope and stayed unconscious until cool-off.

Haggard with exhaustion, Kiev leaned on one elbow above her, staring down into her face, now smoothed out into natural sleep. Teetering on the verge of irresistible unconsciousness himself, he felt in him the strange clearheadedness of utter weariness. She had been right, he thought, about that primitive part in him and all men—the Ancient Enemy. The prospectors did not so much fight the Udbahr males out here as something in themselves that corresponded to its equivalent in the Udbahrs. The lust for killing. A lust that could get you to the point where you no longer cared if you were killed yourself.

Kiev never finished the thought. When he opened his eyes the membrane was down from the entrance and outside was the cool and blessed moonlight.

He crawled out to find Willy and Johnson already packing gear.

"Got to move, Kiev," said Johnson, seeing him. "If Wad and Shanny are alive and headed home we want to take out after them as soon as possible. One long night's walk can put us back at the hotel."

"The hell you say." Kiev was astonished. "They didn't come all the way out with us and then cut that far back to find a digging area."

"No," Johnson said, "but from here we can hit a different pass through the border range. Going back that way makes the hypotenuse of a right triangle. Coming out we would have dog-legged it to reach this point like doing the triangle's other two sides. You understand?"

Within half an hour they were on their way. And within an hour, as they were coming around a high spire of rock, Johnson put out his arm and stopped.

"Wait here, Willy," Johnson said. "Come on, Kiev."

The two men rounded the rock and stopped, staring down into a small open area. They saw the scattered remains of the working equipment and of Wadjik and Shant. At least one day under the open sun had mummified their bodies. Wadjik lay on his back with the broken shaft of a spear through his chest. But Shant had been pegged out and left to die.

Their outerwear and guns were gone.

"I thought I saw sign of at least half a dozen males back there," Johnson said. "Hehog, all right—with help. He must be swinging some real clout with the other males to have kept them from eating these two right away." He glanced hard at Kiev. "And all for you."

Kiev stared.

"Me? You mean Hehog tied Shanny up and left him like that on purpose—just so I could come along and see it?"

"You begin to see what Ancient Enemy means?" he responded. "We're in trouble, Kiev. Two guns missing and one of the local males grown into a real hoodoo. We'll get moving for civilization right now."

"You're going to bury them first," Willy said.

The men swung around. She was standing just behind them, looking at them. Her gaze dropped, fixed on the bodies below. For a second Kiev thought that the sight had sent her completely out of her mind. Then he saw that her eyes were clear and sane.

Johnson said, "We haven't time—and, anyway, the Udbahrs would come back to dig them up again when they were hungry enough."

"He's right, Willy," said Kiev. "We've got to go—fast." He thought of something else and swung back to Johnson. "That pass you talked about—they'll be laying for us there, Hehog and the other males he's got together. It's the straightest route home, you say, and they know prospectors always head straight out of the mountains when they get into trouble."

Johnson shook his head.

"Don't think so," he said. "You're his Ancient Enemy, looking for that one spot where you and he come face to face and one of you gets the word to kill the other. He'll be right around this area, waiting for us to start hunting for him. If we move fast we've got as good a chance as anyone ever had to get out of these mountains alive."

Johnson set a hard pace. Several times—before the nearer moon was high in the sky and the moonflowers were stretching to full bloom—Willy tripped and would have gone down if Kiev had not caught her. But she did not complain. In fact, she said nothing at all. Shortly after midnight, they broke out from under the umbrellas of a clump of moonflower petals and found themselves in the pass Johnson had talked about.

"We made it," said Johnson, stopping. Kiev also stopped. Willy, stumbling with weariness, blundered into him. She clung to him like a child—and at that moment a thin, bright beam came from among the trunks of the moonflowers behind them.

The side of Johnson's outerwear burst in dazzle and smoke.

Johnson lunged forward. Kiev and Willy ran behind him. Three more bright beams flickered around them as they lurched over the lip of the pass, took half a dozen long, staggering, tripping strides down the far side and dived to shelter behind some waist-high chunks of granite.

Male Udbahr voices began to sing on the far side of the pass.

Johnson coughed. Kiev looked at him and Johnson quickly turned his helmet away, so that the face plate was hidden.

"Move out," Johnson said, in a thick voice, like that of a man with a frog in his throat.

"Are you crazy?"

Kiev had his sidearm out. He sighted around the granite boulder before him and sent a beam high into the rock wall beyond the lip of the pass, on the other side. The rock boomed loudly and flew in fragments. The singing stopped. After a moment it started again.

"I can't help you now," Johnson said, still keeping his face turned away. "Move out, I tell you."

"You think I'm going to leave you?"

Kiev sent off another bolt into the rock face beyond the lip of the pass. This time the singing hardly paused.

"Don't waste your charges," Johnson said hoarsely. "Get out. An hour puts you—hotel."

He had to stop in mid-sentence to cough.

"Forget it, partner," said Kiev. "With my gun and yours I can hold that pass until morning. They can't come through."

Johnson gave an ugly laugh.

"What partner?" he asked. "This partnership's dissolved. And what'll you do when dawn comes? Cook? You're still a good hour's trek from the hotel."

Kiev became aware that Willy was tugging at his arm.

She motioned with her head for him to follow her. He did. She slid back down among the rocks until they were a good four meters from where Johnson lay, head toward the pass.

Willy tongued off her intercom and touched her helmet to his.

"He's dying," she said to him through the helmets.

"All right."

Kiev stared at her as if she were Hehog himself.

"You couldn't get him to the hotel in time to save his life even if there weren't any Udbahrs behind us. And we'll never make the hotel unless he stays there and keeps them from following us."

"So?"

She took hold of his shoulders and tried to shake him but he was too heavy and too unmoving with purpose.

"Be sensible." She was almost crying. "Don't you see it's something he wants to do? He wants to save us—"

Kiev stared at her stonily.

"Shanny's dead," Kiev said. "Wad's dead. You want me to leave Johnson?"

She did begin to cry at that, the tears running down her pale face inside her helmet.

"All right, hate me," she said. "Why shouldn't I want to live? This is all your fault—not mine. I didn't kill your partners. I didn't make Hehog your special enemy. All I did was love you. If you were back there I wouldn't leave you, either. But that wouldn't make my staying sensible."

"Go on if you want," he said coldly.

"You know I can't find the hotel by myself!" she said. "You know I'm not going to leave you. Maybe you've got a right to kill yourself—maybe you've even got a right to kill me. But have you got the right to kill me for something that's got nothing to do with me?"

He closed his eyes against the sight of her face. After seconds he opened his eyes, looked away from her, and began to crawl back up the slope until he once more lay beside Johnson.

"It's Willy," he said, not looking at the other man.

"Sure. That's right," said Johnson hoarsely.

A flicker of dark movement came from one side of the pass and his gun spat. The pass was clear of pursuers again.

"Damn you both," Kiev said, emptily.

"Sure, boy," said Johnson. "Don't waste time, huh?"

Kiev lay where he was. The nearer moon was descending in the sky a little above and to the right of the pass.

"I'll leave my gun," Kiev said at last.

"Don't need it," Johnson said.

Kiev reached out and took Johnson's gloved hand in his own. Through the fabric the return pressure of the other man's grip was light and feeble.

"Get out," said Johnson. "I told you I figured on ending out here."

"You told me not for some trips yet."

"Changed my mind." Johnson let go of Kiev's hand and closed his eyes. His voice was not much more than a whisper. "I think instead I'll make it this trip."

He did not say any more. After a long minute Kiev spoke to him again.

"Johnson—"

Johnson did not answer. Only the gun in his hand spat light briefly into the wall of the pass. Kiev stared a second longer, then turned and went sliding down the hill to where Willy crouched.

"We go fast," said Kiev.

They went away without looking back. Twice they heard the sound of a gun behind them. Then intervening rocks cut off whatever else they might have heard. They walked without pausing. After about an hour Willy began to stumble with exhaustion and clung to him. Kiev put his arm around her; they hobbled along to-

gether, leaning into the pitch of the upslopes, sliding in
the loose rock of downslopes.

The moon was low on the stony horizon behind them.
Ahead came the first whitening in the sky that said dawn
was less than two hours away. Willy staggered and
leaned more heavily upon Kiev. Looking down at her
face through the double transparencies of both helmets,
Kiev saw that she was stumbling along with her eyes
tightly closed, her face hardened into a colorless mask
of effort. A strand of hair had fallen forward over one
closed eye and his heart lurched at the sight of it.

Not from the first had he ever thought of her as
beautiful. Now, gaunt with effort, hair disarrayed, she
was less so than ever—and yet he had never loved and
wanted her more. It was because of the mountains, he
thought. And Hehog, Wad, Shanny—and Johnson. Each
time he had paid out one of them for her, the worth of
her had gone up that much. Now she was equal to the
total of all of them together.

She stumbled again, almost lost her footing. A wordless little sound was jolted from between her clenched
teeth, though her eyes stayed closed.

"Walk," he said savagely, jerking her upright and
onward. "Keep walking." They were on the Track, now,
the curving trail that all the prospectors took out of the
valley of the Border Hotel. "Keep walking," he muttered
to her. "Just around the curve there—"

A bolt from a gun behind them boomed suddenly
against the cliff-base to their right. Rock chips rained
down Willy's knees. She lurched toward the shelter of
the nearest boulder.

He jerked her upright.

"Run for it. Run—"

Jolting, stumbling, they ran while bolts from the gun
boomed.

"They can't shoot worth—" Kiev muttered through
his teeth.

He stopped talking. Because at that moment they

rounded a curve and saw the sprawling concrete shape of the Border Hotel and its grounds—and saw Hehog, holding a sidearm, stepping out from behind a rock twenty feet ahead.

In that instant time itself seemed to hesitate. Kiev's weary legs had checked at his sight of Hehog. He started forward again at a walk, half-carrying Willy. Her eyes were still closed.

He thought, *She doesn't see Hehog.*

He marched on. Hehog brought up the gun, aimed it— but he, too, seemed caught in the suspension of time. He wore the helmet he had taken from Kiev two years before and now he also wore the white jacket of Shant's outerwear suit—which almost fit him. He stood waiting, one sidearm in a jacket pocket, one in his hand, aimed.

Kiev stumped toward him, bringing Willy. Kiev's eyes were on the bulging eyes of Hehog. Their gazes locked. The only sound was the noise of Kiev's boots scuffing the rock underfoot. From the hotel in the valley below, no sound. From the other Udbahr males that had been firing at them from behind, no sound.

Kiev marched on, Hehog growing before him. The great eyes danced in Kiev's vision. There was a wild emptiness in Kiev now, an insane certainty. He did not move aside to avoid Hehog. They were ten feet apart— they were five—they would collide—

Hehog stepped back. Without shifting the line of his advance an inch, without moving his eyes to follow Hehog, Kiev marched past him. The trail to the hotel sloped suddenly more sharply under Kiev's feet and now he looked only at what was manmade. All the Udbahrs were behind him. And behind him he heard Hehog beginning to sing softly.

> *Man with a head-and-a-half,*
> *come and get your half-head,*
> *Man with a head-and-a-half,*
> *Come, so I can kill you . . .*

The song faded behind him until his stumbling feet carried him in through the great airdoor of the hotel and all things ended at once.

He was nearly four days recovering and three days after that sitting around the Border Hotel, making plans for the future with Willy. They had adjoining rooms, each with a balcony looking out to the dawnrise side of the hotel. Heavy filterglass doors shut out the sunlight and protected the rooms' air-conditioned interiors during the daytime. Kiev had agreed to go back to the Old Worlds with Willy, to get married and write and tell what he knew. There was nothing wrong with making a living any way you could back on the Old Worlds, even if it meant writing and lecturing. Only once did Willy bring up the subject of the mountains.

"Why did Hehog let us pass?" she asked.

He stared at her.

"I thought that your eyes were closed."

"I opened them when you halted. I closed them when I saw him. I thought it was all over then—and that he was going to kill us both. But you started walking and he let us pass. Why?"

Kiev looked down at the thick brown carpet.

"Hehog's never going to get the message," he said to the carpet.

"What?"

"Ancient Enemies—Johnson told me. Hehog thinks he and I are something special to each other with this Ancient Enemies business. We're doomed to have one of us kill the other. We're supposed to keep coming together until one of us gets the message to kill. Then the other just lets it happen. Because he's doomed—there's nothing he can do about it."

He stopped talking. For a minute she said nothing, either, as if she was waiting for him to go on explaining.

"Hehog didn't get the message when we walked past him?" she asked, at last. "Is that it?"

"He'll never get the message," said Kiev dully. "He had two clear chances at me and he didn't do anything. It means he thinks he's the one who's doomed. He's waiting to die—for me to kill him."

"To kill him? Why would he want you to kill him?"

Kiev shrugged.

"Answer me."

"How do I know?" Kiev said exhaustedly. "Maybe he's getting old. Maybe he thinks it's just time for him to die—maybe his mate's dead."

There was momentary, somehow ugly silence. Then Willy spoke again.

"Kiev."

"What?"

"Look up here," she said, sharply. "I want you to look at me."

He raised his gaze slowly from the thick carpet and saw her face as stiffly fixed as it had been in the helmet on the last long kilometer to the hotel.

"Listen to me, Kiev," she said. "I love you and I want to live with you more than anything else for the rest of my life—and I'll do anything for you I can do. But there's one thing I can't do. I just can't."

He frowned at her, uneasy and restless.

"I can't help it," she said. "I thought we were getting away from it here and that it wouldn't matter. But it does. If I can feel it there in you I go dead inside—I just can't love you any more. That's all there is to it."

"What?" he asked.

Her hands made themselves into ineffective small fists in her lap, then uncurled and lay limp.

"There are so many things I love about you," she said emptily, "I thought I could ignore this one thing. But I can't think so any more. Not since we saw those two dead men—and not since the walk back here. Our love is just never going to work if you still want—want to kill. Do you understand? If you're still wanting to kill it just won't work out for us. Do you understand, Kiev?"

The bottom seemed to fall out of his stomach. He was abruptly sick.

"I told you that's all over!" he shouted furiously at her. "I don't want to kill anything!"

"You don't have to promise." She rose to her feet, her face still tight. "It doesn't matter if you promise. It only matters if you're telling the truth."

She turned and walked to the door of his hotel room.

"It's almost dawn," she said. "I'm going down to see if the authorization for our spaceship tickets has come through for today's flight—before the sun shuts off communications. I'll be back in half an hour."

She went out. The door made no noise closing behind her.

He turned and flopped on the bed, stared up at the ceiling. Everything was wonderful—or was it? He tried to think about the future in safety of the Old Worlds but his mind would not focus. After a bit he rose and walked out to the balcony.

Before him stood the ramparts of the cliffs. On the balcony was an observation scope. He bent over it and fiddled with its controls until the boulders a kilometer away seemed to hang a dozen meters in front of him.

He turned the sound pick-up on.

It was nearly time for the Udbahrs to be hunting their dens for the day but he heard no singing. He panned the scope, searching the rocks. There it came—a faint wisp of melody.

He searched the rock. The stone blurred before him. He lost then found the song again and closed in on it until the image in the screen of the scope locked on the figure of a male Udbahr standing deep between two tall boulders—an Udbahr wearing a transparent helmet and white jacket, with a sidearm in his hand.

The song came suddenly loud and clear.

Ancient, my enemy. Ancient,
my enemy.
No one but ourselves has the
killing of each other . . .
Man with a head-and-a-half,
come and get your half-head.
Man with a head-and-a-half

Kiev stepped back from the scope. His head pounded suddenly. His stomach knotted. His throat ached. A fever blazed through him and his skin felt dry, dusty. He turned and strode across the room to his bag. He plowed through it, throwing new shoes, pants and shirts aside.

His hand closed on the last hard item at the bottom. His gun. He jerked out the weapon, snatched up the long barrel for distance shooting and was snapping it into position on the gun even as he was striding toward the balcony.

He applied the magnetic clamp of the gunbutt to the scope and thumbed up the near lens of the telescope sight. The red cross-hairs wavered, searched, found Hehog. It was a long shot. The lenses of the sight held level on the Udbahr in a straight line; but below them, on their gimbals, the barrel of the automatically sighting weapon was angled so that it seemed to point clear over the cliffs at the day that was coming. Kiev's dry and shaking fingers curled around the butt. His forefinger reached toward the firing button and instantly all the shaking was over.

His grip was steady. His blood was ice but the fever still burned in his brain. As clearly as a vision before him, he saw the mummified figures of Wadjik and Shant —and Johnson as he had last seen the older man.

Kiev pressed the firing button.

From the cliffside came the sound of a distant explosion. A puff of rockdust plumed toward the whitening sky. A rising murmur, a mounting buzz of voices began beyond the walls of his room. People began to appear on the surrounding balconies.

Kiev faded back two steps, silent as a thief. Hidden in the shadows of the balcony he could still see what the others could not.

Hehog lay beside one of the two boulders between which he had been standing. A blackish stain was spreading on the right side of his white jacket and the sidearm had fallen from his grip.

He was plainly dying. But he was not yet dead. He began to sing again.

> Man with a head-and-a-half
> .... come and get your ...
> half-head.
> Man with a head-and-a-...

Through the pick-up of the scope Kiev, frozen in the shadows, could hear the Udbahr's voice weakening. Then the door to the room slammed open behind him.

"Kiev, did you hear it? Someone shot from the Hotel—"

Willy's voice broke off.

He turned and saw her just inside the door. She was gazing past him at the scope with its picture of Hehog and the sound of Hehog's weakening song coming from it. She stared at it. Then, slowly, as if she was being forced against her will, her eyes shifted until they met his.

All the feeling in him that the sight of Hehog had triggered into life went out of him with a rush, leaving him empty as a disemboweled man.

"Willy—"

He took a step toward her. Her face twitched as if with a sudden, sharp, unbearable pain and her hand came up reflexively as if to push him away, though they were still more than a half room apart.

Her throat worked but she made no sound. She struggled for an instant, then shook her head briefly. Still holding up her hand as if to fend him off, she backed away from him. The door opened behind her and let her out.

The door closed, leaving him alone. He swung slowly back to face the scope. Hehog still lay framed in the lens and above that image the ominous light of day was fast whitening the sky.

Hehog was still feebly singing; but the song had changed. Now it was the song Willy had asked Kiev to translate when she had first heard an Udbahr male. Kiev turned and flung himself face down on the bed, his arms over his head to shut out the sound. But the song came through to him.

> *You desert me now, female,*
> *Because I am crippled.*
> *And yet, all my fault was*
> *That I did not lack courage.*
> *Therefore I will go now to the*
> *high rocks to die.*
> *And another will take you . . .*

The slow rumble of the heavy, opaque, thermal glass, sliding automatically across the entrance to the balcony, silenced the song in Kiev's ears. Beyond the dark glass the sun of day broke at last over the rim of the cliffs and sent its fierce light slanting down. There was no mercy in that relentless light and all living things who did not hide before it died.

THE BLEAK AND BARREN LAND

Kent Harmon stepped out into the pitchy blackness of the night and the soft, warm, sulphur-smelling rain of the lowlands on Modor. The darkness wrapped him like some gently odorous cloak as he squelched over the yielding ground to the light of the communications shack and stepped inside.

Tom Schneider, the operator, looked up as Kent banged the door behind him. The by-pass channel direct to Earth was occupying his attention at the moment, but he grinned sympathetically at Kent, and fishing around in the message basket before him with his one free hand, dug out a flimsy from Central Headquarters and handed it up.

"This what you called me about?" asked Kent, taking it. Tom turned his homely pale and boyish face briefly from the controls that were occupying his attention and nodded briefly. A monitor hum squealed suddenly up to the limits of human audibility, and disappeared. Tom relaxed.

"On channel," he said, into the transmitter plate, "receiving. Go ahead, Earth."

The message tape began to click out and Kent looked down at the flimsy. It was an official communication to him from the Central Headquarters Colonial Office. Kent fingered the little black mustache that had once been his pride and joy—back in government circles on Earth where there was someone to see it—and let his mind spell out the single line of code:

CH to Col Rep Modor-Xmas Alert 500
40T 23:76W & 49:40N

The message tape stopped clicking. Tom switched off and stretched in his chair, turning to Kent.

"Something new?" he asked, casually. Then, something odd and rigid in the sharp, almost too-handsome features of the Colonial Representative pricked up his interest. "Bad news?"

"They're letting a colony come in," answered Kent without thinking—and instantly regretted having said it. Tom jerked suddenly upright in his chair.

"You're crazy!" he burst out. Kent, on guard again, smoothed out his face. He shrugged and put the flimsy in his pocket, turning toward the door.

"Hold on, dammit!" Tom reached out a long, skinny arm and caught the sleeve of Kent's jacket, halting him. "A colony? Where?"

"About five hundred kilos west of here," said Kent, distastefully. There was nothing secret about the information, but he would have appreciated being able to think the matter over before releasing it. Now he was committed.

"But that's in the barren land," said Tom incredulously. "What'll the Modorians say? And how come they're letting colonists in anyway?"

"We're open for settlement," answered Kent, sharply, realizing with disgust as he said it that he sounded pompous and official. He jerked his sleeve out of the other's hand, forestalling Tom's flow of questions.

"I can't talk about it now, Tom," he said irritably. "And for God's sake keep as quiet about it yourself as you can. You know what a touchy subject colonists are with the prospectors and the adopted men." He strode to the door.

"But this is *it!*" cried Tom behind him, his high voice squeaking still higher in alarm and excitement. "The Modorians—"

Kent slammed the door of the message shack behind him, cutting off the flow of words.

It was a moment in which he wanted to be alone to think. Here, at the trading post, there would be no opportunity, now that Tom knew the news. The operator was probably broadcasting it now, and inside of an hour, there would be angry prospectors and adopted men—men who had formed working friendships with some Modorian or other—knocking on his door. Kent turned away from the small huddle of buildings and made for the landing field where his flyer stood.

The little machine was silent in the darkness. He crawled inside, set the controls, and bucketed upward into the night.

For several seconds, the flyer seemed to hang in the smoky blackness, then it burst through the overhanging cloud layer above the valley and rode high above in the white moonlight. Kent checked the controls and looked down.

The moon of Modor was close to Modor and the night was brilliant. Below him the valley brimmed with dark clouds, stretching away and down to the sea. To the west and north the hills began and the uplands, stony and bare and clear. He turned the nose of the flyer westward and fled away from the valley, out over the silent landscape.

The cabin of the little flyer was cold with the chill of

high altitude. Kent turned on the heating system, locked
the controls on the five hundred kilos distant area where
the colonist ship was due to land, and sat back, lighting
the pipe that he carried in his jacket pocket, and setting
himself to consider the situation.

The fumes of the pipe rose comfortingly about him as
he dragged the smoke deep into his lungs, and he grinned wryly, remembering how this, too, had been a subject of censure back at Colonial Office on Earth. Kent
was a government career man, and a good one. The only
trouble was that in appearance he was a little too
good—he looked the part.

He was spare and darkly handsome. A little short, by
present day standards; but that did not show up unless
you saw him standing alongside a taller man. What, in
ancient times, would have been called the empire-
builder type of man, he was keen-minded, alert, impec-
cable as to dress and manner—and he smoked a pipe.

Kent chuckled a little sadly, remembering. It had been
the pipe that sent him out here to Modor—the straw, in a
manner of speaking that broke the camel's back.

It was the casual note nowadays in government
circles. Diplomats and representatives, from the least to
the greatest, strove to look like college kids—if they
were young enough—or small businessmen—if they
were too old for the first role. The last thing to look like
was what you were. Kent, of course, had. Couldn't help
himself, in fact. In consequence, he was looked on with
suspicion by his fellows and immediate superiors.
Here's someone trying to show us all up, they said; and
when he began smoking the pipe, that was the final
straw. The pipe was too perfect. It was archaic and
ostentatious. The perfection of Kent Harmon was
ridiculous alongside the careful cultivated lack of
dignity of the Colonial Office. Result—assignment to
Modor.

Well—damn them all—thought Kent, comfortably

sucking in smoke. He enjoyed the pipe, and at least out here he could smoke to his heart's content.

But to get back to this business of colonists—he frowned. It looked as if the disapproval of the Colonial Office was still following him. Letting five hundred Earth-born humans into Modor to settle on the barren land was a fool's trick, and a flat outrage of a sort of unwritten agreement that had existed for over two hundred years between Modorians and humans, ever since the first ship had landed, in fact. Modorians were not the ordinary—by human standard—type of alien.

Kent glanced out through the window of his flyer. Down below, the ground was a tumbled wilderness of rock with only an occasional clump of spiny bush to break the monotony. It looked lifeless and deserted, but Kent knew that somewhere down there there was almost sure to be at least two or three scattered Modorians, sleeping, and probably even some humans, each with his Modorian, the Modorian that had "adopted" him and made it possible for him to roam the wilderness, prospecting or trapping.

No, the Modorians were not the ordinary alien. For one thing, they were the most intelligent race Man had yet discovered on the worlds he had taken over—some said even more intelligent than Man, himself; Kent, after five years on Modor, inclined to that view himself. But that was only the beginning of their uniqueness.

A female Modorian was about three feet high, nervous, suspicious and with about the apparent intelligence and characteristics of a chimpanzee. She resembled the male only in her thinness, the three opposed fingers of her hands, the large tarsier-like eyes and the covering of soft gray fur. She mated for life and rode her male pickaback as he roamed the stony face of his desert-like world.

But the male! Seven feet or more in height when he

was fully grown, inhumanly strong and resourceful, indifferent to extremes of temperature that varied from a hundred and fifty degrees above zero to ninety below, of a different, stranger, steelier flesh than man's, he lived in comfort with nothing more than a steel spear and a few small hand tools on a world where a man without several tons of equipment would have frozen or starved in no time. The Modorians had never built cities because they did not need them—and for another reason.

And this was the strangest part of all. For the one great characteristic of the male Modorian was his utter independence. He needed nothing. He asked for nothing. He could be neither coerced, nor bribed, nor tricked, nor forced. He said and did only what he wished. He was a law unto himself and only to himself. What other living beings did was no concern of his, with the single exception of his own personal female—and, oddly enough, man.

For the Modorians, strangely, seemed to be fascinated by men. They neither needed them, nor objected to them; but they seemed to be eternally confounded by the fact that here were male creatures almost as intelligent as themselves, who could be dependent, and were. Almost anti-social where his own kind was concerned, a male Modorian often "adopted" a human man, watching over him with a sort of puzzled solicitude as the odd, weak creature toiled over the barren land, scrabbling in the burrows of little pack rat-like animals for the precious stones that to the Modorians were not worth a second glance.

Daily the Modorian rescued his prospector from landslide, blizzard, starvation and heat exhaustion, aided him in his search, and, on occasions when they met another of his own kind, discussed his charge gravely in the sonorous tones of the Modorian tongue. It was only through this that men had discovered that the Modorians, beneath the eternal calm and indifference of their exterior, were actually capable of deep and abiding affection and other emotions. And these men, eventually understanding, came to return the liking almost fiercely.

It was these humans, rather than the Modorians themselves, who would be Kent's ostensible problem, now that the news of the coming colonists was out. Central Headquarters on Earth had never made any kind of colonization treaty with the Modorians. To do so would have required an individual agreement with each one of the males, which was impossible, even if every male had proved to be interested in such a treaty. But with an unusual wisdom, the Foreign Office had, until now, restricted any human settlement to the deep valleys, which because of the cloudiness and humidity, the Modorians did not care for.

But, the land area of these valleys was small, and the human civilization was bursting under the pressure of over-population. The day when humans would come into the barren land with their rock pulverizers and fertilizers and farming equipment was inevitable. Sitting alone in his flyer, Kent shivered. The Modorians to date had really never been crossed by humans. What if that icy, infinitely capable mind, inhuman self-control and superhuman determination should be turned against man? What if the icy Modorian logic should decide that man was a pest, and dangerous, instead of an appealing pet? What could you do then against five millions of an enemy whose mind could be altered only by complete extermination?

True—Man, himself was counted now by quintillions —but—Kent shook his head—Central Headquarters had no real idea of how intelligent the Modorians actually were.

A bell on the instrument panel rang suddenly, sharply. Kent put out his hand to bring the flyer to a hovering halt, and looked down. The place where the colonists would land in less than forty hours lay below him, a shallow rocky bowl hemmed by low hills. He sat gazing at it for several minutes, then bit his lips, and turning the flyer, scooted for home. It would be up to him to stop trouble before it got started; and he could think of only one factor that would operate in his favor. The fact that each Modorian worked for himself and alone.

The one to stop, thought Kent grimly, would be the first Modorian who attempted to make trouble for the colony.

Stop the first Modorian—well, it was a good decision, thought Kent as he opened his eyes the following morning, his mind automatically taking up at exactly the point where it had left off the night before. But how? And how would he know when the first Modorian to start something, started something? The pale ghost of fear weaved for a moment through the back of his mind. Familiarity with the Modorians did not breed contempt. Quite the opposite. You were more likely to feel your own good opinion of yourself dwindling on prolonged contact. Maybe he should warn Earth? Ridiculous to expect anything really—he checked himself abruptly. Now with a night's sleep behind him, he was more than ever certain that the Colonial Office had granted the permit with an eye to putting him, personally, on the spot. There was no doubt a strong element that would have liked to get him out of the service completely.

For a moment the memory of green Earth plucked at him with nostalgic fingers. Home. What ninety per cent of the humans on Modor here would give their right arm for—passage back and security on the world of their forefathers, was his for the asking. All he had to do was bow politely out of the Colonial Office and accept a minor position elsewhere with some other governmental branch. Kent shook his head ruefully. Some odd little quirk within him kept him, and would always keep him, from buying on those terms.

He went into the office section of his quarters. On the instrument panel, the red lights for visiphone and doorbell were blinking furiously, and silently, their sound circuits disconnected. Kent grinned briefly at them. There would be angry prospectors and adopted men at the other ends of those circuits, clamoring for him. Well, let them. They had nothing to tell him about their attitude toward the present situation that he didn't know already. He would remain incommunicado until the colony ship came.

Leisurely, he drew a cup of coffee from the wall dispenser and sat down at his desk to draft a full report on the situation as it stood at the present time.

Forty hours, almost to the minute, after the original message had arrived, the ship bearing the colonists flashed radio signal it was entering the atmosphere. Kent rose to its summons and the second morning of his self-incarceration, dressed, and went out to his flyer.

In the dull, cloud-filtered light of day, the valley looked gray and depressing. Water dripped steadily from everything; and not even the careful landscaping with grass and trees and bushes brought in from Earth, nor the carefully colored and designed buildings of the trading station did much to relieve the view. The place looked deserted, now, and probably was—everyone having taken to the air at the first radio signal from the incoming ship. They would be waiting for her—and Kent—at the landing spot five hundred kilometers westward.

Kent climbed into the flyer and took off.

By the time he landed it was nearly mid-morning and the temperature of the open area where the settlement was to be was already shooting up. In the clear brilliant sunlight the ship was down and the scene was a study in harsh beauty, from the yellow dust of the hollow, where four great weather-control pylons and individual shelters were already springing up, to the looming hills, their crowns rust-red against the molten sky. As Kent brought the flyer down he had already spotted the signs of trouble, the prospectors held back from the edge of the camp by armed colonists and milling in an angry group, while their Modorians stood apart, and scattered. As he opened the door of the flyer, the prospectors made a rush and surrounded him.

"Quiet down!" he said crisply, stepping down among them. There was not a man that did not overtop him by two inches or more, and his neatness threw him in dandified contrast to their rough trail clothes. "There's nothing to be done right now, anyhow."

"Listen, Harmon!" said one young giant, shoving his way through his fellows. "You've got to contact Central Headquarters. Tell'm we don't want planters in here."

"I've done it," said Kent, dryly. "I expressed the attitude of you men in the report I sent out yesterday."

"The hell you did!" flared the young giant.

"The hell I didn't, Simmons," said Kent, evenly. "The report's gone in and all you can do is wait and hope that the Colonial Office recommends moving this group."

"We won't wait for that," Simmons threatened. "We're giving these planters twenty-four hours to get out."

The rest took up the cry. "That's right, Branch!" "You tell him!" Kent waited until the clamor died down.

"So you're thinking of using force," he said.

"That's right," retorted Branch Simmons belligerently. Kent snorted contemptuously.

"You're out of your head," he said, incisively. "I'll yank the trading license of the first man that tries anything like that, and blackball him for any attempt he ever makes at Earth citizenship. Do any of you want to risk that?"

His black eyes challenged them, and they looked away. There was not a man facing him who did not hope someday to make a big enough gem find to buy his way back to Earth citizenship.

"Besides," went on Kent. "You've got no grounds for

complaint. The only ones who can protest legally are the Modorians themselves."

"Our boys don't like it," grumbled one of the older prospectors.

"No?" said Kent, turning toward the scattered group of friendly Modorians who stood a little way off. "Let them tell me about it then."

He strode away from the humans and up to the group of gray-furred natives.

"You know me," he said, speaking to all of them. "Have any of you anything to say to me?"

Like lean and silent gods, they rested on their spears, towering over him, gazing down at him with large, inscrutable eyes. Not one of them answered. Kent turned back to the prospectors.

"I'm going down into the settlement," he said. "One of you can go with me, if you like. Now, who's it going to be—you, Branch?"

"Me," said Branch, hitching his gun belt around his waist. "I'll go."

"All right," said Kent, and led the way.

The prospectors waited in a little group apart from the others. Kent and Branch Simmons went down the slope until they reached the perimeter of the settlement area and were halted by two pink-cheeked youngsters, still in their light Earth-surface tunic and kilts, but carrying power-rifles.

"You can't go in," one of them informed Kent and the tall prospector in a high tenor.

"Oh, yes we can," said Kent. "I'm the Colonial Office Representative on this planet, and this man goes with me. I want to talk to your leader." The gun barrels wavered, and Kent strode forward, Branch following.

"Pretty little kids," said Branch contemptuously in Kent's ear. The young prospector was barely into his twenties, himself. Kent ignored him, searching the tangle of rising construction with his eyes.

Evidently the two sentries had orders to remain at their posts, for they did not follow them. The problem of locating the settlement leaders might have been a time-consuming one if their entrance had not attracted notice from the would-be colonists working nearby, and who started at once to yell back the word that outsiders had gotten past the perimeter. A few seconds of this produced a young man as large as Branch himself, and with the perfect muscles of a weight-lifter, and a lighter boy and girl of about the same age, all of whom approached at a run.

"Put your hands up!" roared the weight-lifter, waving a power-rifle at Branch and Kent as they came up.

"Don't point that thing at me, pretty-boy," said Branch, baring his teeth.

"Yes, put it away!" snapped Kent. "I'm the Colonial Office Representative and this man is with me."

"I don't care who—" began the weight-lifter.

"Well, you darn well will," barked Kent, his temper breaking forth, "when you find yourself in a forced labor draft bound for the Frontier Planets. Don't you know what Colonial Representative means? I'm the legal authority on this planet."

The other lowered his gun, but scowled.

"We've got a charter—" he growled.

"The settlement has," said Kent. "But the settlement may have to get along without you, if I decide to have you deported as a troublemaker. Now, put it up!"

Reluctantly, the young man laid his gun aside.

"That's more like it," said Kent, cooling off already and half-ashamed of his heat of a few seconds before. But then, it is never pleasant to look down the barrel of a gun when there is a chance it may be in the hands of a fool who will press the firing button. "You're in authority, here?"

"That's right," said the weight-lifter. "Hord Chalmers is my name."

"No you're not," the girl interrupted. "Dad is. You better wait for him, too."

Branch snorted under his breath and she looked at him unfavorably. She was a pretty little thing, black-haired and thin-featured, almost the twin of the slighter boy that made up the group.

"Then where is he?" asked Kent.

"Right here, sir, right here," said a new voice, somewhat out of breath, and they all turned to see a little, gray-haired, pot-bellied man with a kindly face trot up to the meeting. He came to a winded stop and threw a somewhat stern glance at Hord Chalmers.

"You take too much on yourself, Hord," he said.

"Somebody has to," said Hord, darkly.

"That's enough of that, boy," said the older man sharply. "You're my assistant and nothing more. Now don't you forget it! Sorry, sir—" he turned to Kent. "My name's Peter Lawrence, and these are my son, Bob, and my daughter, Judy. Hord here's my nephew. Did I hear you say you were the Colonial Representative on Modor?"

"That's right," said Kent, dryly. "I'd like to see your charter and talk to you about a few things."

"I've got the charter here," said Peter Lawrence, pulling the little microfilm case from his pocket. "If you'd like to talk privately—"

"That won't be necessary," said Kent. He took the case, flipped up the magnifier, and scanned it. He handed it back. "You seem to be the only one in the whole bunch that's not twenty-one," he said. "Mind telling me about that?" Lawrence looked a little shy.

"Well," he said. "When they came of age, the kids had to leave Earth—you know how it is—" Kent nodded. Overcrowded Earth denied citizenship to even its native-born unless they had certified employment by the time they were twenty-one. "—and so I thought I might just as well come along with them and help them get a start."

Kent nodded, hiding the sympathy he felt. An older man like Lawrence could have stayed safe at home. It was a rare individual nowadays that would go adventuring on a raw new world for the sake of his children when he, himself, was middle-aged.

"They're a good bunch of kids," said Lawrence warmly.

Branch snorted, and Lawrence looked at him in some surprise.

"Oh, yes," said Kent wryly. "Let me introduce Branch Simmons, one of our prospectors, and adopted men. My name is Kent Harmon. Branch is one of the reasons I've come to talk to you."

"How do you do, son," said Peter Lawrence, holding out his hand. Branch ignored it, and after a second the older man let it fall to his side.

"Well!" said the girl.

"Hush, Judy," said Peter Lawrence, automatically. "What about him, Mr. Harmon?"

"Branch," said Kent, "is a representative of the prospectors and adopted men—you know about conditions here on Modor?"

"Yes," said Peter.

"The prospectors feel your settlement is a threat both to their way of life and that of the Modorians—and they've taken it on themselves to speak up for the Modorians."

"Those animals?" said Hord, incredulously.

"Shut your fat mouth," answered Branch, savagely.

"That's enough," said Kent looking at both of them. "For your information, Chalmers, the Modorians are held in rather deep affection by our prospectors—seeing that all of them have owed their lives to a Modorian at one time or another. I feel it my duty to inform you, Lawrence, that in accordance with the wishes of the prospectors, I've registered their protest against your settlement."

"But—why?" burst out the older man, bewilderedly.

"There's millions of miles of empty land here. We're just taking up one tiny spot."

"I know the land looks empty—" began Kent, but the deep voice of Branch interrupted him.

"Let me explain this, Kent," he said, stepping forward. "Listen, Lawrence. If a bear came and pitched a tent in your living room would you be satisfied by his saying there were lots of other living rooms on the planet?" He reached out one long forefinger and prodded the older man on the chest. "You'd say, 'Hell, no!' You'd say, 'I don't care how much room there is, this place is mine.' "

"But look, son—" protested Peter.

"Don't 'son' me," growled Branch, "save that for these hothouse babies you brought along with you."

"—Mr. Simmons"—amended Peter. "Where else is there for us to go? Good God! You don't suppose we'd have picked this place if there was anything else available to us with the money we had? Look at it"—his pudgy arm gestured, widespread, at the rocky and empty land around them. "We've sunk everything we've got into equipment just to make this habitable. Pulverizers, fertilizers, plant food—weather control equipment, passage money. All we've got is here."

"That's your problem," said Branch.

"We can't go," said Peter. "We couldn't if we wanted to and I'm sure Central Headquarters isn't going to force us off Modor." He turned toward Kent. "You don't think they will, do you?"

"No," said Kent, "off the record, I don't think they will."

Hord Chalmers took a half-step forward.

"Anyway," he said to Branch, defiantly. "What business of yours is it, anyway? Let those natives talk for themselves if they want to."

"They won't talk," said Branch, more calmly than he had spoken so far. "They leave the talking up to us. If we can't make you leave, they will."

"Those—" said Chalmers.

"Yes, those!" interrupted Branch fiercely. "If they act, there won't be any more talking, by you or me, ever." And they glared at each other like two strange dogs about to clash.

"The Colonial Office gave me to understand there wouldn't be any trouble with the natives," cried Peter Lawrence a little wildly.

The next morning Kent woke in the shelter that had been assigned to him in the growing settlement. He rolled out of bed, dressed and ate. On the desk in the barren shelter that held his cot, and nothing else beside, there was a small pile of government dispatches that had been flown up early that morning. He lit a cigarette, perched on one corner of the desk, and tore open the envelopes.

Most were routine matters relating to trading and shipping. One was an acknowledgment of his report and an official refusal of the prospector's protest against the settlers. The last was a note from Tichi Marlowe, the daughter of one of his few close friends back on Earth. Tichi was adolescent and fiercely loyal. She had also had a crush on him. He smiled a little sadly and picked up her note.

Darling Kent:
  I wish you were coming back here. Everything is dead and double-dead around here since you shipped out. Daddy never brings anyone home any more but old men with indigestion—and I'm so sick of kids. Anyway, I think about you all the time. Daddy says to give you his best regards, and his wishes that you should come back soon, too. He says he bets you have your hands full with that new colony. I bet so, too. I've been hearing all about it, and I think the whole situation is real gummy.

                                        Lots of love,
                          Tichi (PRSM .2:9 TKMarlowe, Wash.)

Kent whistled and smiled a little grimly. Tichi could be embarrassing, but she could also be useful, with her little girl manner and her childish slang. The words—"real gummy"—were intended to convey to Kent just what he had suspected earlier—that the landing of the colony had been a deliberate attempt by a certain clique in the Office to put him in a discrediting situation. Bless Tichi and her little ears alert to capital gossip!

However—he folded the letter and put it away—there was nothing he could do about it now. He could not quit right in the middle of this situation, even if he wanted to—and he didn't want to.

He went outside and looked up the hills.

What he had expected was there. Singly and in small family groups, during the night they had been drifting in, silently, purposefully, from maybe as far as fifty or a hundred miles away—a Modorian alone could move at amazing speed for surprising lengths of time. And now the heights were scattered with them, lean, gray figures outlined against the horizon, leaning on their spears and looking down on the camp. The wild Modorians—those who had never struck up a partnership with any man, were coming in.

"Mr. Harmon—"

He turned, looking down. The little leader of the colonists was at his elbow, round face worried.

"Are they dangerous?" he asked.

"Yes," said Kent. "Yes, they're dangerous."

"Well, what should I do? Should I arm more of the boys and let the girls handle all the construction?"

"Don't arm anybody," said Kent.

"But what if they start something? They've got those spears. I know they're only savages—"

"Mr. Lawrence," Kent interrupted wearily. "They're not savages. If you and your bunch of youngsters would just get that through your heads, you'd be a lot safer." He pointed. "Those up there on the hills are Modorians who've never had more than an occasional contact with people. But you won't find one of them who can't talk your own language as well or better than you can, and doesn't know as much or more about the Universe and the human race as you do. They're not savages, and they're not fools. You're making the common mistake of most newcomers when you think that the intelligence of a race can be measured by its technology."

"But can't we do something?" cried Peter. "Maybe I can pay them for the land. We have a little money left."

"They've no use for money," said Kent. "This desert that is no good to you without a lot of work, is a Garden of Eden to them. The only thing they want from you is what you've taken from them—land."

"But they've got so much land!"

"They want it all," said Kent. "And why not—it was all theirs to start with."

"Well," said Peter hopelessly. "What can we do?"

"You can't do anything," said Kent. He took a step backward, reached in through the door of his shelter and picked up his jacket. He shrugged his arms into it. "But maybe I can. I don't know. Wait here and keep all your kids inside the limits of the settlement. I'm going up and see if any of them will talk to me."

"But—" cried Peter again. But Kent ignored him, walking away. The little man trotted behind him for a few steps, but, finding himself outdistanced, slowed down and gave up; and stood staring in doubt and indecision after the Colonial Representative's trim back as it dwindled away in the distance, climbing the hillside.

Kent walked along the crest of the encircling hills. For several hours he had been going, now, stopping in front of each Modorian in hope that the tall creature would speak to him. So far none had. Some ignored him. Some looked at him gravely, then looked away again, down into the hollow. A few were talking together like orators, declaiming in their own, sonorous incomprehensible tongue, and these he did not even bother to approach. The sun was climbing and its naked rays were coming down hot on the hillside when finally he found one who would talk.

The Modorlan was tall and unusually gaunt. As with most Modorians, there was nothing about him to mark his age, but something about his pose as he leaned on the spear gave Kent an impression of great age. As Kent came up and stood before him, the other tilted his head downward and looked at the man with his large, dark, incurious eyes.

"Which man are you?" he said.

The voice was high-pitched, a tenor by human standards, but a certain monotonous and mechanical style of delivery kept it from the reediness that would have been apparent in a like human voice.

"Kent Harmon," said Kent. "Colonial Representative. Do you have a name I can call you by?"

The Modorian looked away from him and down at the settlement.

"Call me Maker," he said. For a moment he stood gazing in silence, then he turned his head back to Kent.

"This land," he said, "from pole to pole, from ocean to ocean, and across the ocean, is mine. Do you understand that, man?"

"I understand," said Kent.

"But they down there do not understand," said Maker.

"No," said Kent. There was another brief silence.

"To know and understand are two different things," went on Maker. "Do they know this?"

"They've been told," said Kent. "But they haven't any choice, Maker. There's no room on any other world for them so they have had to come here."

"Man," said Maker, "you lie to me. There are more worlds in the universe than men, and more than there will ever be of men, should each man be given a world of himself."

"But not livable worlds."

"Yes, livable worlds," said Maker. "There are more worlds on which men can live than men will ever occupy. If you do not know this, man, I tell you now."

Kent shrugged.

"I will tell you the truth, Kent Harmon, and you can deny it if you can. There is more than enough room for men. But men go where it is closest and easiest. Hear me. Those below come here because fear keeps them from other worlds unknown, where savage races live. They come here rather than to go beyond what men call their Frontier in space. Is this true or not?"

Kent bowed his head.

"It is true," said Maker. "Fear is all they know. Let them fear me."

He turned his gaze back to the settlement below. Twice more Kent spoke to him, without getting an answer. The Modorian had withdrawn into his own thoughts. Kent turned and went down the hill to the colonists.

"Well," he said grimly to Peter Lawrence, "at least I know which one the trouble is going to come from."

The second day there were more than a thousand Modorians on the hillsides. Maker had dug down through the loose rock to the solid granite bedrock and cleared a space there several yards in area. It would have been an inconceivable amount of work for a single man to perform in even a week, but the Modorian had done it easily in less than one day and a night.

Kent went back up to see him again.

"Maker," he said. "What you're doing is foolish. I and all of the men except the prospectors will combine to stop you if you create anything dangerous."

Maker looked up from the bottom of the pit where he stood.

"Look, man," he said. "It is to be settled here whether I will drive men from my land, or whether they will drive me from it. You may meet my blow, but not avoid it; or all others like me will say to themselves—'This is not settled' and try it for themselves."

"I don't understand," said Lawrence, puzzled, when Kent repeated this statement to him, Hord Chalmers and Peter's two youngsters.

"He was pointing out a fact," said Kent wryly. "If I wanted to risk the lives of half a dozen men, I could take him into custody. If I wanted to violate Colonial Office directives, I could shoot him, just on suspicion, although all I have against him so far is that he's dug a hole in the ground. But that wouldn't settle anything. Conceivably, what he's doing, any other male Modorian can do, and if I stopped him, they'd all be trying."

"A skinny native playing in the dirt and you all get the wind up—" Hord Chalmers, who was standing by his uncle, burst into a sudden sarcastic laugh.

It was echoed suddenly by the deep-throated laughter of Branch. He was striding toward them, and the sound of his laughing was carefree on the thin air. He came up to them and stopped, grinning, his thumbs hooked into his gunbelt.

"Getting worried, eh?" he said.

"Who let you in here?" demanded Peter with a frown. But before Branch could answer, Hord had cut in.

"Worried!" he snorted. "Of that fleabag up on the hills? I thought he was just digging a hole to hide in."

But Branch's face did not lose its cheerfulness.

"You can't make me mad, today, Buster," he said. "Things are going too well."

"Branch—" interrupted Kent sharply. "If you know what Maker is planning to do, it's your duty to let us know." Branch sobered, but his eyes did not soften as he looked down at Kent.

"Harmon," he said. "I kind of like you, and most of the boys do, too. But I'll see you damned in hell before I'll tell you anything that might help these dirt-grubbers—besides, I don't know."

He looked stolidly at the Colonial Representative; but
before Kent had a chance to answer, the big prospector
was attacked from a quarter so unexpected that they
were all taken by surprise. It was little Judy Lawrence
who spoke up in sudden, furious anger, her delicate
face, now burned and peeling from the merciless sun,
taut with emotion.

"Do you know what's wrong with you?" she cried.

"Judy—" stammered Peter.

"Oh, leave me alone!" she cried. "None of you has
guts enough to tell him what he really is—but I will."
She turned like a small ferocious terrier on the tall
young bulk of Branch, and Kent was suddenly, fleetingly
reminded of Tichi as she tore into him. "I'll tell you what
you are. You're a dog in the manger. You can't really do
anything with this desert. You can't make it grow and
turn green and beautiful, or build homes, or have
children—and you don't want anybody else to have them
either. You want them all to be just as miserable and
just as ugly and savage as you are!" Branch's face
whitened. For a moment the youth beneath his hard
competent shell showed through and the rest could
glimpse a boyish hurt and rage.

"You can talk!" he cried. "You can talk about
homes—" he choked on his swelling emotion and took a
sudden blind, half-step toward her. His round face
lighting up, Hord moved suddenly between them. Wildly, Branch turned on him. There was an eye-blurring
flash of movement, the thud of a blow, and the heavier,
Earth-born human lay stretched on the ground. Branch
faced them over the fallen man, half-crouched, his fists
knotted, his face contorted, something mad about his
twisted features.

"Get out!" said Peter, sharply. The little middle-aged
man moved forward on the big prospector, and Kent
saw Branch tense as the older man came within reach.
Swiftly he reached forward and yanked him back.

"Come on," said Branch, wildly, his voice scaling up,

"the whole fat, lousy, stinking crew of you!" Kent shoved Peter aside and confronted the staring young man himself.

"Branch!" he said in a calm, steady voice. "Branch."

"Homes!" half-sobbed Branch, his voice shaking, "cute little—boxy little—"

"Branch!" snapped Kent. "Branch!"

Gradually, the young man began to relax, and the insane light died slowly from his eyes. The tenseness drained out of him and he straightened, his calmness regained, but somehow empty. He sighed and shivered. Kent felt hardness underneath his right hand, and, glancing down, saw his hand was cramped around his gun butt. He let go and flexed the aching fingers.

"You better go, Branch," he said.

Branch shook himself like a big dog coming out of water.

"I'll go," he said, emptily. "It doesn't matter. They won't be here long anyway."

"You—" began Judy, but Kent's hand clamped down sharply on her slim arm and the sudden pain made her gasp. Her twin brother spoke up.

"Never mind, Judy," said Bob. "It's all a bluff. Like Hord says, a dirty savage digging a hole in the ground."

Branch looked at him, but his eyes were withdrawn and his voice when he answered was remote and disinterested.

"Go ahead and dream," he said, turning away. "You'll learn. When a Modorian starts to throw his weight around—the earth moves."

They watched his slim figure shorten in the distance. Peter Lawrence spoke up.

"Bob!" he said sharply. "Look after Hord. And I want you to talk to the boys on guard and make sure that young man never gets in here again."

"Why he—he's insane!" said Judy, fascinatedly. Kent released her arm and looked at her somewhat sardonically. An evil genius impelled him to speak.

"You're probably right, Miss Lawrence," he said. "In fact, I wouldn't be a bit surprised if you were. You see, Branch is one of the Reclaimed—one of the kids that was recaptured from a raiding alien life-form when we cleaned them out of the Sagittarius section of our Frontier. He was just old enough to remember the raid that killed off his parents and he was a prisoner for nearly a dozen years. When you were going out on your first date back on Earth, Branch was living in a cage."

Judy's mouth fell open, and the hand with which she had been massaging her bruised arm stopped abruptly.

Kent smiled at her and turned away.

There was not a great deal of technical help to be had on Modor, since the planet was primarily a trading station. But, such as it was, Kent corralled it from all the inhabited valleys, ordered it to the settlement site with all possible speed. On the third day after the landing of the colonists, men began to arrive, and Kent spent a weary day tramping up the hillside with geologists, mining engineers, weather station men and chemical engineers—all of whom looked at what Maker was doing, shook their heads, shrugged their shoulders, and left the Colonial Representative just as wise as he had been before.

Nor could he really blame them, thought Kent, moodily, standing on the edge of Maker's pit as the sunset lengthened, and a biting chill came in over the darkening land. Maker's creation looked like the fantastic building of some powerful, aberrant child.

By main strength, Maker had sunk the steel shaft of his twelve-foot spear half its length into the solid granite. Around this he had built a sort of crude framework of long narrow splinters of rock, gummed together with a sort of soft clay—and inside this framework he was creating a strange crystalline structure by the medium of dissolving certain minerals in water and pouring them along the rock splinters.

At first, progress had been slow, most of the mineral solution running off the splinters and being wasted. But as the little bit that remained dried, forming adhering crystals, the thing began to grow rapidly, until now a rough, globular mass appeared within the framework, covering and completely enclosing the exposed end of the steel spear-shaft.

Now that phase of the construction seemed to be finished. Maker had turned away from the crystal and stone and was seated off to one side and fashioning what appeared to be a very long, light bow, using wood from one of the stunted bushes and a tendon from one of the small burrowing animals he had killed. He had somehow stretched the tendon enormously over a fire, and now he was engaged in binding it to the wooden arc.

Kent went down the side of the pit with a rush and rattle of loose stones, and approached him.

"You've been working two days and nights straight, Maker," he said. "Don't you ever sleep?"

He had not really expected an answer, and he was surprised when the other replied.

"Sleep is death," said the Modorian, not looking up from what his hands were doing.

Above the mouth of the pit, the first breath of the evening wind moaned abruptly, sending a chill down Kent's back. He shivered.

"You don't really believe that, Maker," he said, half-jokingly to throw off the sudden feeling of depression.

"Man," said Maker, "you talk like a fool."

Kent got out his pipe and bit hard on the stem. His hands searched his pockets for tobacco, but found none. He stayed with the empty pipe clamped between his teeth, looking down at the squatting Modorian, who worked on in the gathering gloom without looking up.

"You know," volunteered Kent. "There's still time for me to send an official protest from you to Central Headquarters."

"Words are for men," said Maker. "I do not play with my mouth. Nor will I tell you, Harmon, what you want to know. What I am going to do, I will keep to myself."

Darkness thickened around them. Kent strained to see, while the larger pupils of the Modorian dilated easily to take advantage of the waning light.

"Tell me this, anyhow," said Kent. "Will what you have in mind involve the killing of people? If worse comes to worst, I would rather move them against orders than have anyone die."

"It is to the death," said Maker.

His last words were lost in blackness as the final rays of the sun fell behind the hill.

"Thanks, Maker," said Kent.

There was no answer from the obscurity. Kent turned and climbed his way back up to the edge of the pit. At the top he turned and looked down again. A spark leaped suddenly into being in the shadows and a little flame flared up, illuminating the pit. By its light Kent saw Maker rise to his feet and cross over to the crystalline mass, the now-completed bow in his hand. He reached out into the structure and with one slow, soft movement, drew the bow-string across the jagged facets around the hidden spear-shaft.

An odd, discordant, musical note cried sharply out on the night air. It pierced Kent, seeming to shiver in his very bones; and he turned swiftly, going away down the hillside toward the settlement, while behind him the crystals cried, again and again, every time in a different note, like the devil tuning up his violin. Lonesome, questioning, the varied discordant notes of Maker laboring over his creation followed him as he walked among the houses, but dying, dying in the distance, until at last the slam of his door shut them from his ears entirely.

Kent lay awake in the dark, his tired mind searching. Like the sad montage of a dream, faces moved through

his mind—the desperate young features of Branch, and
Maker's inscrutable huge dark eyes. The serious,
worried face of Peter, and Hord's beefy handsome
countenance. In his mind's eye he saw them circling his
bed, looking down at him, all of them waiting, looking to
him for a solution, an answer.

They crowded around him. There was Bob's tense,
thin features, and the delicate beauty of his sister Judy,
her eyes frightened and haunting. By them they evoked
the golden-haired image of Tichi, looking on and wondering, and all the host of peoples, human and alien
alike, the knowledge of whose existence lived within his
consciousness. To his tired mind the immediate
problem swelled and grew enormously, until it blotted
out all other problems in the Universe, until it was The
Problem—the great question that must eventually be
answered if any human and any alien were ever to exist
permanently side by side.

And somehow, it was all up to him. Under the scourge
of his conscience, Kent's hard body twisted in the
narrow bed. He was the administrator, the trained
executive. His was the ethical and the moral responsibility. To stop Maker by force meant blood on his
hands. To let him go ahead with the strange creation of
his alien mind meant blood on Kent's hands—the blood
of the colonists. Why must it always end in killing? Why
must there always be no choice? Branch had no choice
but to stick by the Modorians. The colonists had no
place else to go. The Modorians, seeing the future
clearly—humans flooding in to take the land that was all
in all to them—had no choice but to resist. There must
be an answer—and there was no answer. The tension
built up, reached an unendurable pitch—and broke.

In the darkness Kent laughed in sudden bitter irony
and sat up, swinging his legs over the side of the bed. He
lit the lamp, reached for his pipe, filled and lit it. As
always, at the last minute, an odd, cold sense of humor
came to save him from himself—and this time it had

been a wishful mental picture of himself washing his hands. He laughed again, and sighed deeply. It had been a mistake to let himself think—his sphere was action.

In the end like goes to like, when a side must be chosen—and Kent was human. For all his admiration for Modorians in general and sympathy with Maker in particular, he realized that he must protect and maintain the colony at the cost of any native sacrifice. He pulled on the pipe and white smoke streamed up around him, past his head and out the ventilator above his bed. If necessary, he would call in the Space Guard. Whatever Modor's instrument was capable of doing, either above ground or below—

He caught himself suddenly, in midthought. Inspiration had suddenly come to him.

Charlie Colworth did not like being gotten up in the middle of the night; but when the Colonial Representative pounds at your very door, which is halfway across the planet from where you saw him last, you are forced to rise to the occasion. Cursing to himself, he pulled clothes onto his skinny body and wandered, yawning, into the front room of his quarters, where Kent was waiting.

Kent handed him a cup of his own coffee. "Here," he said. "You'll need it."

Charlie complied, and shuddered. The stuff was black, and he was a strong cream-and-sugar man.

"I suppose it's about that colony mess," he grumbled.

"That's right," said Kent.

"Well, now what?" said Charlie, dropping on the couch. "And what's it got to do with me?" Kent grinned.

"Sorry, Charlie," he said. "But you know that area best of any of the geologists we have here. I want to know what's under that granite Maker anchored his gadget in."

"More granite," said Charlie sourly, "now can I go back to bed?"

"I don't think so," said Kent. "What's under the more granite?"

"Hell," said Charlie. "It's a capstone. Magma, probably."

"By magma I take it you mean molten rock—lava?"

"It's only called lava after it comes out on the surface," said Charlie, grumpily.

"What would happen if the granite was split open?" asked Kent. "Would this magma rise up and flow over the surface?"

"If the pressure was—what in hell are you talking about?" said Charlie. "That's one of the most stable areas on this planet's surface. The K'tabi Shield. It's at least two miles thick and may be as much as fifty. Something like that doesn't split open."

"Charlie," said Kent, "what do you know about vibrations in rock?"

"As much as a well-brought-up earthquake," answered Charlie. "Now, are you going to tell me what all this is about, or do I go back to sleep?"

"I'll show you," said Kent. "Right now I want you to put on some outer clothes, pick up detector equipment and come out with me to find out what effect Maker's gadget is having on the K'tabi Shield."

"Good God, is *that* it?" said Charlie.

They were climbing the hillside outside the settlement in the early dawn, Charlie and Kent. With them was a man loaded down with detector equipment, and the Wonder Boy, as Karl Mencht, the ace troubleshooter for Modor's only spaceship repair yard was called. What had drawn the exclamation from Charlie's lips was the varying sound emanating from Maker's equipment as the sleepless Modorian continued to draw his bowstring across it.

"Interesting," said the Wonder Boy in his customary clipped tones, cocking his boyish head on one side to listen.

"That's what you say," grunted Charlie. "It sends shivers down my back."

"Subsonics," said the Wonder Boy.

"Go to hell," said Charlie. He stopped abruptly. "Here," he said, "if there's anything going on at all, we're plenty close enough to pick it up, now. And there's an outcropping of granite here I can tie into. Set it down."

Gently, the man carrying the equipment lowered it into place and set it up. Charlie fiddled with the dials.

"Now we'll see," he said. "Just as I thought—nothing—Holy Hannah!"

Coincidental with a squeak from Maker's distant bow, a needle on one of the dials had jumped clear across the scale and out of sight. It returned to rest in the same moment that the sound died away.

"But he can't do that—" said Charlie, fascinated. They watched the needle for a moment in which the squeaks continued, then the needle jumped again.

"He just hits it by accident every so often," said Charlie, in an awed voice. "But when he does—*wow*!"

"What's he doing, exactly?" asked Kent.

"He must be making this whole area of the shield vibrate," said Charlie. "And he can't do that. I must be seeing things."

"Nonsense," said the Wonder Boy. "You can vibrate anything."

"By rubbing a crystal on a rod just touching the surface on an area this size? You'd have to amplify—why you'd have to amplify—"

"Ever stop to think?" said the Wonder Boy. "Using area as sounding board. Don't know rocks myself, but makes sense."

" 'Makes sense'—you're nuts," said Charlie. The Wonder Boy shrugged.

"All right," said Kent, crisply. "Going on the assumption that my hunch was right and Maker can vibrate the rock underneath here enough to cause either a volcanic eruption or an earthquake—have either of you any ideas about how to stop him?"

"Smash his gadget," said Charlie.

"If I did that, what's to stop every other Modorian from trying it where I can't see him? Anyway that's not it. It's my belief that the rest of the Modorians—" he gestured to the ridge of the hills around them where the pink dawnlight was beginning to pick out the lean gray shapes that watched in silence—"are looking on this as sort of a test-case. If I beat Maker at his own game, they'll give up and leave the colony alone. If I don't, every single one of them will take his individual and particular swing at every settlement group that comes along after this."

"Ruin your career," said the Wonder Boy.

"Wonder Boy," said Charlie. "You've got a filthy mind. For half a credit I'd kick your pretty white teeth down your throat."

"Never mind that," said Kent. "Any ideas?"

Charlie shrugged.

"Interesting problems," said Wonder Boy. "Fight fire with fire, maybe."

"How?" asked Kent.

"Damp his vibration. Counter-vibrations. Could do it —got crews—equipment down at the repair yard. Engineering feat, be interesting. Very."

"The Modorian might beat you anyway. Embarrassing. Very," mocked Charlie.

"Try it," said the Wonder Boy, to Kent. "Up to you."

"Of course," said Kent. "You go ahead with it as fast as you can. Charlie, what actually is liable to happen if Maker cracks the shield?"

"Possibly the lava flow you were worried about," said Charlie. "But more probably a landslip."

"Either way, the settlement is in danger of being destroyed?"

Charlie grimaced.

"I'd use the word 'obliterated,' " he said.

"Then I've got to get those people out of there. Charlie, you help Karl here as much as you can; and Karl—rush it."

"Course!" said the Wonder Boy; and "Hell, yes!" said Charlie. Kent turned and went plunging off down the hillside toward the camp.

He went down the hill in a blind rush—so intent on what he was doing, in fact, that he had run on Branch and Judy Lawrence almost before he realized they were in his way. He skidded to a halt to avoid bumping into them and for a second the three of them looked at each other in not-too-friendly surprise. Kent was the first to recover his tongue.

"Good Lord," he said, "what are you doing out here?" She looked at him a little defiantly.

"I came out to apologize to Branch," she said.

"Oh?" said Kent, and looked from her to the tall young prospector, who colored slightly. "Well, don't let me interrupt you," Kent said, stepping around them.

Judy reached out a hand and caught at his arm.

"Oh, Mr. Harmon—"

"What?" demanded Kent, wheeling to face her with a touch of exasperation at being delayed.

"We're all through talking. I wonder if we could go back to the settlement with you?"

"Why not?" said Kent, turning away again. But then a hint of something odd struck him. "But, come to think of it, why?"

She still met his eyes somewhat defiantly.

"Well you see," she said. "I went out looking for Branch last evening. And night comes down so quickly, here. Well—we got lost."

"Lost?" said Kent, incredulously, looking at Branch.

"That's right," said the young man with dogged belligerence. "We got lost. She hasn't been home since last night."

They both stared at him. And suddenly understanding

struck him, bringing a rich sense of humor in its wake. Here was their personal world about to blow up and all these two babies could find time to worry about—

"All right," said Kent, the hint of a grin twisting his lips in spite of himself. "Come on, both of you, and I'll see if I can't put in a good word for you with your father, Judy. I take it you have the instincts of an honest man, Branch?"

"What?" said Branch, uneasily.

"Never mind," said Kent. "Come on—and hurry!"

Kent did not speak on the walk back.

"Judy!" cried Peter Lawrence, when he first caught sight of them. And—"What are you doing here, Simmons? I gave orders—"

"I brought him, Daddy," said Judy, putting her arm through his.

"You might as well reconcile yourself, Lawrence," said Kent. "These things happen quickly on the Outer Worlds."

"What?"

"Yes," said Kent abruptly, without any excess courtesy. "And now that that's settled, I've got something important to talk to you about. We've found out what Maker's doing—and it's dangerous. I'm rushing equipment up here to try and save the settlement, but it may not get here in time; and I want you to evacuate all your people."

"Evacuate?" cried Peter, spinning to face Kent. "Why?"

"Because," snapped Kent, "I say so. We may have anything from an earthquake to an active volcano taking place here within the next minute. Get your kids out. You can have reasons later."

"Why, this is some kind of a trick—" cried Peter, his face purpling.

"Don't be a fool," said Kent.

"I won't move until I know just what you mean by this high-handed order."

"Give me that," said Kent, exasperatedly, reaching out and yanking off the button mike that was fastened to Peter's tunic. He thumbed the switch, and loudspeakers all over the settlement bellowed his voice.

"All right," they boomed. "This is the Colonial Representative speaking. Everybody come to the Headquarters Building. Everybody. That means everybody, sick and well alike. As fast as you can. No loitering."

Kent cut off the mike. Peter made an unsuccessful grab for it. Kent fended him off and put it in his pocket.

"Stand aside, and keep quiet," he said.

"I will not!" raved the little man. "Ever since we landed, everyone's been trying by hook or crook to get us out of the land that the charter guaranteed us. We haven't given it up yet, and we won't. Now you're turning against us."

"Look, Lawrence," said Kent, "I tell you this whole area may be buried under rock or lava at any moment. Do you want to lose your lives as well as your possessions?"

"Why not?" cried Peter Lawrence. "Why not? Everything we own is here. How could we live without it?"

"Other people have," said Kent, coldly.

"Savages. Scum." The area in front of the Headquarters Building was beginning to fill up with hurrying youngsters, and Peter half-swung toward them, addressing them as well as Kent. "Not people like us who've been gently brought up on a civilized world. We'd die out there—" and he extended a shaking hand toward the hills where, rank on silent gray rank, the Modorians stood watching.

"Shut up!" snapped Kent. The area before the building was almost full now, and he took the button from his pocket, snapping the switch and lifting it to his lips. The loudspeaker on the roof of Headquarters blasted forth his voice.

"Listen, all of you!" he said. "This is a direct order. You will pick up warm clothing and evacuate this settlement at once. Head for any open space beyond the hills, and when you get there institute a check to see nobody has been left behind. Now, move!"

But the crowd rocked hesitantly, murmuring to itself and looking toward Peter.

"Don't listen to him!" cried the little man, almost hysterically. "Don't move. Don't believe him. Go back to work! It's just another trick to get us out of here. Go back to what you were doing."

The crowd murmur rose and broke. The group eddied and began to disintegrate. On every side, people began to drift away.

"Come back, you idiots!" thundered the loudspeakers, with Kent's voice. "Will you let him shove all your heads into a noose? Do I have to order up a platoon of police to move you out by force?"

But the crowd was dispersing rapidly.

"Let him try it," screamed Peter. "We'll fight for our rights."

The last few members of the crowd broke and ran for the protection of nearby buildings. Defeated, Kent lowered the phone button and stuck it in his pocket. Peter crowed his triumph. Kent turned on him.

"May God have mercy on your soul!" he said savagely.

Peter grinned wildly; but before he could answer, the two youngsters drew both men's attention.

"*You* aren't staying!" said Branch to Judy.

"What do you mean?" she answered, between surprise and anger, "I certainly will stay if the rest of them do."

"That's what you think," said Branch bluntly. "I know Harmon knows what he's talking about. Let the rest be dumb if they want to. You and me are going where it's safe."

"I certainly will not!" said Judy; but the words were barely out of her mouth before he seized the collar of her tunic with one large hand and began to march her off in the direction of the perimeter.

"Stop!" screamed Judy. "Daddy! Help!"

Peter made an inarticulate sound in his throat and dived for a power-rifle that was leaning against the side of Headquarters. He was bringing the weapon up to his shoulder when Kent seized it and wrested it out of his hands. A single blast went skyward.

"You—" choked Peter, scrabbling desperately for the gun. "Give it back!"

"Not on your life," said Kent, grimly, pushing him away. He nodded in the direction of the dwindling pair of figures. "There go two more lives off my conscience." He held the little man off until a distant building hid Judy and Branch from sight.

Abruptly Peter stopped struggling. He stood forlorn, as if all the strength had gone out of him, looking in the direction the two had disappeared. There were sudden tears in his eyes. The tears of an old man.

"My baby," he said, brokenly. "With that—that—savage."

Kent was not feeling any sympathy for him.

"Worse things have happened to women," he said harshly.

Kent stood on the hillside opposite Maker's pit, watching as a sweating crew of technicians from the repair yard struggled to sink a fifty-foot steel rod four feet in diameter deep into the rocky crust beneath his feet. Beside them an even larger crew labored to hook up an oversize generator and sounding equipment for the broadcasting of counter-vibrations through the rod.

At ten other intervals in a circle around the camp a similar job was being carried on, under the gimlet eye of the Wonder Boy, who flitted from group to group like some cherubic slave driver. The day was well advanced, and every available man with technical knowledge had been pressed into service.

Kent turned and walked away to where Charlie had set up a sort of seismographic headquarters. He was about to speak to him when he felt someone tap his elbow. He turned and saw Tom Schneider, the skinny space-communications operator.

"What is it, Tom?" he asked. The other held out a flimsy.

"Urgent," he said.

Kent turned away again.

"Stick it in your pocket, Tom," he said. "I haven't time for anything like that now." Tom reached out and grabbed him.

"I think you better read it, Kent." Kent turned an exasperated face toward him.

"Can't you take 'no' for an answer?" he demanded. "I said I didn't want to be bothered."

"You better read it," said Tom, stubbornly.

Kent sighed, and took the thing. He had expected some coded top secret dispatch from Central Headquarters. But it was nothing like that. It was from Tichi—and written out in plain language for all the world to see.

Dearest Kent:

I've got two things to tell you. And neither one is the sort of thing that can be put very well in schoolgirl slang.

(Kent blinked and looked at the first two sentences again. This didn't sound like Tichi.)

The first I might as well put down in plain words, since it isn't even an open secret around here any more. The Colonial Office has been keeping itself informed of how things have been going for you since the colony landed—and on the strength of what's happened so far alone, a Central Headquarter's Investigation has already been started. Apparently, this business is bigger than we thought. It seems that for some time now there's been a lot of public pressure from the Outer Planets on Central Headquarters—demanding that our supreme authorities clean house in the Colonial Office—and somebody has to be thrown to the wolves. They've made up their minds it's to be you.

There's one way out of this mess; and in defiance of all polite convention I'm naming it. That is that you marry me. As son-in-law of a Supreme Council Senator, you'd be too hot to handle, and they'd have to find some other scapegoat if they have to have one.

The second is this: Do you remember the birthday party I had when I was twelve years old? You came because you were a friend of Dad's and you brought me one of those big Centaurian dolls that walk around by themselves. I was too big for dolls and I was horribly embarrassed; but I loved you so much I hid the way I felt. That same party I got you alone and asked you to wait for me to grow up so I could marry you. And you laughed and said you would and gave me a phone chip and told me to call you up in half a dozen years if I still felt the same way. You were joking, but I wasn't. All my life you've acted as if I'd never grown up, and all my life I've loved you. Well, I have grown up and the six years have gone by. I'm using the phone chip—with a little extra, since you're farther away than you thought you'd be—

(Good lord! Six years already. Why that would make Tichi eighteen, thought Kent. It wasn't possible.)

—and now you know. I just want you to understand that I'm not offering this marriage deal in a burst of childish self-sacrifice. I want you more than anything in the Universe, and you're all I've ever wanted. I'm not a child, and I'm not shelteredly ignorant—I could even tell you a few things as far as *this* world goes. And—this will rock you back on your heels—Dad agrees with me. He thinks I'd be good for you, though he won't say a word to you about it.

I would never have said a word to you, my darling. I would have gone on play-acting that I was the little girl in pigtails, if this investigation hadn't come up with only one way out of it. And now that it has, and I've spoken out, I'm almost glad; because whatever happens, at least now I know that you know....

All my love

Tichi (PRSM .7:3 TKMarlowe, Wash.)

Profoundly disturbed, Kent folded the flimsy and put it in his pocket. Tichi eighteen! And this marriage stunt. Why, damn it all, he was—how old was he now?—thirty-two . . . double her age. Who would have thought she felt like that!

"Any answer?" said Tom.

Shocked back to the present, Kent stared at him.

"No," he said. "No, Tom. No answer."

"I think maybe you ought to answer," said Tom. Kent's lips thinned angrily. This was the worst of living on a sparsely populated world where everybody knew your private business and felt himself qualified to pass judgment upon it.

"No!" he snapped explosively, and turned away toward Charlie.

"I'll be around in case you change your mind," said Tom behind his back.

Kent ignored him. He was leaning over Charlie's shoulder. The lean geologist felt his presence and turned a strained face away from his instruments.

"He hits the pitch oftener all the time," said Charlie.

"It's a matter of holding it. I'll guess that if he can hold it steady for ten minutes we're done for."

"That bad!" said Kent.

"Can't you feel the vibration through your feet from the rock?" Kent hesitated.

"No," he said truthfully. Charlie wiped his forehead.

"Well, maybe it's my imagination," he said. "But I don't see how we've much time left."

"Oh? How much?" It was the clipped voice of Wonder Boy, who had just come up. Charlie turned toward him.

"At a guess," he said, "two hours at the most."

"Close," said the Wonder Boy, with a sharp jerk of his head. "Take us that long at least." Charlie, sweating under the hot sun, and worried, glared at the dapper young man.

"How do you manage to stay so cool?" he said.

"I?" said Wonder Boy, calmly, turning away. "Low blood pressure." And he was gone on his way to incite his crews to greater effort.

"What is it?" said Charlie, looking after him. "Has he got steel guts or is it that he just isn't human? You tell me, Kent."

Kent did not answer him. He was thinking what the investigating committee would do to him on the basis of the first blood he spilled, and looking out over the hollow. Down below, the settlement was silent and empty. The colonists had all gone to earth inside their buildings and the hills beyond were thick with watching Modorians. Kent made a quick estimate and whistled. There must be fifteen thousand of them waiting to see what happened now.

Kent hitched up his belt and started down the side of the hill.

"Where are you going?" called Charlie.

"Maker," called back Kent, without turning his head. "I'm going to delay him, if I can. If I can't—well, one way or another I'll give us time to get the equipment set up."

And his hand went half-unconsciously to the holstered gun at his side.

Kent went down the hillside and into the as yet unpaved streets of the settlement. It was like walking into a ghost town. The doors of the buildings were shut and there was no sound of life from within. Tools near the uncompleted buildings lay scattered where they had been dropped, and the general scene gave an impression of a place long deserted.

But the impression was only a surface one. Beneath it, Kent could sense the deep terror of the colony. Fear panted soundlessly like the breathing of a hunted animal couched in its lair. He went quickly through the settlement and breasted the hill on the far side.

The minute he came out on the hillside, he knew that something was wrong—but dared not hesitate; and so he was forced to figure it out as he walked forward. It was this that he saw—there were too many Modorians between him and Maker.

When or how they had moved to cluster around the pit, he did not know. It was possible that they had been this way for some time, and he just had not noticed. It was equally possible that they had seen him start from Charlie's station and had moved while he was among the houses of the settlement. One way or another, they now barred his path—not obtrusively, but casually, by their very presence and closeness to one another.

He saw all this as he walked the thirty or more yards from the perimeter of the settlement to a spot about a third of the way up the hill, where their ranks started. They leaned on their spears, looking not at him, but down at the settlement and over at the crews toiling under the blazing heat of the afternoon sun. They did not move as he came toward them and he saw that they must either give way, or he must shove them aside, if he was to get through to Maker at all, for there was room, but not enough room to squeeze through, between them.

Yet he could not stop and wait. He must walk forward, assuming that they would give at the last minute. He was five steps away down the hill, then he was four, then three. . . .

He walked hard against the two foremost Modorians and rebounded from them as if they had been two statues. There was not even the yielding when he touched, that softer human flesh would have given.

It was only then that one of them deigned to notice him. The Modorian on his left tilted his head downward and his enormous eyes seemed to swim dizzyingly before Kent's face.

"Man," he said. "Go back."

It was the final utterance. It was the conclusion, a statement beyond protest. The wild Modorians would not let him through. The knowledge that he had kept to himself ever since this conflict started had proved itself. The Modorians were individuals. Each one made up his mind for himself and they did not work together. But— and this Kent had realized silently in his heart—when the last came to the last, there was nothing to stop them all from getting the same idea and acting together, though independently. Each of the Modorians before him had made up his mind that he would not allow Maker to be interfered with. What did it matter that these were a hundred separate decisions, instead of one overall conclusion? The result was the same.

He turned away and went back down the hillside, back through the settlement and back to Charlie and the Wonder Boy. His mouth was dry and his heart pounded in his chest so strongly that he could feel and seem to hear the thud of the blood in his ears, as he walked through the silent streets. For the first time, Kent was clearly, nakedly, and unequivocally, afraid.

The afternoon was well advanced and the sun was hot upon them.

"Feel it now?" said Charlie tautly.

"Thrumming," said the Wonder Boy. "A buzzing."

"The vibrations are growing as he holds the pitch longer," said Charlie.

"How much longer with the crews?" asked Kent.

"Minutes," said the Wonder Boy. "A few."

"There!" said Charlie. His face was taut and sweat glistened on it in little beads in the lines of his brow. "See the houses quiver."

Kent looked. The settlement shimmered slightly.

"They'll be coming out soon," said Charlie. "Maybe on the next tremor. I've seen people in houses during earthquakes before."

The sun beat down, long-angled rays now, late afternoon and hot. The faces of the men were ruddy in the glare. The heat waves danced.

"I don't get it," said Charlie. The vibration coming up through the rock seemed to get into his voice, so that it appeared he buzzed the words in a monotone. "The Modorians. They'll go too. The whole area," said Charlie, "dozens of miles. Bound to collapse—Lord, you can hear it now."

They listened. Something was thrumming on the air. Was it the sound of Maker's bow, magnified and distorted by the great sounding board of the rock, or something else?

"I don't think they mind," said Kent. "The land will still be here."

"Yeah," said Charlie, hummingly, "the land."

The vibration was everywhere now. The rock, the air, the very individual molecules of each man's body seemed to dance to its tune. The eye struggled to focus and failed. Vision played tricks. The solid ground seemed to ripple and wave like water.

"They're coming out of the buildings," said Charlie, as if from a long distance off.

A weak, distant and ragged cheer came to their ears.

"Number two's hooked up," clipped Wonder Boy, his voice now strangely torn and distorted.

"Good," gasped Kent. "What about the others?"

"Coming in," vibrated Wonder Boy. "There go five and seven."

Kent tilted his head and fought his eyes to a fleeting focus on the settlement below. The colonists had indeed come out of their buildings, but the vibrations must be stronger down there, for they seemed unable to stand. They were lying flat and some were crawling. Faint screams came drifting up to the three men, wailing and distant.

The ground was really moving now. It seemed to swell and retreat under their feet and even up here on the hillside the men had to struggle to keep upright.

"One, three, four and six," buzzed Wonder Boy, distantly. He was standing over the master controls, and holding on.

The wailing from the shifting mass of color that was the village below was like the sounds from Dante's *Inferno*. The vibration tore and ground with angry fingers as if it would shake human flesh from human bones. Dust began to rise everywhere in great clouds, filling the air.

"—and all the rest," said Wonder Boy conclusively. "Now I'll throw the power in." His hands quivered, dancingly, as he fought with the master controls.

A new note swelled up to them from the torn and shaken ground beneath their feet. Unheard, but felt, it rose up like a wall to meet the tidal wave of vibration from Maker's instrument and the two clashed and fell to worrying each other like monstrous dogs. In their meeting and conflict there was no relief, for the earth still shook, but raggedly now, and out of tune.

"Hold on!" yelled Charlie thinly through the gathering storm of vibration, clinging valiantly to his instruments, calling to Wonder Boy. It was the ancient human battle cry in modern words. "Hold on! You're stopping him!"

And Wonder Boy, clinging limpet-like to his own controls, echoed it back.

"I'm holding!"

Dust clouds rose more thickly from the quivering ground, isolating each one from the rest by a burning, opaque yellow cloud. The counter-vibrations screamed and fought, the world reeled, and then—

A break, a sudden lessening in the battle.

"Quit it!" yelled Charlie, lost in the dust. "He's stopped."

Abruptly, silence and peace returned. And they were so welcome and strange after the battle that for a moment the shaken people could not believe them and felt them somehow unreal. Then they pulled themselves together and stared through the thinning haze.

"Don't move until the dust rises," said Charlie.

Like mist from the face of a magic mirror that draws aside like a veil in fairy stories to reveal unknown things, the dust thinned and passed from the face of the hollow and the distant rim of watching hills. Like a ghost growing solid and more real, the settlement came back into being before their watching eyes, the marked out streets, the buildings, the weather pylons; and it was all there, all standing and all whole.

In the streets a few people wandered dazedly, but all seemed to be on their feet and none were hurt.

Kent lifted his eyes from this to the hills beyond where, rank on rank and spears in hand, the Modorians still stood immovable and inscrutable. If any had fallen during the battle, they had gotten up again. And they waited now.

"I guess," said Kent. "It's up to me."

He went away down the hillside, loosening his gun in its holster by his side. He stepped into the settlement, and walked along its streets where the people gave him a wide berth. And he came out on the hill beyond, where the phalanx of wild Modorians had shielded Maker from him before.

They were still there; and he walked toward them.

They parted before him.

He walked through. He climbed up the narrow lane between them with the tall gray figures on each side no more than an arm's length away. He came to a little open space on the high ground around the pit, where Maker stood alone, his weapon below and behind him, glittering like some discarded toy in the rays of the late afternoon sun, gazing on the settlement below.

"Well, Maker?" said Kent, halting before him.

The Modorian did not answer, nor look down at him. His great dark eyes ate up the settlement and nothing else.

"Well, Maker?" repeated Kent, more loudly, his voice sounding blatant and huge in the silence of the waiting gray-furred crowd around them. Silence stretched out and tenseness grew brittle and thin between them. Then, slowly, without moving, the Modorian spoke.

"I will turn aside for no man, or men," he said—and, as if the words had been a talisman, he turned swiftly, his great body cat-like with the sinuous grace of his race, and flung himself at Kent, his steely arms wrapping around the man, crushing him, hurling him down the hillside.

The crowd, the ground, the rocks, the sky, whirled in one mad maelstrom around Kent as he went tumbling down the hillside between the leaping gray-furred legs of the Modorian host, and fighting for his life. The ground beat at his body with many hammers. Maker's arms crushed the breath from him and he struggled to free his right arm and draw his gun.

Hopelessly, instinctively, he fought during that wild fall down the hillside, knowing Maker was more than a physical match for any man that lived, knowing the odds were against him, but fighting anyhow. And, by some miracle, he did it; his arm came free, his hand closed

about the gun butt; and, as they rolled at last toward a
stop in the smothering yellow dust their fall had raised,
on the level ground at the bottom of the hill, he shoved
the muzzle hard against the rock-hard Modorian's side,
and squeezed the button, twice.

Once more they rolled, through sheer momentum, but
when they came at last to a standstill, Maker did not
move, but lay limp and heavy above him. Kent fought for
breath and was suddenly aware of hands that pulled the
gray-furred body free.

It came away above him and he looked up to see Charlie and the Wonder Boy.

"You hurt, Kent?" cried Charlie.

"Guns!" croaked Kent, desperately, struggling to his
feet and turning to face the dust cloud that obscured the
hillside in front of him. "They're coming! Get out your
guns!"

He faced into the wavering dust pall, his gun weaving
in his hand, and the other two, tense suddenly with the
implication of his words, snatched out their sidearms
and stood beside him, knowing the futility of their stand,
three men against thousands of Modorians, but not
knowing what else to do, and acting with the direct instinct of desperation.

So they stood, expecting each next second to be their
last. And the dust pall thinned before them, revealing
the hillside. Even after it was gone, they still stood tense
for a long minute, after all the fear and labor of the past
hours, unable to trust their eyes. Then, wonderingly,
they put their guns back and looked at each other as if
for enlightenment.

For the slope was empty before them and the hilltops
beyond were clearing like the bottom of a pond when a
school of minnows melts away from a spot where the
food has all been eaten. The wild Modorians, with the
strange logic of their kind, were giving up, were retreating to the barren reaches yet untouched by man,

were going away for good and leaving the human settlement alone.

Kent stood on the hillside the next morning, beside his
waiting flyer, and looked down on the settlement below.
To the eye it was as peaceful as it had ever been. The
terrors, the troubles, the host of threatening Modorians
had vanished like the night and the hills were wide and
empty above it. Buildings were going up and streets
were being surfaced. The weather pylons were working
at last, and an artificial climate held the little hollow.
Far below him he could see colonists thronging the
streets in light tunics and kilts, and among them the
occasional rough clothing of a prospector.

Kent grinned. One of those would certainly be Branch,
for all Peter Lawrence might have to say about it. But
the others would be men who three days ago were ready
to turn their guns against the people they talked with.
Still, their change of attitude was inevitable. Like calls
to like with the strongest call in the Universe, and the
men below were starved for male and female com-
panionship and the social structure of their kind. For
them the settlement was a small bit of the Earth they
longed for. They would inter-marry, and in time, settle
down, as the civilized portions of the planet were extended.

Kent shook his head, and a sudden realization came to
him of the inevitability of the whole proceeding. The
situation which had loomed so large yesterday, now appeared as an incident, doomed to be forgotten in time as
the march of civilization went on. He grinned a little ruefully. Now that it was all over, he felt completely useless. Modorian and colonist alike had turned away from
him to their own small immediate affairs—and Maker
was dead.

He frowned a little, remembering. Now that the heat
had gone from his mind, he could look back and wonder
on the chance that had enabled him to survive—first, the

embrace of a full grown male Modorian and second, a tumble down a sixty-foot slope. The whole thing was a little too good to be true. Now, looking back on it, realization came to him. There had been no miracle about his winning. The Modorian had failed, and having failed, wanted to die. He had merely put the taking of his life in Kent's hands.

Kent was suddenly very weary. The smallness of his own importance—even to the people nominally under his control—and the greatness of the Universe came back to him. What if the Colonial Representative had been someone else? What if Maker had won and the colonists had died? The end would have been the same In the long run the individualist always loses to the organization. What difference whether Maker or Kent wins? Man will win, and Modorian lose—as far as the races are concerned, when the last chips are added up on each side.

Kent moved slightly, and the flimsy Tom had given him crackled in his pocket. He took it out, unfolded it and looked again at Tichi's words. The investigation committee—well, they could do little to him now, the way things had turned out. Tichi—that was something else. . . .

The great aching nostalgia of the space-weary came over him. Sooner or later everybody feels it and turns toward his home. Earth's green hills were pretty much of a myth now, as the sprawling cities ate up the open space—but there was yet a little of stream and forest and mountain untouched, and Kent felt in his heart a longing for them, too deep to be expressed.

There was nothing more for him to do here. The great first fight was over and the rest of history here would be a succession of niggling brawls and troubles. Why bother with it, when what he wanted of Earth was his for the asking?

And Tichi?

Kent laughed suddenly, out loud, at himself.

"I'm an old man," he said, to the empty Modorian landscape. "It's high time I retired."

Still chuckling, he swung himself into the flyer, drove it up the ground and across the hollow to where Tom was setting up a subsidiary communications center.

"Hi!" said the communications man, popping out of the half-constructed building as Kent set the flyer down.

"Hi, Tom," said Kent. "You can send an answer to that message for me now."

Tom's homely face grinned.

"Right," he said. "What'll I say?"

"Just say everything's all right and that I'm coming home."

"That's all?" asked Tom. Kent frowned.

"Add 'love' to that," he said.

Tom still lingered.

"Nothing more. Kent?"

"Oh, hell!" said Kent, climbing back into his flyer. "Tell her I've just become convinced of the inevitability of things. That should keep her busy wondering—unless she starts putting her own interpretation on it.

"—but that's just what she'll probably do," he muttered half-pessimistically to the controls. Smiling, he slammed the door of the flyer behind him and lifted the machine into the air. Into the bright sky of morning, Kent Harmon headed east—and home. . . .

STEEL BROTHER

"We stand on guard."
—MOTTO OF THE FRONTIER FORCE

"... *Man that is born of woman hath but a short time to live and is full of misery. He cometh up and is cut down, like a flower; he fleeth as it were a shadow and never continueth in one stay—*"

The voice of the chaplain was small and sharp in the thin air, intoning the words of the burial service above the temporary lectern set up just inside the transparent wall of the landing field dome. Through the double transparencies of the dome and the plastic cover of the burial rocket the black-clad ranks could see the body of the dead stationman, Ted Waskewicz, lying back comfortably at an angle of forty-five degrees, peaceful in death, waxily perfect from the hands of the embalmers, and immobile. The eyes were closed, the cheerful, heavy features still held their expression of thoughtless dom-

245

inance, as though death had been a minor incident, easily shrugged off; and the battle star made a single blaze of color on the tunic of the black uniform.

"*Amen*." The response was a deep bass utterance from the assembled men, like the single note of an organ. In the front rank of the Cadets, Thomas Jordan's lips moved stiffly with the others', his voice joining mechanically in their chorus. For this was the moment of his triumph, but in spite of it, the old, old fear had come back, the old sense of loneliness and loss and terror of his own inadequacy.

He stood at stiff attention, eyes to the front, trying to lose himself in the unanimity of his classmates, to shut out the voice of the chaplain and the memory it evoked of an alien raid on an undefended city and of home and parents swept away from him in a breath. He remembered the mass burial service read over the shattered ruin of the city; and the government agency that had taken him—a ten-year-old orphan—and given him care and training until this day, but could not give him what these others about him had by natural right—the courage of those who had matured in safety.

For he had been lonely and afraid since that day. Untouched by bomb or shell, he had yet been crippled deep inside of him. He had seen the enemy in his strength and run screaming from his spacesuited gangs. And what could give Thomas Jordan back his soul after that?

But still he stood rigidly at attention, as a Guardsman should; for he was a soldier now, and this was part of his duty.

The chaplain's voice droned to a halt. He closed his prayerbook and stepped back from the lectern. The captain of the training ship took his place.

"In accordance with the conventions of the Frontier Force," he said, crisply, "I now commit the ashes of Station Commandant First Class, Theodore Waskewicz, to the keeping of time and space."

He pressed a button on the lectern. Beyond the dome, white fire blossomed out from the tail of the burial rocket, heating the asteroid rock to temporary incandescence. For a moment it hung there, spewing flame. Then it rose, at first slowly, then quickly, and was gone, sketching a fiery path out and away, until, at almost the limits of human sight, it vanished in a sudden, silent explosion of brilliant light.

Around Jordan, the black-clad ranks relaxed. Not by any physical movement, but with an indefinable breaking of nervous tension, they settled themselves for the more prosaic conclusion of the ceremony. The relaxation reached even to the captain, for he about-faced with a relieved snap and spoke to the ranks.

"Cadet Thomas Jordan. Front and center."

The command struck Jordan with an icy shock. As long as the burial service had been in progress, he had had the protection of anonymity among his classmates around him. Now, the captain's voice was a knife, cutting him off, finally and irrevocably from the security his life had known, leaving him naked and exposed. A despairing numbness seized him. His reflexes took over, moving his body like a robot. One step forward, a right face, down to the end of the row of silent men, a left face, three steps forward. Halt. Salute.

"Cadet Thomas Jordan reporting, sir."

"Cadet Thomas Jordan, I hereby invest you with command of this Frontier Station. You will hold it until relieved. Under no conditions will you enter into communications with an enemy nor allow any creature or vessel to pass through your sector of space from Outside."

"Yes, sir."

"In consideration of the duties and responsibilities requisite on assuming command of this Station, you are promoted to the rank and title of Station Commandant Third Class."

"Thank you, sir."

From the lectern the captain lifted a cap of silver wire mesh and placed it on his head. It clipped on to the electrodes already buried in his skull, with a snap that sent sound ringing through his skull. For a second, a sheet of lightning flashed in front of his eyes and he seemed to feel the weight of the memory bank already passing on his mind. Then lightning and pressure vanished together to show him the captain offering his hand.

"My congratulations, commandant."

"Thank you, sir."

They shook hands, the captain's grip quick, nervous and perfunctory. He took one abrupt step backward and transferred his attention to his second in command.

"Lieutenant! Dismiss the formation!"

It was over. The new rank locked itself around Jordan, sealing up the fear and loneliness inside him. Without listening to the barked commands that no longer concerned him, he turned on his heel and strode over to take up his position by the sally port of the training ship. He stood formally at attention beside it, feeling the weight of his new authority like a heavy cloak on his thin shoulders. At one stroke he had become the ranking officer present. The officers—even the captain—were nominally under his authority, so long as their ship remained grounded at his Station. So rigidly he stood at attention that not even the slightest tremor of the trembling inside him escaped to quiver betrayingly in his body.

They came toward him in a loose, dark mass that resolved itself into a single file just beyond saluting distance. Singly, they went past him and up the ladder into the sally port, each saluting him as they passed. He returned the salutes stiffly, mechanically, walled off from these classmates of six years by the barrier of his new command. It was a moment when a smile or a casual handshake would have meant more than a little. But protocol had stripped him of the right to familiarity;

and it was a line of black-uniformed strangers that now
filed slowly past. His place was already established and
theirs was yet to be. They had nothing in common any
more.

The last of the men went past him up the ladder and
were lost to view through the black circle of the sally
port. The heavy steel plug swung slowly to, behind them.
He turned and made his way to the unfamiliar but well-
known field control panel in the main control room of
the Station. A light glowed redly on the communications
board. He thumbed a switch and spoke into a grill set in
the panel.

"Station to Ship. Go ahead."

Overhead the loudspeaker answered.

"Ship to Station. Ready for take-off."

His fingers went swiftly over the panel. Outside, the
atmosphere of the field was evacuated and the dome slid
back. Tractor mechs scurried out from the pit, under remote control, clamped huge magnetic fists on the ship,
swung it into launching position, then retreated.

Jordon spoke again into the grill.

"Station clear. Take-off at will."

"Thank you, Station." He recognized the captain's
voice. "And good luck."

Outside, the ship lifted, at first slowly, then faster on
its pillar of flame, and dwindled away into the darkness
of space. Automatically, he closed the dome and pumped
the air back in.

He was turning away from the control panel, bracing
himself against the moment of finding himself completely isolated, when, with a sudden, curious shock, he
noticed that there was another, smaller ship yet on the
field.

For a moment he stared at it blankly, uncomprehend-
ingly. Then memory returned and he realized that the
ship was a small courier vessel from Intelligence, which
had been hidden by the huge bulk of the training ship.
Its officer would still be below, cutting a record tape of

the former commandant's last memories for the file at
Headquarters. The memory lifted him momentarily
from the morass of his emotions to attention to duty. He
turned from the panel and went below.

In the triply-armored basement of the Station, the
man from Intelligence was half in and half out of the
memory bank when he arrived, having cut away a
portion of the steel casing around the bank so as to
connect his recorder direct to the cells. The sight of the
heavy mount of steel with the ragged incision in one
side, squatting like a wounded monster, struck Jordan
unpleasantly; but he smoothed the emotion from his
face and walked firmly to the bank. His footsteps rang
on the metal floor; and the man from Intelligence, hearing them, brought his head momentarily outside the
bank for a quick look.

"Hi!" he said, shortly, returning to his work. His voice
continued from the interior of the bank with a friendly,
hollow sound. "Congratulations, commandant."

"Thanks," answered Jordan, stiffly. He stood, somewhat ill at ease, uncertain of what was expected of him.
When he hesitated, the voice from the bank continued.

"How does the cap feel?"

Jordan's hands went up instinctively to the mesh of
silver wire on his head. It pushed back unyieldingly at
his fingers, held firmly on the electrodes.

"Tight," he said.

The Intelligence man came crawling out of the bank,
his recorder in one hand and thick loops of glassy tape
in the other.

"They all do at first," he said, squatting down and
feeding one end of the tape into a spring rewind spool.
"In a couple of days you won't even be able to feel it up
there."

"I suppose."

The Intelligence man looked up at him curiously.

"Nothing about it bothering you, is there?" he asked.

"You look a little strained."

"Doesn't everybody when they first start out?"

"Sometimes," said the other, noncommittally. "Sometimes not. Don't hear a sort of humming, do you?"

"No."

"Feel any kind of pressure inside your head?"

"No."

"How about your eyes. See any spots or flashes in front of them?"

"No!" snapped Jordan.

"Take it easy," said the man from Intelligence. "This is my business."

"Sorry."

"That's all right. It's just that if there's anything wrong with you or the bank I want to know it." He rose from the rewind spool, which was now industriously gathering in the loose tape; and unclipping a pressure-torch from his belt, began resealing the aperture. "It's just that occasionally new officers have been hearing too many stories about the banks in Training School, and they're inclined to be jumpy."

"Stories?" said Jordan.

"Haven't you heard them?" answered the Intelligence man. "Stories of memory domination—stationmen driven insane by the memories of the men who had the Station before them. Catatonics whose minds have got lost in the past history of the bank, or cases of memory replacement where the stationman had identified himself with the memories and personality of the man who preceded him."

"Oh, those," said Jordan. "I've heard them." He paused, and then, when the other did not go on: "What about them? Are they true?"

The Intelligence man turned from the half-resealed aperture and faced him squarely, torch in hand.

"Some," he said bluntly. "There's been a few cases like that; although there didn't have to be. Nobody's trying to sugarcoat the facts. The memory bank's nothing but a storehouse connected to you through your silver cap—a gadget to enable you not only to remember everything you ever do at the Station, but also everything anybody else who ever ran the Station, did. But there've been a few impressionable stationmen who've let themselves get the notion that the memory bank's a sort of a coffin with living dead men crawling around inside it. When that happens, there's trouble."

He turned away from Jordan, back to his work.

"And that's what you thought was the trouble with me," said Jordan, speaking to his back.

The man from Intelligence chuckled—it was an amazingly human sound.

"In my line, fella," he said, "we check all possibilities." He finished his resealing and turned around.

"No hard feelings?" he said.

Jordan shook his head. "Of course not."

"Then I'll be getting along." He bent over and picked up the spool, which had by now neatly wound up all the tape, straightened up and headed for the ramp that led up from the basement to the landing field. Jordan fell into step beside him.

"You've nothing more to do, then?" he asked.

"Just my reports. But I can write those on the way back." They went up the ramp and out through the lock on to the field.

"They did a good job of repairing the battle damage," he went on, looking around the Station.

"I guess they did," said Jordan. The two men paced soberly to the sally port of the Intelligence ship. "Well, so long."

"So long," answered the man from Intelligence, activating the sally port mechanism. The outer lock swung open and he hopped the few feet up to the opening without waiting for the little ladder to wind itself out. "See you in six months."

He turned to Jordan and gave him a casual, offhand

salute with the hand holding the wind-up spool. Jordan returned it with training school precision. The port swung closed.

He went back to the master control room and the ritual of seeing the ship off. He stood looking out for a long time after it had vanished, then turned from the panel with a sigh to find himself at last completely alone.

He looked about the Station. For the next six months this would be his home. Then, for another six months he would be free on leave while the Station was rotated out of the line in its regular order for repair, reconditioning, and improvements.

If he lived that long.

The fear, which had been driven a little distance away by his conversation with the man from Intelligence, came back.

If he lived that long. He stood, bemused.

Back to his mind with the letter-perfect recall of the memory bank came the words of the other. Catatonic—cases of memory replacement. Memory domination. Had those others, too, had more than they could bear of fear and anticipation?

And with that thought came a suggestion that coiled like a snake in his mind. That would be a way out. What if they came, the alien invaders, and Thomas Jordan was no longer here to meet them? What if only the catatonic hulk of a man was left? What if they came and a man was here, but that man called himself and knew himself only as—

Waskewicz!

"No!" the cry came involuntarily from his lips; and he came to himself with his face contorted and his hands half-extended in front of him in the attitude of one who wards off a ghost. He shook his head to shake the vile suggestion from his brain; and leaned back, panting, against the control panel.

Not that. Not ever that. He had surprised in himself a weakness that turned him sick with horror. Win or lose; live or die. But as Jordan—not as any other.

He lit a cigarette with trembling fingers. So—it was over now and he was safe. He had caught it in time. He had his warning. Unknown to him—all this time—the seeds of memory domination must have been lying waiting within him. But now he knew they were there, he knew what measures to take. The danger lay in Waskewicz's memories. He would shut his mind off from them—would fight the Station without the benefit of their experience. The first stationmen on the line had done without the aid of a memory bank and so could he.

So.

He had settled it. He flicked on the viewing screens and stood opposite them, very straight and correct in the middle of his Station, looking out at the dots that were his forty-five doggie mechs spread out on guard over a million kilometers of space, looking at the controls that would enable him to throw their blunt, terrible, mechanical bodies into battle with the enemy, looking and waiting, waiting, for the courage that comes from having faced squarely a situation, to rise within him and take possession of him, putting an end to all fears and doubtings.

And he waited so for a long time, but it did not come.

The weeks went swiftly by; and that was as it should be. He had been told what to expect, during training; and it was as it should be that these first months should be tense ones, with a part of him always stiff and waiting for the alarm bell that would mean a doggie signaling sight of an enemy. It was as it should be that he should pause, suddenly, in the midst of a meal with his fork halfway to his mouth, waiting and expecting momentarily to be summoned; that he should wake unexpectedly in the nighttime and lie rigid and tense, eyes fixed on the shadowy ceiling and listening. Later—they had said in training—after you have become used to the Station, this constant tension will relax and you will be left at ease, with only one little unobtrusive corner of your mind unnoticed but forever alert. This will come with time, they said.

So he waited for it, waited for the release of the coiled springs inside him and the time when the feel of the Station would be comfortable and friendly about him. When he had first been left alone, he had thought to himself that surely, in his case, the waiting would not be more than a matter of days; then, as the days went by and he still lived in a state of hair-trigger sensitivity, he had given himself in his own mind, a couple of weeks—then a month.

But now a month and more than a month had gone without relaxation coming to him; and the strain was beginning to show in nervousness of his hands and the dark circles under his eyes. He found it impossible to sit still either to read, or to listen to the music that was available in the Station library. He roamed restlessly, endlessly checking and rechecking the empty space that his doggies' viewers revealed.

For the recollections of Waskewicz as he lay in the burial rocket would not go from him. And that was not as it should be.

He could, and did, refuse to recall the memories of Waskewicz that he had never experienced; but his own personal recollections were not easy to control and slipped into his mind when he was unaware. All else that he could do to lay the ghost, he had done. He had combed the Station carefully, seeking out the little adjustments and conveniences that a lonely man will make about his home, and removed them, even when the removal meant a loss of personal comfort. He had locked his mind securely to the storehouse of the memory bank, striving to hold himself isolated from the other's memories until familiarity and association should bring him to the point where he instinctively felt that the

Station was *his* and not the other's. And, whenever
thought of Waskewicz entered in spite of all these precautions, he had dismissed them sternly, telling himself
that his predecessor was not worth the considering.

But the other's ghost remained, intangible and invul-
nerable, as if locked in the very metal of the walls and
floor and ceiling of the Station; and rising to haunt him
with the memories of the training school tales and the
ominous words of the man from Intelligence. At such
times, when the ghost had seized him, he would stand
paralyzed, staring in hypnotic fascination at the screens
with their silent mechanical sentinels, or at the cold
steel of the memory bank, crouching like some brooding
monster, fear feeding on his thoughts—until, with a
sudden, wrenching effort of the will, he broke free of the
mesmerism and flung himself frantically into the duties
of the Station, checking and rechecking his instruments
and the space they watched, doing anything and everything to drown his wild emotions in the necessity for
attention to duty.

And eventually he found himself almost hoping for a
raid, for the test that would prove him, would lay the
ghost, one way or another, once and for all.

It came at last, as he had known it would, during one
of the rare moments when he had forgotten the im-
minence of danger. He had awakened in his bunk, at the
beginning of the arbitrary ten-hour day; and lay there
drowsily, comfortably, his thoughts vague and formless,
like shadows in the depths of a lazy whirlpool, turning
slowly, going no place.

Then—the alarm!

Overhead the shouting bell burst into life, jerking him
from his bed. Its metal clangor poured out on the air,
tumbling from the loudspeakers in every room all over
the Station, strident with urgency, pregnant with disaster. It roared, it vibrated, it thundered, until the walls
themselves threw it back, seeming to echo in sympathy,

acquiring a voice of their own until the room rang—until the Station itself rang like one monster bell, calling him into battle.

He leaped to his feet and ran to the master control room. On the telltale high on the wall above the viewer screens, the red light of number thirty-eight doggie was flashing ominously. He threw himself into the operator's seat before it, slapping one palm hard down on the switch to disconnect the alarm.

The Station is in contact with the enemy.

The sudden silence slapped at him, taking his breath away. He gasped and shook his head like a man who has had a glassful of cold water thrown unexpectedly in his face; then plunged his fingers at the keys on the master control board in front of his seat— Up beams. Up detector screen, established now at forty thousand kilometers distance. Switch on communications to Sector Headquarters.

The transmitter purred. Overhead, the white light flashed as it began to tick off its automatic signal. "Alert! Alert! Further data follows. Will report."

Headquarters has been notified by the Station.

Activate viewing screen on doggie number thirty-eight.

He looked into the activated screen, into the vast arena of space over which the mechanical vision of that doggie mech was ranging. Far and far away at top magnification were five small dots, coming in fast on a course leading ten points below and at an angle of thirty-two degrees to the Station.

He flicked a key, releasing thirty-eight on proximity fuse control and sending it plunging toward the dots. He scanned the Station area map for the positions of his other mechs. Thirty-nine was missing—in the Station for repair. The rest were available. He checked numbers forty through forty-five and thirty-seven through thirty to rendezvous on collision course with enemy at seventy-five thousand kilometers. Numbers twenty to thirty to rendezvous at fifty thousand kilometers.

Primary defense has been inaugurated.

He turned back to the screen. Number thirty-eight, expendable in the interests of gaining information, was plunging towards the ships at top acceleration under strains no living flesh would have been able to endure. But as yet the size and type of the invaders was still hidden by distance. A white light flashed abruptly from the communications panel, announcing that Sector Headquarters was alerted and ready to talk. He cut in audio.

"Contact. Go ahead, Station J-49C3."

"Five ships," he said. "Beyond identification range. Coming in through thirty-eight at ten point thirty-two."

"Acknowledge." The voice of Headquarters was level, precise, emotionless. "Five ships—thirty-eight—ten—thirty-two. Patrol Twenty, passing through your area at four hours distance, has been notified and will proceed to your station at once, arriving in four hours, plus or minus twenty minutes. Further assistance follows. Will stand by here for your future messages."

The white light went out and he turned away from communications panel. On the screen, the five ships had still not grown to identifiable proportions, but for all practical purposes, the preliminaries were over. He had some fifteen minutes now during which everything that could be done, had been done.

Primary defense has been completed.

He turned away from the controls and walked back to the bedroom, where he dressed slowly and meticulously in full black uniform. He straightened his tunic, looking in the mirror and stood gazing at himself for a long moment. Then, hesitantly, almost as if against his will, he reached out with one hand to a small gray box on a shelf beside the mirror, opened it, and took out the silver battle star that the next few hours would entitle him to wear.

It lay in his palm, the bright metal winking softly up at him under the reflection of the room lights and the small movements of his hand. The little cluster of diamonds in its center sparked and ran the whole gamut of their flashing colors. For several minutes he stood looking at it; then slowly, gently, he shut it back up in its box and went out, back to the control room.

On the screen, the ships were now large enough to be identified. They were medium sized vessels, Jordan noticed, of the type used most by the most common species of raiders—that same race which had orphaned him. There could be no doubt about their intentions, as there sometimes was when some odd stranger chanced upon the Frontier, to be regretfully destroyed by men whose orders were to take no chances. No, these were *the enemy*, the strange, suicidal life form that thrust thousands of attacks yearly against the little human empire, who blew themselves up when captured and wasted a hundred ships for every one that broke through the guarding stations to descend on some un-protected city of an inner planet and loot it of equipment and machinery that the aliens were either unwilling or unable to build for themselves—a contradictory, little understood and savage race. These five ships would make no attempt to parley.

But now, doggie number thirty-eight had been spotted and the white exhausts of guided missiles began to streak toward the viewing screen. For a few seconds, the little mech bucked and tossed, dodging, firing defen-sively, shooting down the missiles as they approached it. But it was a hopeless fight against those odds and sud-denly one of the streaks expanded to fill the screen with glaring light.

And the screen went blank. Thirty-eight was gone.

Suddenly realizing that he should have been covering with observation from one of the doggies further back, Jordan jumped to fill his screens. He brought the view from forty in on the one that thirty-eight had vacated

and filled the two flanking screens with the view from
thirty-seven on his left and twenty on his right. They
showed his first line of defense already gathered at the
seventy-five kilometer rendezvous and the fifty thousand kilometer rendezvous still forming.

The raiders were decelerating now, and on the wall,
the telltale for the enemy's detectors flushed a sudden
deep and angry purple as their invisible beams reached
out and were baffled by the detector screen he had
erected at a distance of forty thousand kilometers in
front of the Station. They continued to decelerate, but
the blockage of their detector beams had given them the
approximate area of his Station; and they corrected
course, swinging in until they were no more than two
points and ten degrees in error. Jordan, his nervous
fingers trembling slightly on the keys, stretched thirty-
seven through thirty out in depth and sent forty through
forty-five forward on a five-degree sweep to attempt a
circling movement.

The five dark ships of the raiders, recognizing his
intention, fell out of their single file approach formation
to spread out and take a formation in open echelon.
They were already firing on the advancing doggies and
tiny streaks of light tattooed the black of space around
numbers forty through forty-five.

Jordan drew a deep and ragged breath and leaned
back in his control seat. For the moment there was
nothing for his busy fingers to do among the control
keys. His thirties must wait until the enemy came to
them; since, with modern automatic gunnery the body at
rest had an advantage over the body in motion. And it
would be some minutes before the forties would be in
attack position. He fumbled for a cigarette, keeping his
eyes on the screens, remembering the caution in the
training manuals against relaxation once contact with
the enemy has been made.

But reaction was setting in.

From the first wild ringing command of the alarm until the present moment, he had reacted automatically, with perfection and precision, as the drills had schooled him, as the training manuals had impressed upon him. The enemy had appeared. He had taken measures for defense against them. All that could have been done had been done; and he knew he had done it properly. And the enemy had done what he had been told they would do.

He was struck, suddenly, with the deep quivering realization of the truth in the manual's predictions. It was so, then. These inimical others, these alien foes, were also bound by the physical laws. They as well as he, could move only within the rules of time and space. They were shorn of their mystery and brought down to his level. Different and awful, they might be, but their capabilities were limited, even as his; and in a combat such as the one now shaping up, their inhumanness was of no account, for the inflexible realities of the universe weighed impartially on him and them alike.

And with this realization, for the first time, the old remembered fear began to fall away like a discarded garment. A tingle ran through him and he found himself warming to the fight as his forefathers had warmed before him away back to the days when man was young and the tiger roared in the cool, damp jungle-dawn of long ago. The blood-instinct was in him; that and something of the fierce, vengeful joy with which a hunted creature turns at last on its pursuer. He would win. Of course he would win. And in winning he would at one stroke pay off the debt of blood and fear which the enemy had held against him these fifteen years.

Thinking in this way, he leaned back in his seat and the old memory of the shattered city and of himself running, running, rose up again around him. But this time it was no longer a prelude to terror, but fuel for the kindling of his rage. *These are my fear*, he thought, gazing unseeingly at the five ships in the screens *and I will destroy them*.

The phantasms of his memory faded like smoke around him. He dropped his cigarette into a disposal slot on the arm of his seat, and leaned forward to inspect the enemy positions.

They had spread out to force his forties to circle wide, and those doggies were now scattered, safe but ineffective, awaiting further directions. What had been an open echelon formation of the raiders was now a ragged, widely dispersed line, with far too much space between ships to allow each to cover his neighbor.

For a moment Jordan was puzzled; and a tiny surge of fear of the unexplicable rippled across the calm surface of his mind. Then his brow smoothed out. There was no need to get panicky. The aliens' maneuver was not the mysterious tactic he had half-expected it to be; but just what it appeared, a rather obvious and somewhat stupid move to avoid the flanking movement he had been attempting with his forties. Stupid—because the foolish aliens had now rendered themselves vulnerable to interspersal by his thirties.

It was good news, rather than bad, and his spirits leaped another notch.

He ignored the baffled forties, circling automatically on safety control just beyond the ship's effective aiming range; and turned to the thirties, sending them plunging toward the empty areas between ships as you might interlace the fingers of one hand with another. Between any two ships there would be a dead spot—a position where a mech could not be fired on by either vessel without almost aiming at its right- or left-hand companion. If two or more doggies could be brought safely to that spot, they could turn and pour down the open lanes on proximity control, their fuses primed, their bomb loads activated, blind bulldogs of destruction.

One third, at least, should in this way get through the defensive shelling of the ships and track their dodging prey to the atomic flare of a grim meeting.

Smiling now in confidence, Jordan watched his mechs

approach the ships. There was nothing the enemy could do. They could not now tighten up their formation without merely making themselves a more attractive target; and to disperse still further would negate any chance in the future of regaining a semblance of formation.

Carefully, his fingers played over the keys, gentling his mechs into line so that they would come as close as possible to hitting their dead spots simultaneously. The ships came on.

Closer the raiders came, and closer. And then—bare seconds away from contact with the line of approaching doggies, white fire ravened in unison from their stern tubes, making each ship suddenly a black nugget in the center of a blossom of flame. In unison, they spurted forward, in sudden and unexpected movement, bringing their dead spots to and past the line of seeking doggies, leaving them behind.

Caught for a second in stunned surprise, Jordan sat dumb and motionless, staring at the screen. Then, swift in his anger, his hands flashed out over the keys, blasting his mechs to a cruel, shuddering halt, straining their metal sinews for the quickest and most abrupt about face and return. This time he would catch them from behind. This time, going in the same direction as the ships, the mechs could not be dodged. For what living thing could endure equal strains with cold metal?

But there was no second attempt on the part of the thirties, for as each bucked to its savage halt, the rear weapons of the ships reached out in unison, and each of the blasting mechs, that had leaped forward so confidently, flared up and died like little candles in the dark.

Numb in the grip of icy failure, Jordan sat still, a ramrod figure staring at the two screens that spoke so eloquently of his disaster—and the one dead screen where the view from thirty-seven had been, that said nothing at all. Like a man in a dream, he reached out his right hand and cut in the final sentinel, the *watchdog*, that mech that circled closest to the Station. In one short breath his strong first line was gone, and the enemy rode, their strength undiminished, floating in toward his single line of twenties at fifty thousand with the defensive screen a mere ten thousand kilometers behind them.

Training was strong. Without hesitation his hands went out over the keys and the doggies of the twenties surged forward, trying for contact with the enemy in an area as far from the screen as possible. But, because they were moving in on an opponent relatively at rest, their courses were the more predictable on the enemy's calculators and the disadvantage was theirs. So it was that forty minutes later three ships of the alien rode clear and unthreatened in an area where two of their mates, the forties and all of the thirties were gone.

The ships were, at this moment, fifteen thousand kilometers from the detector screen.

Jordan looked at his handiwork. The situation was obvious and the alternatives undeniable. He had twenty doggies remaining, but he had neither the time to move them up beyond the screen, nor the room to maneuver them in front of it. The only answer was to pull his screen back. But to pull the screen back would be to indicate, by its shrinkage and the direction of its withdrawal, the position of his Station clearly enough for the guided missiles of the enemy to seek him out; and once the Station was knocked out, the doggies were direction-less, impotent.

Yet, if he did nothing, in a few minutes the ships would touch and penetrate the detector screen and his Station, the nerve center the aliens were seeking, would lie naked and revealed in their detectors.

He had lost. The alternatives totaled to the same answer, to defeat. In the inattention of a moment, in the smoke of a cigarette, the first blind surge of self-confidence and the thoughtless halting of his by-passed doggies that had allowed the ships' calculators to find them stationary for a second in a predictable area, he had failed. He had given away, in the error of his pride, the initial advantage. He had lost. Speak it softly, speak it gently, for his fault was the fault of one young and untried. He was defeated.

And in the case of defeat, the actions prescribed by the manual was stern and clear. The memory of the instructions tolled in his mind like the unvarying notes of a funeral bell.

"*When, in any conflict, the forces of the enemy have obtained a position of advantage such that it is no longer possible to maintain the anonymity of the Station's position, the commandant of the Station is required to perform one final duty. Knowing that the Station will shortly be destroyed and that this will render all remaining mechs innocuous to enemy forces, the commandant is commanded to relinquish control of these mechs, and to place them with fuses primed on proximity control, in order that, even without the Station, they may be enabled to automatically pursue and attempt to destroy those forces of the enemy that approach within critical range of their proximity fuse.*"

Jordan looked at his screens. Out at forty thousand kilometers, the detector screen was beginning to luminesce slightly as the detectors of the ships probed it at shorter range. To make the manual's order effective, it would have to be pulled back to at least half that distance, and there, while it would still hide the Station, it would give the enemy his approximate location. They would then fire blindly, but with cunning and increasing knowledge and it would be only a matter of time before they hit. After that—only the blind doggies, quivering, turning and trembling through all points of the stellar compass in their thoughtless hunger for prey. One or two of these might gain a revenge as the ships tried to slip past them and over the Line; but Jordan would not be there to know it.

But there was no alternative—even if duty had left him one. Like strangers, his hands rose from the board and stretched out over the keys that would turn the doggies loose. His fingers dropped and rested upon them—light touch on smooth polished coolness.

But he could not press them down.

He sat with his arms outstretched, as if in supplication, like one of his primitive forebearers before some ancient altar of death. For his will had failed him and there was no denying now his guilt and his failure. For the battle had turned in his short few moments of inattention, and his underestimation of the enemy that had seduced him into halting his thirties without thinking. He knew; and through the memory bank—if that survived—the Force would know. In his neglect, in his refusal to avail himself of the experience of his predecessors, he was guilty.

And yet, he could not press the keys. He could not die properly—*in the execution of his duty*—the cold, correct phrase of the official reports. For a wild rebellion surged through his young body, an instinctive denial of the end that stared him so undeniably in the face. Through vein and sinew and nerve, it raced, opposing and blocking the dictates of training, the logical orders of his upper mind. It was too soon, it was not fair, he had not been given his chance to profit by experience. One more opportunity was all he needed, one more try to redeem himself.

But the rebellion passed and left him shaken, weak. There was no denying reality. And now, a new shame came to press upon him, for he thought of the three alien vessels breaking through, of another city in flaming ruins, and another child that would run screaming from his destroyers. The thought rose up in him, and he writhed internally, torn by his own indecisions. Why couldn't he act? It made no difference to him. What would justification and the redeeming of error mean to him after he was dead?

And he moaned a little, softly to himself, holding his hands outstretched above the keys, but could not press them down.

And then hope came. For suddenly, rising up out of the rubble of his mind came the memory of the Intelligence man's words once again, and his own near-pursuit of insanity. He, Jordan, could not bring himself to expose himself to the enemy, not even if the method of exposure meant possible protection for the Inner Worlds. But the man who had held this Station before him, who had died as he was about to die, must have been faced with the same necessity for self-sacrifice. And those last-minute memories of his decision would be in the memory bank, waiting for the evocation of Jordan's mind.

Here was hope at last. He would remember, would embrace the insanity he had shrunk from. He would remember and be Waskewicz, not Jordan. He would be Waskewicz and unafraid; though it was a shameful thing to do. Had there been one person, one memory among all living humans, whose image he could have evoked to place in opposition to the images of the three dark ships, he might have managed by himself. But there had been no one close to him since the day of the city raid.

His mind reached back into the memory bank, reached back to the last of Waskewicz's memories. He remembered.

Of the ten ships attacking, six were down. Their ashes strewed the void and the remaining four rode warily, spread widely apart for maximum safety, sure of victory, but wary of this hornet's nest which might still have some stings yet unexpended. But the detector screen was back to its minimum distance for effective concealment and only five doggies remained poised like blunt arrows behind it. He—Waskewicz—sat hunched before the control board, his thick and hairy hands lying softly on the proximity keys.

"Drift in," he said, speaking to the ships, which were cautiously approaching the screen. "Drift in, you. Drift!"

His lips were skinned back over his teeth in a grin—but he did not mean it. It was an automatic grimace, reflex to the tenseness of his waiting. He would lure them on until the last moment, draw them as close as possible to the automatic pursuit mechanisms of the remaining doggies, before pulling back the screen.

"Drift in," he said.

They drifted in. Behind the screen he aimed his doggies, pointing each one of four at a ship and the remaining one generally at them all. They drifted in.

They touched.

His fingers slapped the keys. The screen snapped back until it barely covered the waiting doggies. And the doggies stirred, on proximity, their pursuit mechs activated, now blind and terrible fully armed, ready to attack in senseless directness anything that came close enough.

And the first shells from the advancing ships began to probe the general area of the Station asteroid.

Waskewicz sighed, pushed himself back from the controls and stood up, turning away from the screens. It was over. Done. All finished. For a moment he stood irresolute; then, walking over to the dispenser on the wall, dialed for coffee and drew it, hot into a disposable cup. He lit a cigarette and stood waiting, smoking and drinking the coffee.

The Station rocked suddenly to the impact of a glancing hit on the asteroid. He staggered and slopped some coffee on his boots, but kept his feet. He took another gulp from the cup, another drag on the cigarette. The Station shook again, and the lights dimmed. He crumpled the cup and dropped it in the disposal slot. He dropped the cigarette on the steel floor, ground

it beneath his boot sole; and walked back to the screen
and leaned over it for a final look.

The lights went out. And memory ended.

The present returned to Jordan and he stared about
him a trifle wildly. Then he felt hardness beneath his
fingers and forced himself to look down.

The keys were depressed. The screen was back. The
doggies were on proximity. He stared at his hand as if he
had never known it before, shocked at its thinness and
the lack of soft down on its back. Then, slowly, fighting
reluctant neck muscles, he forced himself to look up and
into the viewing screen.

And the ships were there, but the ships were drawing
away.

He stared, unable to believe his eyes, and half-ready to
believe anything else. For the invaders had turned and
the flames from their tails made it evident that they
were making away into outer space at their maximum
bearable acceleration, leaving him alone and unharmed.
He shook his head to clear away the false vision from
the screen before him, but it remained, denying its false-
ness. The miracle for which his instincts had held him in
check had come—in the moment in which he had bor-
rowed strength to deny it.

His eyes searched the screens in wonder. And then, far
down in one corner of the watch dog's screen and so distant still that they showed only as pips on the wide
expanse, he saw the shape of his miracle. Coming up
from inside of the Line under maximum bearable acceleration were six gleaming fish-shapes that would
dwarf his doggies to minnows—the battleships of Patrol
Twenty. And he realized, with the dawning wonder of
the reprieved, that the conflict, which had seemed so
momentary while he was fighting it had actually lasted
the four hours necessary to bring the Patrol up to his
aid.

The realization that he was now safe washed over him

like a wave and he was conscious of a deep thankfulness swelling up within him. It swelled up and out, pushing aside the lonely fear and desperation of his last few minutes, filling him instead with a relief so all-encompassing and profound that there was no anger left in him and no hate—not even for the enemy. It was like being born again.

Above him on the communication panel, the white message light was blinking. He cut in on the speaker with a steady hand and the dispassionate, official voice of the Patrol sounded over his head.

"Patrol Twenty to Station. Twenty to Station. Come in Station. Are you all right?"

He pressed the transmitter key.

"Station to Twenty. Station to Twenty. No damage to report. The Station is unharmed."

"Glad to hear it, Station. We will not pursue. We are decelerating now and will drop all ships on your field in half an hour. That is all."

"Thank you, Twenty. The field will be clear and ready for you. Land at will. That is all."

His hand fell away from the key and the message light winked out. In unconscious imitation of Waskewicz's memory he pushed himself back from the controls, stood up, turned and walked to the dispenser in the wall, where he dialed for and received a cup of coffee. He lit a cigarette and stood as the other had stood, smoking and drinking. He had won.

And reality came back to him with a rush.

For he looked down at his hand and saw the cup of coffee. He drew in on the cigarette and felt the hot smoothness of it deep in his lungs. And terror took him twisting by the throat.

He had won? He had done nothing. The enemy ships had fled not from him, but from the Patrol; and it was Waskewicz, *Waskewicz*, who had taken the controls from his hands at the crucial moment. It was Waskewicz who had saved the day, not he. It was the memory bank.

The memory bank and Waskewicz!

The control room rocked about him. He had been betrayed. Nothing was won. Nothing was conquered. It was no friend that had broken at last through his lonely shell to save him, but the mind-sucking figment of memory-domination insanity. The memory bank and Waskewicz had seized him in their grasp.

He threw the coffee container from him and made himself stand upright. He threw the cigarette down and ground it beneath his boot. White-hot, from the very depths of his being, a wild anger blazed and consumed him. *Puppet*, said the mocking voice of his conscience, whispering in his ear. *Puppet*!

Dance, Puppet! Dance to the tune of the twitching strings!

"No!" he yelled. And, borne on the white-hot tide of his rage, the all-consuming rage that burnt the last trace of fear from his heart like dross from the molten steel, he turned to face his tormentor, hurling his mind backward, back into the life of Waskewicz, prisoned in the memory bank.

Back through the swirling tide of memories he raced, hunting a point of contact, wanting only to come to grips with his predecessor, to stand face to face with Waskewicz. Surely, in all his years at the Station, the other must sometime have devoted a thought to the man who must come after him. Let Jordan just find that point, there where the influence was strongest, and settle the matter, for sanity or insanity, for shame or pride, once and for all.

"Hi, Brother!"

The friendly words splashed like cool water on the white blaze of his anger. He—Waskewicz—stood in front of the bedroom mirror and his face looked out at the man who was himself, and who yet was also Jordan.

"Hi, Brother!" he said. "Whoever and wherever you may be. Hi!"

Jordan looked out through the eyes of Waskewicz, at the reflected face of Waskewicz; and it was a friendly face, the face of a man like himself.

"This is what they don't tell you," said Waskewicz. "This is what they don't teach in training—the message that, sooner or later, every stationman leaves for the guy who comes after him.

"This is the creed of the Station. *You are not alone*. No matter what happens, *you are not alone*. Out on the rim of the empire, facing the unknown races and the endless depths of the universe, this is the one thing that will keep you from all harm. As long as you remember it, nothing can affect you, neither attack, nor defeat, nor death. Light a screen on your outermost doggie and turn the magnification up as far as it will go. Away out at the limits of your vision you can see the doggie of another Station, of another man who holds the Line beside you. All along the Frontier, the Outpost Stations stand, forming a link of steel to guard the Inner Worlds and the little people there. They have their lives and you have yours; and yours is to stand on guard.

"It is not easy to stand on guard; and no man can face the universe alone. But—*you are not alone*! All those who at this moment keep the Line, are with you; and all that have ever kept the Line, as well. For this is our new immortality, we who guard the Frontier, that we do not stop with our deaths, but live on in the Station we have kept. We are in its screens, its controls, in its memory bank, in the very bone and sinew of its steel body. *We are the Station*, your steel brother that fights and lives and dies with you and welcomes you at last to our kinship when for your personal self the light has gone out forever, and what was individual of you is nothing any more but cold ashes drifting in the eternity of space. *We are with you and of you, and you are not alone*. I, who was once Waskewicz, and am now part of the Station, leave this message for you, as it was left to me by the man who kept this guard before me, and as you will leave it in your turn to the man who follows you, and so on down the centuries until we have become an elder race and no longer need our shield of brains and steel.

"*Hi, Brother! You are not alone!*"

And so, when the six ships of Patrol Twenty came drifting in to their landing at the Station, the man who waited to greet them had more than the battle star on his chest to show he was a veteran. For he had done more than win a battle. He had found his soul.

LOVE ME TRUE

On the way to the colonel's office, Ted Holman asked the MP to take him around by the laboratories so he could get a look at Pogey.

"You think I'm nuts?" said the MP. "I can't do that. Anyway we haven't got time. And anyway, they wouldn't let you in there. All we could do is look through the door."

"All right. I can see him through the door, anyway," said Ted. The MP hesitated. He was a lean, dark young kid from Colorado; and he looked older than Ted, who was a tow-headed, opened-faced young blond soldier of the type who never looks quite grown up. But Ted had been to Arcturus IV and back; while the MP had never been farther than Washington, D.C.

So they went to the laboratories; and the MP stood to one side while Ted peered through the wire and glass of the small window set high in the door to the experimental section. Inside were cages with white rats, and rabbits, some rhesus monkeys and a small, white-

haired, terrier-looking bitch. The speaker grille above
the door brought to Ted's ears the rustling sound of the
creatures in their cages.

"I can't see him," said Ted.

"In the corner," said the MP.

Ted pressed closer to the door and caught sight of a
cage in the corner containing what looked like some
woman's silver fox fur neckpiece, including the black
button nose and the bead-eyes. It was all curled up.

"Pogey!" said Ted. "*Pogey!*"

"He can't hear you," said the MP. "That speaker's one
way, so the night guards can check, in the labs."

A white-coated man came into the room from a far
door, carrying a white enamel tray with fluffy cotton
and three hypodermic syringes lying in it. The little
bitch and Pogey were instantly alert and pressing their
nose to the bars of their cages. The bitch wagged her
stub tail and whined.

"Love me?" said Pogey. "Love me?"

The white-coated man paid no attention. He left his
tray and went out again. The bitch whined after him.
Pogey dropped. Ted's hands curled into fists against the
slick metal face of the door.

"He could've said something!" said Ted. "He could've
spoke!"

"He was busy," said the MP nervously. "Come on—we
got to get going."

They went on over to the colonel's office. When they
came to the door of the outer office, the MP slid his gun
around on his belt so it was out of sight under his jacket.
Then they went in. A small girl with startlingly beautiful
green eyes in a blue summer-weight suit, a civilian, was
seated on one of the hard wooden benches outside the
wooden railing, waiting. She looked closely at Ted as he
and the MP came through the railing.

"He's waiting for you. Go on in," said the lieutenant
behind the railing. They passed on, through a brown
door and closed it behind them, into a rectangular office

with a good-looking dark wood desk, a carpet and a couple of leather chairs this side of the desk.

"You can wait outside, Corporal," said the colonel, from behind the desk. The MP went out again, leaving Ted standing stiff and facing the desk. "You fool, Ted!" said the colonel.

"He's mine," said Ted.

"You just get that notion out of your head," said the colonel. "Get it out right now." He was a dark little man with a nervous mustache.

"I want him back."

"You're getting nothing back. It's tough enough as it is. All right, we all went to Arcturus together, and we're the first outfit to do something like that and so we're not going to let one of our own boys get slapped by regulations when we can handle it among ourselves. But you just get it straight you aren't getting that antipod back."

Ted said nothing.

"You listen to me good now," said the colonel. "Do you know what they can do to you for striking a commissioned officer? Instead of getting out, today, you could be starting fifteen years hard labor. Plus what you'd get for smuggling the antipod back."

Ted still said nothing.

"Well, you're lucky," said the colonel. "You're just plain lucky. The whole outfit went to bat for you. We got the necessary papers faked up to make the antipod an experimental animal the outfit brought back—not you, the outfit. And Curry—*Lieutenant* Curwen, Ted, you might remember—is going to pretend you didn't try to half-kill him when he came to take the antipod away from you. I was going to make you go over and apologize to him; but he said no, he didn't blame you. You're just lucky."

He stopped and looked at Ted.

"Well?" he said.

"You don't understand," said Ted. "They die if they don't have somebody to love them. I was at that weather observation point all by myself for six months. I know. Pogey'll die."

"Look . . . oh, go out and get drunk, or something!" exploded the colonel. "I tell you we've done the best we can. Everybody's done the best they can; and you're lucky to be walking out of here with a clean record." He picked up the phone on his desk and began punching out a number. "Get out."

Ted went out. Nobody stopped him. He went to the temporary barracks the expedition had been assigned to, changed into civilian clothes and left the base. He was in about his fifth bar that evening when a woman sat down on the stool next to him.

"Hi there, Ted," she said.

He turned around and looked at her. Her eyes were as green as a well-watered lawn at sunset, her hair was somewhere between brunet and blond and she wore a tailored blue suit. Then he recognized her as the girl in the colonel's outer office. With her face only a foot or so away she looked older than she had in the office; and she saw he saw this, for she leaned back a little from him.

"I'm June Malyneux," she said, "from *The Recorder*. I'm a newspaperwoman." Ted considered this, looking at her.

"You want a drink, or something?" he said.

"That'd be wonderful," she said. "I'd like a Tom Collins."

He bought her a Tom Collins; and they sat there side by side in the dim bar looking at each other and drinking.

"Well," she said, "what did you miss most when you were twenty-three and a half quadrillion miles from home?"

"Grass," said Ted. "That is, at first. After a while I got used to the sand and the creepers. And I didn't miss it so much any more."

"Did you miss getting drunk?"

"No," said Ted.

"Then why are you doing it?"

He stopped drinking to look at her.

"I just feel like it, that's all," he said. She reached out and laid a hand on his arm.

"Don't be mad," she said. "I know about it. It's pretty hard to keep secrets from newspaper people. What are you going to do about it?"

He pulled his arm out from under her hand and had another swallow from his glass.

"I don't know," he said. "I don't know what to do."

"How'd you happen to get the . . . the—"

"Antipod. When they hunch their back to walk it looks like the front pair of legs're working against the back pair."

"Antipod. How'd you make a pet of it in the first place?"

"I was alone at this weather observation point for a long time." Ted was turning his glass around and around, and watching the rim revolve like a hoop of light. "After a while Pogey took to me."

"Did any of the other men make pets out of them?"

"Nobody I know of. They'll come up to you; but they're real shy. They scare off easy. Then after that they won't have anything to do with you."

"Did you scare any off?" June said.

"I must have," he shrugged, "—at first. I didn't pay any attention to them for a long time. Then I began to notice how they'd sit and watch me and my shack and the equipment. Finally Pogey got to know me."

"How did you do it?" she asked.

He shrugged again.

"Just patient, I guess," he said.

The bar was filling up around them. A band had started up in the supper club attached, and it was getting noisy.

"Come on," June said. "I know a quieter place where we can hear ourselves talk." She got up; and he got up and followed her out.

They took a taxi and went down to a place on the beach called Digger's Inn. It had a back porch overlooking the surf which was washing upon the sand, some fifteen feet below. The porch had a thatched roof; and the small round tables on it were lit by candles and the moonlight coming in across the waves. They had switched to rum drinks and Ted was getting quite drunk. It annoyed him; because he was trying to tell June what it had been like and his thickened tongue made talking clumsy.

"... The farther away you get," he was saying. "I mean—the farther you go, the smaller you get. You understand?" She sat, waiting for him to tell her. "I mean ... suppose you were born and grew up and never went more than a block from home. You'd be real big. You know what I mean? Put you and that block side by side, like on a table, and both of you'd show." He drew a circle and a dot with his forefinger on the dampness of the table between them to illustrate. "But suppose you traveled all over the city, then you'd look *this* big, side by side with it. Or the world, or the solar system—"

"Yes," she said.

"... But you go some place like Alpha Centauri, you go twenty-three quadrillion, four hundred trillion miles from home, and"—he held up his thumb and forefinger nails pinched together—"you're all alone out there for months, what's left of you then?" He shook his thumb and forefinger before her eyes. "You're that small. You're nothing."

She glanced from his pinched fingers to his face without moving anything but her eyes. His elbow was on the table, his thumb and forefinger inches before her face. She reached up and put her own hand gently over his fingers.

"No, listen—" he insisted, shaking his hand loose. "What's left when you're that small? What's left?"

"You are," she said.

He shook his head, hard.

"No!" he said. "I'm not. Only what I can do? But what can I do when I'm that high?" He closed his hand earnestly around her arm. "I'm little and I do little things. Everything I do is too little to count—"

"Please," she was softly prying at his fingers with her other hand, "you're hurting—"

". . . I can love," he said. "I can give my love."

Her fingers stilled. They stopped trying to loosen his. She looked up at him and he looked drunkenly down at her. Her eyes searched his face almost desperately.

"How old are you?" she whispered.

"Twenty-five," he said.

"You don't look that old. You look—younger than I am," she said.

"Doesn't matter how old I am," said Ted. "It just matters what I can do."

"Please," she said. "You're squeezing too hard. My arm—"

He let go of her.

"Sorry," he said. He went back to his drinking.

"No, tell me," she said. Her right hand massaged the arm he had squeezed. "How did you get him out?"

"Pogey?" he said. "We practiced. I wrapped him around my waist, under my shirt and jacket."

"And he didn't show? And you got him on the ship that way when you came back."

"They weighed us on," said Ted, dully. "But I'd thought of that. I'd taken off twelve pounds. And exercised so I wouldn't look gaunted down. Pogey weighs just about eleven."

"And they didn't know it until you got here?"

"Sneak inspection. To beat the government teams to it, so nobody'd be embarrassed. Colonel ordered it; but Curry pulled it—Lieutenant Curwen—and he found him, and—" Ted ran down staring at his glass.

"What would you have done?" June said. "With—Pogey, I mean?"

He looked over at her, surprised.

"I would have kept him. With me. I would have taken care of him." He looked at her. "Don't you understand? Pogey *needs* me."

"I understand," she said. "I do." She moved a little toward him, so that her shoulder rubbed against the sleeve of his arm. "I'll help you get him out."

"You?" he said.

"Oh, yes!" she said quickly. "Yes, I can!"

"How?" he said. And then—"Why? We've been talking here all this time; and now all of a sudden you want to help Pogey and me. Why? It isn't that newspaper of yours—"

"No, *no!*" she said. "I didn't really care at first, that was it. I mean it was a good story, that was all. Just that. And then, something about the way you talk about him . . . I don't know. But I changed sides, all of a sudden. Ted, you believe me, don't you?"

"I don't know," he said thickly.

"Ted," she said. "Ted." She moved close to him, her head was tilted back, her eyes half-closed. He stared stupidly down at her for a moment; then, clumsily, he put his arms around her and bent his own head and kissed her. He felt her tremble in his arms.

He let her go at last. She drew back a little from him and wiped the corners of her eyes, with her forefinger.

"Now," she said shakily, "do you believe me?"

"Yes," he said. He watched her for a second as she got out handkerchief, lipstick and compact. "But how're we going to do it? They've got him."

"There're ways," she said, sliding the lipstick around her upper lip carefully. She rolled her upper lip against the lower, and blinked a little, examining the result in the mirror. "I'm quite good, you know," she said to the compact. "I can manage all sorts of things. And I . . . I want to manage this for you."

"How?" he said.

"You have to know what's going on." She folded the compact and put it away with a sharp snap. "That expedition of yours to Alpha Centauri cost forty billion dollars."

"I know," he said. "But what's that got to do—"

"The military's sold on the idea of further stellar exploration and expansion. They want a program of three more expeditions of increasing size; one that would cost a hundred and fifty billion during the next twenty years." She glanced at him the way a schoolteacher might. "That's a lot of money. But now's the ideal time to ask for it. All of you have just got back. Popular interest is high . . . so on."

"Sure," he said. "But what's that got to do with Pogey?"

"They don't want a fuss. No scandal. Nothing that'll start an argument at this stage in the game. Now tell me," she turned to face him, "you're released from service now, aren't you?"

"Yes." Ted nodded, frowning at her, "they signed me out today before they took me to see the colonel. I'm a civilian."

"All right. Fine," she said. "And you know where Pogey is. Can you go get him and get him outside the base?"

"Yeah," he said. "Yeah, I thought of that. But I was saving it for last—if I couldn't think of a better way where they couldn't come after us."

"They won't. You leave that part of it to me. Pogey was your pet; and his kind was listed harmless by the expedition when they were on Alpha Centauri. There's enough of a case there to make good weepy newspaper copy. I'll have a little talk with your colonel and some others."

"But what good'll that do if they just take him back anyway?"

"They won't. Legally, they've got you, Ted. But they'll let you get away with it rather than risk the publicity.

Wait and see."

"You think so?" he said, his face lighting up. "You really think they will?"

"I promise," she answered, watching him. He surged to his feet. The little round table before them rocked. "I'll go get him right now."

"You better have some coffee first."

"No. No. I'm sober." He took a deep breath and straightened up; and the fuzziness from the liquor seemed to burn out of his head.

"You'll need some place to bring him," she said. "I've got an apartment—" He shook his head.

"I'll call you," he said. "We may just move around. I'll call you tomorrow. When'll you be seeing the colonel?" He was already backing away from her.

"First thing in the morning." She got up hurriedly and came after him. "But wait—I'm coming."

"No . . . no!" he said. "I don't want you mixed up in it. I'll call you. Where'll I call you?"

"Parketon 5-45-8321—the office," she called after him. And then he was gone, through the entrance to the interior bar of the Inn. She reached the entrance herself just in time to see his tow head and square shoulders moving beyond the drinkers at the bar and out the front door of the place.

Outside, Holman called a cab.

"Richardson Space Base," he told the driver. His permanent pass was good to the end of the week; and they passed through the gates of the base, when they reached them, with only a nod and a yawn from the guard.

He left the cab outside the laboratories and stepped off into the shadows. He followed along paths of darkness until he came to the section where Pogey was being kept. A night guard came out of the door just before he reached it, swinging his arm with the machine pistol clipped to one wrist, and looking ahead down the corridor with the sleepy young face of a new recruit. Ted stood still in the shadows until the door of the next section had swung to behind the guard, then went inside.

He found the door he had looked through earlier. A light burned inside the room and most of the animals in the cages were curled up with their heads tucked away from the glare of it. The door was locked, but there was an emergency handle under glass above it. Ted broke the glass, turned the handle and went in; and the animals woke at the noise and looked at him wonderingly.

He opened the door to Pogey's cage.

"Pogey . . . Pogey . . ." he said; and the antipod leaped up and came into his arms like a child and clung there. Together they went out into the night. When he got back into the cab, Ted bulged a little around the waist under his shirt; but that was all.

The sky was paling into dawn as they got back into the city. Ted paid off the cab and took the public tubes. Wedged into a corner seat, he drowsed against the soft cushions, feeling Pogey stir warmly now and again around his waist; until, waking with a start he looked at the watch on his wrist and saw that it was after eleven a.m. He had been shuttling back and forth beneath the city for seven hours.

He got stiffly off the tubes and phoned the number June had given him. She was not in, they told him at the other end, but she should be back shortly. He hung up and found a restaurant and had breakfast. When he called for the second time, he heard her voice answer him over the phone.

"It's all right," she said. "But you better stay out of sight for a while anyway. Where can I meet you?"

He thought.

"I'm going to get a hotel room," he said. "I'll register under the name of—William Wright. Where's a good hotel where they have individual entrances and lobbies for the room groups?"

"The Byngton," she said. "One hundred and eighty-seventh and Chire Street—fourth level. I'll meet you there in half an hour."

"All right," he said, and hung up.

He went to the Byngton and registered. He had just gone up to his room and let Pogey out on the bed, when the talker over the door to the room told him he had a visitor.

"There she is—" he said to Pogey; and went out alone, closing the door of the room carefully behind him. June was waiting for him in the bright sunlight of the little glassed-in lobby a dozen yards from his door; and she ran to him as he appeared. He found himself holding her.

"We did it! We did it!" She clung to him tightly. Awkwardly, but a little gently, he disengaged her arms so that he could see her face.

"What happened?" he said.

"I phoned ahead—before I went out at nine this morning," she said, laughing up at him. "When I got there, your colonel was there, and General Daton—and some other general from the United Services. I told them you'd taken Pogey—but they knew that; and I told them you were going to keep him. And I showed them some copy I'd written." She almost pirouetted with glee. "And oh, they were angry! I'd stay out of their way for a long time, Ted. But you can keep him. You can keep Pogey!"

She hugged him again. Once more he put her arms away.

"It sounds awful easy. You sure?" he said.

"You've got to keep him quiet. You've got to keep him out of sight," she said. "But if you don't bother them, they'll leave you alone. The power of the Fourth Estate—of course it helps if you're on the national board of the Guild."

"Guild?"

"Newspaperman's Guild," she said. "Didn't I tell you, darling? Of course, I didn't. But I've been northwestern sector representative to the Guild for fourteen"—she stumbled suddenly, caught herself on the word, and the animation of her face crumpled and fled—"years," she finished, barely above a whisper, her eyes wide and palely watching upon his face.

But he only frowned impatiently.

"Then it's set for sure," he said. "I mean—from now on they'll leave us alone?"

"Oh, yes!" she said. "Yes! You and Pogey are safe, from now on."

He sighed so deeply and heavily that his shoulders heaved.

"Pogey's safe then," he murmured. Then he looked back at her. He took her hand in his. "I . . . don't know how to thank you," he said.

She stared at him, pale-faced, wide-eyed.

"Thank me!" she said.

"You did an awful lot," he said. "If it hadn't been for you . . . but we had to have faith somebody'd come through." He shook her hand, which went lifelessly up and down in his. "I just can't thank you enough. If there's ever anything I can do to pay you back." He let go of her hand and stepped backward. "I'll write you," he said. "I'll let you know how we make out." He took another step backward and turned toward the door of his room. "Well, so long—and thanks again."

"*Ted*!" Her voice thrust at him like an icepick, sharply, bringing him back around to face her. "Aren't you," she moved her lips stiffly with the words, "going to invite me in?"

He rubbed the back of his neck with one hand, clumsily.

"Well," he said. "I was up all night; and I had all those drinks . . . and Pogey is pretty shy with strangers—" He turned a hand out toward her. "I mean, I know he'd like you; but some other time, huh?" He smiled at her wooden face. "Give me a call tomorrow, maybe? I tell you, I'm out on my feet right now. Thanks again."

He turned and opened the door to his room and went in, closing it behind him, leaving her there. Once on the inside he set the door on lock and punched the DO NOT DISTURB sign. Then he turned to the bed. Pogey was still curled up on it, and at the sight of the antipod Ted's face softened. He knelt down by the side of the bed and put his face down on a level with Pogey's. The antipod humped like an otter playing and shoved its own nose and bead-eyes close to his.

"Love me?" said Pogey.

"Love you," breathed Ted. "We're all right now, Pogey, just like we knew we'd be, aren't we?" He put his face down sideways on the coverlet of the bed and closed his eyes. "Love Pogey," he whispered. "Love Pogey."

Pogey put out a small pink tongue and stroked Ted's forehead with it.

"What now?" murmured Ted, sleepily.

Pogey's bead-eyes glowed like two small flames of jet.

"Now," Pogey said, "we go to Washington—for more like you."